Romance Along the Rails

Joyce Valdois Smith

TALLGRASS
MEDIA

Columbia, South Carolina

Romance Along the Rails

Published by Tallgrass Media
Columbia, South Carolina
books@tallgrass.media
www.tallgrass.media

Cover and interior book design by Kelly Smith.
Cover photograph by Rozann Hickey.

This is a work of fiction. Names, characters, places, and incidents either are the products of the author's imagination or are used fictitiously. Any resemblance to actual persons, living or dead, businesses, companies, events, or locales is entirely coincidental.

Printed in the United States of America
First Printing, 2018

ISBN-13: 978-0-9997626-0-8

To Bob, my loving and patient husband, who has remained by me in this process of publication, when it seemed it would never come to fruition.

To my children and their spouses: Kelly & Joice, Janna & Michael, Annette & Andrew, and Holly & Erik. You have always encouraged and believed in me.

To the most amazing grandchildren in the world: Gabby, Isaiah, Rylee, Aidan, Ridge, Sophie, April, Michaela, Sonja, Carenza, Blakeney and Dani. I love you more than I can tell you.

I give all the glory and honor to my Lord and Savior, Jesus Christ. "I can do all things through Christ who strengthens me."

Philippians 4:13 KJV

In memory of my daddy and mama, Harry and Lucile Valdois. Thank you so much for the Christian heritage you gave our family.

and

My dear friend and encourager, Ruth Montgomery. You believed in me when I had barely begun to believe in myself.

I know I will see you all again soon, in Heaven.

ACKNOWLEDGEMENTS

Karen Wingate — You were an early encourager who believed in me and pushed me to be better. Our friendship has remained strong through the years in spite of the miles between us.

Ginny Pohlenz — What an invaluable friend you are. I have thoroughly enjoyed our time together as you critiqued and edited this book. You did an amazing job.

Peggy Lee Manoogian, Barbara Warren, Kaye Calkins, Connie Baker, and Shirley King McCann — Thank you for reading, editing and making helpful suggestions. You have all had an important part in this process.

Rozann Hickey — your photographic skills brought the cover to life. *Janna Wiseley* — You helped gather the props and with the composition of the cover. *Kelly Smith* — You have been my encourager and motivator. You created the cover, formatted and edited the manuscript and published the book through Tallgrass Media. Thank you so much.

Kansas Historical Society — For the permission to use the Harvey Girl photograph on the cover. I started writing this book about fifteen years ago. Through the years I have lost track of the names of those who helped with my early research, but I want to thank everyone who assisted me.

Most of the historical information about the Harvey Girls came from *The Harvey Girls; Women who opened the West* by Lesley Poling-Kempes and *The Harvey House Cookbook; Memories of Dining Along the Santa Fe Railroad* by George H. Foster and Peter C. Weiglin.

"Thou preparest a table before me..."

PSALM 23:5 KJV

Chapter 1

April 11, 1885
Pickens, Missouri

"No money?" The half-whispered words hung like wisps of vapor in the air. Elise's hands trembled in her lap. Her shoulder and neck muscles tensed and pain radiated into the back of her head. "Papa said there would be enough money to live on."

"There was, six months ago. He expected to be back in half that time." Mr. Brownley, the family lawyer, shifted his ample weight in the wingback chair. "If your father had carried out his business plans while in France, it would have increased the family income substantially. Unfortunately, his robbery and death prevented that."

The lawyer mopped his forehead with a worn handkerchief and looked around the farmhouse parlor at the six young people. "Your parents' will divides the assets among you, but your father borrowed heavily against the farm to finance his trip to France. There isn't enough to make the next farm payment." He cleared his throat and adjusted his glasses on his nose. "Ben Davison, president of the bank, is prepared to advance enough money to buy seed for spring crops. He'll also extend the farm payment deadline until January first of next year."

Arnaud stepped from the fireplace where he'd leaned against the mantle. He pulled a straight back chair up to the sofa and straddled it. "Have you been in contact with the authorities in France? Is there any progress in the investigation into Pa's death?"

Mr. Brownley shook his head. "I'm afraid not. The last I heard, there was no trace of the murderer or money."

Elise studied the reactions of her stunned siblings. Justine sat next to her husband, Paul LaFayette on the loveseat. They'd been married less than two months when the family received the news of Papa's death last fall. A small house that belonged to Paul's family provided them a home near the Dumond farm.

Sixteen-year-old Marie, at the far end of the sofa, hugged a pillow Mama had embroidered. Impressed with her high school academics, the school board had offered her the country school's teacher position for next fall.

Jule, only fourteen and set to graduate from eighth grade,

sat on the footstool. He and Elise had lived together the last sixteen days since Mama's horrible death from an intestinal infection. Her throat constricted and tears stung her eyes as she watched his sad face, so like their father's. She wanted to hug him but knew he'd be embarrassed.

Her gaze returned to Arnaud. When he received the news of Mama's death, he'd taken a short leave of absence as engineer on the Santa Fe railroad. She was glad he was home. As the oldest he took charge and made things seem better, even if they weren't. Everyone, including her, sat motionless for several moments until Arnaud leaned forward, his brown eyes intense.

"January, you say — and the payment is three hundred and fifty dollars?" He drummed his fingers on his knee and stared thoughtfully across the room. "That gives us nine months and includes harvest. If we all pitch in to help, we can do it." He looked at each sibling. "At least I think we should give it a try. I'll save what I can from my paychecks."

He looked at Paul. "Can you keep the farm going with Jule's help?" At Paul's nod, he continued. "You and Justine could move back into this house. You'd be closer."

Justine squeezed Paul's arm. "We could, couldn't we, Paul? I can take in washing and ironing." She smiled at her little brother. "Jule will be a huge help."

Jule straightened to his full height. "Sure! Paul and I can take care of everything."

Elise slumped back in the rocker. Tears pricked behind her eyelids and a hard lump formed in her chest. *Three hundred and fifty dollars. How would they ever come up with that much money?*

"Elise, you could marry August Perret. The way he's been hanging around, I'm sure he'd be willing. Then he could help with the farming." Justine's teasing words cut across her thoughts.

She glared at her older sister while the others laughed. "Don't start that, Justine. I've already told you I'm not getting married, not to August or any other man! Not now, anyway." She clenched her fists in her lap. She wanted to get married and have children, eventually, but she wasn't ready to settle down yet.

A familiar blanket of frustration settled around her shoulders. Everyone else appeared to take the news in stride. Why couldn't she find her place in it all? If Justine and Paul moved back into the farmhouse there wouldn't be a need for her to stay. Marie would be here to help during the school summer break.

She put her hand over the lump of pain in her chest. She needed to find a job, but the only positions in town were housekeepers or nannies. Not what she wanted for her life. If she were a man, she'd seek work on the railroad like Arnaud.

Elise stood and walked to the large front window. The warmth from the fireplace and closeness of the air threatened to suffocate her. She leaned her forehead against the cool damp glass and grasped the lace curtain. A deluge of rain pelted the yard from swirling clouds overhead.

The voices of the lawyer and her siblings droned on behind her as they discussed crops and possible solutions to the dilemma. She should be in the conversation, but her brain refused to function rationally.

Elise blinked against tears. In the last few weeks she'd shed enough to fill the rain barrel. She needed fresh air. She rushed to the front door.

Outside, she leaned against the rough surface of the front porch pillar and gazed around the farmstead, her home for the last twelve years. She'd been seven when the family moved from France to these Missouri hills.

She loved the large gray barn with the oak and buck brush grove in the background. The spring rain caused the new green leaves to glow in the half-light of early afternoon.

Elise closed her eyes as the rain dampened her clothes and formed droplets in her hair. Grief surged through her. The pain of Papa and Mama's deaths had consumed her thoughts, and now her family might lose the farm as well. She pounded her fist against the pillar in fear and frustration. How could God be so cruel? She wasn't sure she could ever forgive Him.

She opened her eyes and peered at the overcast sky. She half expected a bolt of lightning to strike her for her thoughts. God was an integral part of their family life. Papa had made sure they'd attended church every Sunday, and she'd given her life to God at an early age. Why had He allowed so many bad things to happen?

Movement at the end of the drive ended Elise's reverie. A horseman rode up the lane toward the barn. He wore a great-coat, his hat pulled low over his face.

Sudden fear gripped her midsection. It must be bad news for someone to come out in this thunderstorm. She clung to the post and braced herself against the pain. "God," she whispered. "Please don't let anything else happen. I can't stand it."

She glanced through the parlor window. The others were occupied inside. She'd find out who this man was. She gathered her skirt, pulled it above her shoe tops and hurried down the steps.

She picked her way across the soaked yard. The rain had let up, but a stream of water trailed down the middle of the lane between her and the barn. She hesitated, stepped back, hiked her skirt a few inches further and took a running leap.

Her foot slipped in the slimy mud, and her shoe filled with water. A cold shiver ran through her. She dropped her skirt and flailed her arms wildly, as she tried to regain her balance. Certain she would sprawl in the muddy stream, she was surprised when two strong hands caught and pulled her to more solid ground.

"Th—thanks." Elise looked up at her rescuer as she struggled to regain her balance. "Wha—who?" Amazement and consternation flooded through her. He pushed his hat away from his face revealing deep blue eyes, which brimmed with laughter. Several strands of sandy blond hair had fallen across his tanned forehead, and an intriguing dimple lodged in his strong square chin.

She took a step back and pulled her arm from his grip. Warmth crept up her neck and into her face at her undignified behavior and greeting. What must this stranger think?

He chuckled as she tried to regain her composure. "I didn't anticipate such a greeting. Obviously, I'm not who you were expecting."

"In this rain? I wasn't expecting anyone." The words were sharp. She softened her voice and relaxed her face. "I thought you might be bringing news—"

He removed his hat, his blue eyes serious. "I'm Daniel Gilbertson, a friend of Arnaud Dumond. We work together on the railroad."

Elise stared at him; her face grew warmer with embarrassment. "Oh, yes, Arnaud did say you might be coming." She glanced down. Her dress was splattered with mud from her sprint across the yard. Suddenly self-conscious, she became aware of his broad shoulders and ruggedly tanned face. Arnaud would be mortified to know she had welcomed his friend in such a manner.

"Let's go in the barn. We can't talk out here in the rain." She lifted her damp skirts and hurried ahead of him. She needed to gather her wits.

He reached the door first, pushed it open for her then dashed back to lead his horse into the warmth of the barn. Elise stood inside and watched as he wrapped the reins around the post of the nearest stall.

He turned his attention toward her, a bit uncertain. "I hope I haven't caught you at an inconvenient time." He paused. "This is Arnaud's home, isn't it? He invited me to come from Columbia, where I visited my sister's family, so we could travel to Kansas City together."

"Yes, he's here. And, we're glad you've come, in spite of my ungracious welcome. I couldn't imagine why anyone would ride out in this weather unless they brought bad news." Elise looked at him, a half smile on her face. "I'm glad I was wrong. Arnaud will be happy to see you."

Daniel grinned. His eyes searched her face. "You must be his sister. Elise?"

"How did you know?"

He chuckled. "You resemble him, but even more, because he talks a lot about you." A smile lit Daniel's face and laugh lines radiated from the corners of his eyes. "He said, of all his sisters, Elise was the most adventurous, the most like him. I figured that had to be you."

She sucked in her breath. *Arnaud talked about her to this stranger?* She crossed her arms and glared at him. What else did he know? "I'm sure he gave you a list of my other unflattering qualities, as well."

His laughter was replaced by seriousness. "I'm sorry. I didn't mean to offend you. Arnaud wouldn't do that. He talks highly of you." Daniel stepped toward her, his hand outstretched. "I guess I got ahead of myself, Miss Dumond."

She deserved the comment about being adventurous after her impetuous dash across the yard. Maybe she was being too hard on him. Her lips curved into a smile as she placed her hand in his. "I'm sorry. You don't have to call me Miss Dumond. Elise is fine. Any friend of Arnaud's is my friend, too."

At that moment, Daniel's horse shook his head and gave a loud neigh followed by a snort. The sounds were answered by a whiny farther back in the barn.

Elise dropped Daniel's hand and turned. "Oh, my. That's Star. I forgot about her. She's due to foal anytime." She glanced back to see Daniel throwing off his coat as he followed her toward Star's stall. "Arnaud checked her just before Mr. Brownley came."

Daniel was immediately beside her. He pushed open the stall door where Star lay. Moving slowly, he knelt by her side and ran his hand along her distended side. Elise noticed how gentle his touch was.

"It's her time."

"You know about horses?"

He smiled, took his hat off and laid it in the straw. "I grew up on a ranch. I've seen mares foal many times. She's doing fine."

"Should I go get Arnaud and Jule?"

Shaking his head, Daniel stood and stepped back. "No time. Have you ever attended an animal giving birth?"

Her heart raced, and she stared at him wide-eyed. Anxiety welled up in her chest. She shook her head. "I've seen kittens being born, but Papa and the boys always took care of the bigger animals."

Daniel knelt beside the mare. "Looks like you'll have the opportunity now, if you want it."

She forced a nod, but was frozen in place. What was she to do next?

"Get down by Star's head and talk to her, keep her quiet."

Elise willed her knees to bend, lowered herself onto the straw and watched Daniel check Star's progress. The soft mewing of the mother cat accompanied the rain that once again peppered against the wall, and a hen scratched in the corner. The cool air penetrated her damp clothing.

Star whinnied and began to thrash her legs. Elise leaned over, wrapped her arms around the horse's neck and spoke softly in her ear. Star relaxed as she talked.

She leaned her head against Star's warm body and smiled as she watched Daniel, aware of his confident strength. His cowboy hat had left a damp ring around his head causing an indentation in his hair, and the firm muscles in his arms rippled as he moved. Elise was relieved that Daniel had taken charge of the situation. No wonder Arnaud had chosen him as a friend.

A loud whiny, from Star, caused her to lift her head. Daniel looked up with a grin. "The front legs are coming and the nose. We're going to have a baby in a few minutes."

"Good girl. You can do it." She sat forward in anticipation and stroked Star's neck. With the next two muscular contractions the foal was born.

"It's a girl." Daniel sat back.

She stared in wonder as the tiny filly scrambled its way to freedom, then lay resting on the straw. After a short time, the foal clumsily attempted to get to her feet. She toppled over twice before she succeeded. Just then, Star stood up and nearly knocked Elise backward.

She turned toward Daniel. He was watching her with admiration and amusement. Suddenly, she became aware that she and this handsome man were alone in the barn and had just shared the intimate experience of observing a birth. Embarrassment spiraled through her. "Daniel...er, Mr. Gilbertson. Oh, I'm sorry. This is no way to treat a guest. I...I should have gotten Arnaud or Jule."

Daniel's intense gaze captured hers and caused her breath to catch in her throat. "It's alright. I don't think either of us had much choice in the matter. Don't call me Mr. Gilbertson, though. If you're Elise, then I'm Daniel."

Elise nodded as he reached for her hand and pulled her up.

Daniel glanced back at the foal. "Do you know what you're going to name this little rascal?"

She watched the colt nurse hungrily. "I don't know. I hadn't thought..." A white blaze streaked from the filly's forelocks to her nose. "We could name her Star Fire, after her mother."

Daniel nodded. "That sounds good."

Elise turned back to Daniel and placed her hand on his arm. "Thank you, Daniel. I don't know what I would've done if something had happened to either of them."

"I didn't do anything. Star did all the work, with God's help." Daniel grinned as he took her hand in his. "Come on, let's get my horse taken care of then go tell the rest of the family."

Chapter 2

The rain had eased to a light sprinkle when Elise and Daniel stepped from the barn. Rays of sun shone through the clouds in the west, causing the farmstead to shine with unusual intensity. Elise stared in amazement as the house glowed in the afternoon light. She drew a deep breath. "Don't you just love the smell of a spring rain? This is my favorite time of year."

Daniel nodded, pointing east. "Look, there's a rainbow."

The double rainbow stretched across the sky and embraced the farm. Its full spectrum of color from yellow to violet filled her with awe. "Beautiful," she whispered. "God's promise."

Voices from the front porch of the house caught her attention. She turned to see Arnaud and Justine walk Mr. Brownley to his carriage. Elise cringed. They would be upset she'd left. "We better go. They'll wonder where we've been." She stopped, looked at Daniel and giggled. "At least they'll wonder about me. They don't know you're here."

Daniel's eyes twinkled as he took her arm and helped her step across the puddles. The rivulet she had nearly fallen into had slackened to a mere trickle.

Arnaud and Justine walked toward them as Mr. Brownley drove away. A smile of welcome lit Arnaud's face. "Daniel, my man, how long have you been here?" Arnaud thrust out his hand for a handshake. He looked around for Daniel's horse. "Did you come during the rainstorm?"

Daniel nodded and smiled at his friend. "It hadn't rained much when I left town, but it poured on my way here."

Arnaud turned to Justine. "This is my friend, Daniel Gilbertson. We met and worked together on the railroad line when I first went west."

Justine nodded a welcome to Daniel. "Glad to have you, Daniel." She grinned. "I see Elise didn't waste any time making your acquaintance."

Elise felt her face grow warm. "When he rode up the lane I thought he was someone from town or one of the neighbors."

Daniel chuckled. "It's a good thing Elise came to the barn to meet me. Star has a new filly, born just a few minutes ago."

Justine let her breath out in surprise. "Star had her colt? Elise, why didn't you come get Arnaud and Jule? That's quite a welcome for our guest."

14

Elise glared at her sister. "There wasn't time. We barely got into the barn before Star foaled."

"Are they alright? Did Star have any trouble?" Arnaud edged toward the barn.

"They're fine. No trouble at all. Come see for yourself!" Daniel punched Arnaud lightly on the shoulder. "Come on, Elise. Let's show them."

Justine gestured toward the barn. "You go on. Paul will be ready to leave. We have to get the chores done before dark." She backed away. "See you tomorrow at church."

Elise nodded and followed Arnaud and Daniel. She needed to see Star Fire and make sure she was alright once more before she fixed supper.

The next afternoon Daniel slipped out of the farmhouse and walked to the swing at the end of the front porch. It had been some time since he'd taken a Sunday afternoon nap, but it refreshed him. Arnaud and Elise hadn't awakened yet and Jule was off on an adventure somewhere,

He seated himself on the swing and set it in motion with his foot. The rain had freshened the air. A cool, crisp breeze caused him to pull his coat tighter in spite of the bright sun making its way into the western sky. A few brave daffodils and tulips clustered by the front porch, and the large maple in the front yard hinted at new growth of green leaves.

Daniel laid his folded newspaper beside him and casually viewed the neatly kept farmstead. In less than twenty-four hours, he'd grown to appreciate the farm and the family who lived here. He'd accompanied them to church in the small town of Pickens that morning then enjoyed the noon meal prepared by Elise and Justine. Marie had stayed in town with relatives after church so she could attend school through the week. She had a month before graduation.

Daniel watched the tiny filly, Star Fire, cavorting around her mother's legs in the corral beside the barn. He was gratified to have shared the occasion of her birth with Elise. The expression of joy on Elise's face was priceless.

With a glance at the door, Daniel stood, left the porch and walked across the yard to the corral. He rested his foot on the bottom rung of the fence and reached to scratch Star between the ears. Arnaud had told him they could lose the farm. How much could one family endure?

The crunch of gravel on the drive behind him made Daniel turn. Elise walked toward him. Golden light in the depths of her green eyes glimmered beneath well-shaped eyebrows and thick dusky eyelashes. The afternoon sun burnished her silky, dark brown hair with auburn highlights. He'd felt he knew Arnaud's family from their many conversations, but he'd not been prepared for Elise's unaffected beauty. *Get a grip on yourself, man. There's no place in your life for a woman right now.*

Elise stared at Daniel's back as she walked toward the corral. Tall and muscular, his broad shoulders filled out the width of his coat. He stood with the wind rifling through his hair. Her pulse quickened as he turned. Was he married? She couldn't recall hearing Arnaud say.

"Hello, Daniel." Elise smiled as she joined him. "It's a beautiful spring day isn't it?" She reached through the fence to touch Star Fire. "Thank you for your help with Star and Star Fire yesterday afternoon." She lowered her eyes. "And thanks for not telling my family about my undignified behavior."

"You were worried, justifiably so, considering the news you'd received." Daniel lowered his foot from the fence and turned toward her. "Arnaud told me what happened with your family."

Elise nodded and pulled her cloak around her. "The news about the farm was hard to take after everything else. We'll make it, though." She shrugged as she cleared her throat. "That's enough about us. Tell me about you; about your job. I know you work for the railroad, but you aren't an engineer like Arnaud, are you? Didn't you meet at work on the line?"

Daniel leaned against the top rail of the fence. "When he first went to work for the railroad he joined the line crew in Kansas, where I was assigned. We hit it off right from the start and became good friends. Been friends ever since even though our jobs have changed."

Elise leaned over, pulled a handful of the new grass that grew along the fence and held it for Star to nibble. "What do you do now?"

"I work on a survey crew and as a negotiator for a possible merger with another railroad." Daniel ran his hand through his hair and pushed back the strands that had blown down over his forehead. "We have to find the best route for the railroad. I'm going to be on a crew from Kansas to Texas. That's the direction the Santa Fe plans to expand next."

Elise stood and turned toward him. "Isn't that through the Indian Territory? Can the railroad build there?"

"Yes. The government has passed legislation that encourages the building of a railroad. The plan is to open the Oklahoma territory to settlers in the next few years, and they want the railroad there."

"On our map at school, that looks like pretty rugged country. Did you find a route?" Elise rested her hand on the fence.

Daniel straightened. "It is rugged. Not much there but jack-rabbits and red hills." He grinned. "Actually, we did find a possible route, along an old cattle trail. There's a small struggling railroad based at Galveston, Texas. If the Santa Fe can merge with them, we would have a route to the Gulf that would use their existing line. I've been in Galveston the last six months to negotiate with the owners of the other railroad."

Elise studied his earnest face. Enthusiasm radiated from

the azure depths of his eyes. His lips parted over evenly spaced teeth and the small dimple had reappeared in the cleft of his chin. A subtle tinge of envy shimmered through her. "You enjoy your job, don't you?"

"Most of the time, I do." He hesitated. "Of course, it's not all fun. I don't like the long periods of time away from my family."

Elise nodded and looked toward the corral. Star and Star Fire had moved away from the fence. His family. Did that include a wife? She glanced at him then turned back toward the horses. What did she care? She wasn't interested.

She watched as Jule emerged from the trees beside the creek then turned back toward Daniel. "I have to find a job to help with the farm payment. I wish I could find one I enjoyed doing. There aren't any positions around here suitable for women except housecleaning or a nanny." She wrinkled her nose. "If I was a man, I'd go work on the railroad."

Daniel studied her, his face serious. "Maybe you can."

Elise gave a burst of laughter, "What do you mean? I couldn't work on the railroad. I was joking."

"Not on the railroad itself, but as a Harvey Girl." Daniel pushed away from the fence.

Elise frowned. "A Harvey Girl? What's that?"

"They work as waitresses in dining rooms called Harvey Houses along the Santa Fe line."

19

Elise's eyes grew large with shock, and she reached out to grab the fence. "Waitresses? That's not safe is it? I've heard those places aren't for...ladies."

Daniel shook his head. "No, no. The Harvey Houses aren't anything like regular railroad eating houses or saloons. They're different, very different. The young women who work there are respectable, beyond reproach." His face was serious. "Fred Harvey has started several of them in towns along the Santa Fe. They're in or near the railroad depot, and they have a lunchroom and dining room. Some of them even have hotels with them. Mr. Harvey has strict rules for the houses and for the ladies he employs. I've eaten in several of them in my travels across Kansas. Topeka has a Harvey House. There isn't a hotel in it, but there's a first-rate lunchroom and dining room."

He motioned toward the house. "As a matter of fact, I noticed his ad in the St. Louis paper I was reading. I'll get it for you when we go in."

Elise frowned again. "Now that I think about it, I believe I saw an ad about them in Aunt Victorine's *Harper's Bazaar*." She looked at him for reassurance. "Are you sure it's respectable?"

Daniel nodded as they headed back across the yard. "Why don't you ask Arnaud? He's eaten in more of them than I have."

"Ask me about what?" Arnaud stood from his seat on the porch steps as they approached.

Daniel motioned toward his friend. "About the Harvey

Houses and Harvey Girls; I just suggested that Elise might consider it as a job opportunity."

"Hey, that's a capital idea." Arnaud's eyes lit up as he turned toward her. "You'd be perfect as a Harvey Girl." He clapped Daniel on the shoulder. "Why didn't I think of that?"

Elise leaned against the porch pillar. "Wait a minute. Not so fast." She held up her hand. "I need a lot more information before I make a decision like that."

Arnaud sobered. "Of course you would, but I do think you'd enjoy it. There are girls from all over the Eastern United States who work for Fred Harvey. It would sure beat being a teacher or a housekeeper, and I'd get to see you more often."

Daniel handed Elise the newspaper he'd laid on the swing. "Here's the ad. We can send you more information when we get back to Topeka."

Elise took the newspaper and read the small ad.

Wanted: Young women of good character, attractive and intelligent, ages 18 to 30, to work in Harvey Eating Houses on the Santa Fe railroad in the West. Generous salary plus room and board. Contact Fred Harvey, Kansas City, Missouri.

She sucked in her breath. What would Justine and Marie think? What would Aunt Victorine and all the women in town say? Suddenly, Elise didn't care as certainty flowed through her. This was what she wanted! She could make money for the farm payment and enjoy some adventure as well.

Elise released her breath as she looked up. "Please, send more information about this. I'm interested." She held the newspaper against her chest as she glanced at the sun sinking in the west. "Right now, though, I better fix supper."

Elise and Jule stood on the porch steps the next morning as Arnaud and Daniel fastened their satchels to the back of their saddles. Elise pulled her cloak around her and shivered in the early morning chill. The sky had begun to lighten in the east with streaks of pink and orange painting the horizon.

Daniel checked the cinch then walked back to the porch. "Thank you for everything, Elise. I've enjoyed my stay." He held out his hand to her.

"You've been a blessing. I'm glad you came. It helped keep our minds off our problems." Elise placed her hand in his. "Thank you, most of all, for being there when Star and I needed you. I'll never forget it."

"Neither will I. Glad I could help."

Arnaud pounded him on the back. "Well, old man, we better be on our way if we are going to meet our train."

Daniel pulled his gaze away from Elise's face and turned to shake Jule's hand.

Elise gave Arnaud a hug. "I wish you and Daniel didn't have to leave so soon."

"I know, Elise. I wish we didn't have to go, either, but you know the railroad. Trains have to be on schedule and they won't run without an engineer." Arnaud touched his finger to her nose. "I'll send you the information about the Harvey Girls as soon as I get back."

Elise smiled. "I'll be waiting."

As Elise watched Daniel and Arnaud disappear behind the trees at the end of the drive a wild urge to run after them nearly overtook her. If only she could go along. Placing her hand in her pocket, she felt the newspaper ad Daniel had given her. She had to get that job. She had to help save the farm.

CHAPTER 3

Daniel stretched his legs into the aisle. He'd chosen a seat by himself when he got on the train at Emporia. Still, there wasn't enough room for his lanky frame. Railroad passenger cars weren't built for the comfort of anyone over six feet tall.

He removed an envelope from the side pocket of his valise and looked at the return address: Atchison, Topeka and Santa Fe. The enclosed letter was written on official stationery instructing him to return to Topeka and make his report to the Santa Fe president who had just returned from California. Anticipation flowed through Daniel. He planned to spend this summer in the Indian Territory and the wilderness of Texas. Once President Strong chose the best route to the Gulf, a survey crew would have to map it. He planned to be on that crew.

The weeks since he'd returned from the Texas negotiations hadn't been wasted. He'd spent time with his sister and her family in Columbia. Then he'd traveled to Pickens to spend a few days with Arnaud and his family on the Dumond farm. He admired those young people who were determined to work together to save their home. He'd returned to Kansas and spent the next week and a half on his father's ranch in Emporia riding roundup with his brother, Thomas, and the other ranch hands. He was proud of the Lazy G Ranch. His father had worked hard to bring it to its present prominence.

Daniel flipped the Santa Fe envelope over and studied the name he had scrawled across the back — Elise Dumond. Why had she affected him so profoundly? After his visit to the farm, she had invaded his thoughts often. She was beautiful and vulnerable, so in need of comfort. She had elicited his protective nature.

With a frown, he returned the envelope to his valise. His job and women didn't mix. He'd found that out soon after he began with the railroad. Lila Baxter, the neighboring rancher's daughter, had jilted him. She'd promised to wait for him while he worked on the railroad. But when he came home for Christmas, four months later, she confessed she was marrying Chet Paulson, his best friend. Daniel's jaw set in determination at the reawakened feelings of betrayal. He hadn't given women a thought since then. He wouldn't start now.

He looked out the train window. A horse and carriage traveled along a road beside the track. Scattered farmsteads had given way to clusters of house, which indicated that they were almost to Topeka. Daniel lifted his satchel and placed it beside the valise on the seat as he prepared to disembark.

When he stepped from the train, the metallic clang of a gong rang across the train yard. A bellboy, standing on the platform of the large two-story, wood frame depot, announced, "Fred Harvey dining room right this way." The words were nearly obscured by the clamor of passengers.

The famed Harvey House dining room and lunchroom would be crowded for at least an hour. Daniel made his way around the horses, buggies and wagons parked by the depot. As he started to walk up the street toward the Windsor Hotel he heard someone call his name. He turned to see Arnaud hurry toward him, bobbing through the crowd of people.

"Hey, Arnaud, were you engineering this thing?"

"Sure was." Arnaud clasped Daniel's outstretched hand. "Finally making your report to Strong?"

Daniel nodded.

Arnaud gestured toward the depot. "Want to meet for supper? What time is your meeting? I don't have to leave until morning."

"I'm not sure. I expect there will be a message at the hotel." He pulled out his pocket watch. "It's four fifteen now. How about six-thirty? I should be finished by then."

"Sure. Sounds good." Arnaud turned back toward the depot.

Daniel headed up the street. In the lobby, he dropped his bags on a chair by the stairs and strode to the registration desk. "Need a room for two nights."

The desk clerk watched as he signed the registration book. "Mr. Gilbertson! Good to see you. I have a message for you." Taking a folded paper from a pigeonhole behind him, he handed it to Daniel along with a key. "Room 206."

"Thanks." Daniel grabbed his luggage and headed up the stairs two at a time. He let himself into the room, set down his bags and tossed his coat on a chair. Then he walked to the window and opened the curtain. He broke the seal on the note and held it up to the afternoon light.

April 21, 1885

Mr. Gilbertson

Please come to the office as soon as possible. Albert Robinson arrived today. We are looking forward to your report.

Daniel sat on the bed. He opened his valise, took out the large envelope he'd brought from the directors of the Texas railroad and flipped through the papers inside. They appeared to be in order. He was pleased with the results of the negotiations. Would Strong and Robinson think he'd done enough? Daniel stood, grabbed his coat and made his way back down the stairs.

At the depot, he sauntered across the lobby, ascended the staircase and walked down the short hall to the Santa Fe offices. He pushed the door open and stepped into the outer office. A young clerk glanced up from the ledger on his desk. "Mr. Gilbertson?" At Daniel's nod, he waved toward the door behind him. "Go on in. Mr. Strong is expecting you."

A spirited conversation ensued when he entered. A huge walnut desk sat in front of a bay window that overlooked the city. It was covered with open books, piles of paper and a plaque bearing the name, "William Strong". Two men studied a huge railroad map draped across a large table. A dozen or more rolled maps stood in the corner.

"Mr. Gilbertson! Daniel, isn't it?" William Strong stepped toward Daniel, his hand outstretched. Long white hair and sideburns flowed into a massive beard that covered the lower portion of his face. "We've been awaiting your report." With a wave he included the other man. "Have you met our chief engineer, Albert Robinson?"

Daniel nodded as he grasped the other man's hand. A strong scent of cigar smoke wafted around him. Mr. Strong continued. "I'm sorry we weren't here when you arrived. We were in California to finish the railroad through Cajon Pass." He sighed, pulled his handkerchief from his pocket and wiped his brow. "I'll be glad when we get that line through to the Pacific."

Albert Robinson stepped forward. Tall and distinguished,

he, too, was a large man with a full head of white hair and a well-groomed mustache. "Did the negotiations go well in Texas?"

Daniel set his valise on a chair and took out the envelope. "The Gulf, Colorado and Santa Fe Railway is in financial trouble again. In fact, the president, George Sealy, is practically begging us to merge; but his stockholders haven't given their approval yet. I'm sure it's just a matter of time." He handed the parcel to William Strong. "Here's a communiqué he sent."

Strong scanned the top sheet before he looked up. "Good work. You've done well on our behalf."

Robinson walked to the corner where the rolls of maps leaned against the wall. He selected one and spread it over the other map on the table, tracing a line with his finger. "We've decided to take the Santa Fe south from Arkansas City, Kansas, across the Cherokee lands and into the Oklahoma unassigned territory, then into Texas to meet the Gulf, Colorado and Santa Fe at Gainesville." He looked at Daniel. "Later this summer, we want you to get a survey team together and finish the mapping so we'll be ready to build when the merger is final."

Daniel straightened and turned toward Robinson. "Me? You want me to lead a survey team?"

"As you know, our chief surveyor, H. L. Marvin is occupied in California, so he won't be able to lead this team." Albert Robinson stepped away from the table. "He has highly recommended you. Said you were the best surveyor he had on his crew; that you learn quickly and retain what you learn. We trust his judgment."

Daniel grasped the table. "Thank you. I'll do my best."

"Good! We'll help you organize a team and get the equipment together when the time comes."

Daniel nodded as he looked at the map and frowned in concentration. "When do you want me to start?"

"There's no hurry." William Strong rolled up the map. "We have to finish the rail line to the Pacific before we start serious negotiations with the GCSF. Take a couple of months off. Spend time with your family. We'll be in touch."

"Thank you, sir." Daniel was dazed as he shook hands with the two men and made his way out of the office. Would he be able to lead a survey crew? That was a lot of responsibility.

As he entered the Harvey dining room, the aroma of roast beef and fresh apple pie assailed his senses. He could hear the quiet hum as the diners visited while they ate their meals.

Two couples ahead of him waited to be seated. Daniel looked around, impressed by the precise order in the room. White linen tablecloths and napkins adorned each table; silverware gleamed, polished to perfection, and crystal glassware sparkled in the glow of gaslights. The Harvey Girls, all dressed in black and white uniforms, moved through the room with a professional air. Daniel knew the standards of the Harvey eating-houses allowed for nothing less.

Daniel watched the head waitress greet the couples. She exuded a friendliness and charm, which made customers feel welcome. Her blonde hair pulled into a proper bun on the back of her head, she looked neat and professional in the modest uniform. He knew from previous visits that her name was Millie Petersen.

Millie met him with a warm smile. "Hello, Mr. Gilbertson. It's good to have you back."

Daniel grinned, amazed at her ability to remember his name. "It's good to be back." He glanced around the dining room. "Is Arnaud Dumond here?" The question barely passed his lips when he saw his friend at a table near the window.

Arnaud signaled for Daniel to sit with him as Millie led him across the busy room.

Daniel folded his lanky frame into the chair opposite Arnaud and thanked Millie as she handed him the menu. He ordered coffee and waited until she turned his coffee cup right side up before he turned to Arnaud.

"How did your meeting go?" Arnaud asked as he placed his napkin in his lap.

"Strong and Robinson were pleased with the report." Daniel pushed his chair back and crossed his right ankle over his left knee. "Did you have a good trip?"

"Uneventful. A lot of folks have returned from the West. It's been a hard winter." He sat back in his chair. "Of course, with spring here, more are headed west. The grass is always greener on the other side of the fence, you know."

Daniel studied the menu as the Harvey Girl approached to take their orders. "I'll have the roast prime rib dinner with some apple pie and ice cream for dessert." He smiled as she removed the menu then waited while another girl filled his cup with coffee.

Arnaud ordered his meal then leaned forward and propped his elbows on the table. "You look about to burst with news. What happened in that meeting?"

"They asked me to head a survey team to map the route into Texas. H.L. Marvin, the chief surveyor, recommended me." Daniel lowered his leg and sat forward.

"That's great, man. I'm impressed." Arnaud sat up as the Harvey Girl approached with their meals.

After she left, both men bowed their heads for a short thanks, then began to eat.

"So, when will you head back to Texas?"

Daniel shook his head. "It won't be for a couple of months. Everyone is more interested in finishing the railroad line through the Cajon Pass to the Pacific Ocean." He buttered a slice of bread. "I thought I'd be on the crew, but I never dreamed they'd ask me to lead it."

"Ah, you'll do fine. Will you stay at your father's ranch in the meantime?"

Daniel nodded. "I'll ride round-up with the ranch hands. They can always use help this time of year. Have you heard anything from your family?"

Arnaud looked up. "I received a letter from Elise today."

Daniel leaned forward. "You did? How are things on the ranch? Is she alright?"

"They're all still trying to recover. Justine and Paul moved into the farmhouse." Arnaud reached for his dessert. "Elise is fine. I need to get the information about the Harvey Girls sent to her. I didn't have time before I left last week."

Daniel glanced at the young woman who hurried by their table. "I hope it works out for her." He could easily imagine Elise dressed in the Harvey Girl uniform; her gold-flecked, green eyes shining with life and her silky, brown hair framing the classic features of her face. The thought made his heart beat faster. He wanted to see her again, even if a relationship was impossible.

CHAPTER 4

Elise stared out the kitchen window. A cardinal warbled its spring song in the newly leafed elm tree. Scent of honeysuckle drifted through the window as the warm spring breeze ruffled the calico curtains. Star Fire frolicked beside her mother in the pasture. She and Daniel had worked well together when Star gave birth to her foal that terrible day when everything else had gone wrong. The colt was growing fast.

She gazed at the risen bread dough in the large crockery bowl on the sideboard, then punched her fist into the smooth, rounded surface and watched it deflate and collapse. Why hadn't Daniel and Arnaud sent the information about the Harvey Girls? If she was going to try for the job, she needed to get started. She sighed as she scattered flour on the wooden surface, placed the ball of dough on it and divided it to make loaves.

She stared out the window again, her hands idle. It was hard to believe it had been twelve years ago that her family had left France to come to America. She could still recall the dampness in the air as she climbed the gangplank holding tightly to her big brother's hand. They were headed to a wonderful new life. Uncle Henri and Aunt Victorine, who had already been in America for seven years, had described the area around Pickens, Missouri, as a beautiful wonderland with hills and trees much like their home in France.

After the difficult ocean crossing, the ordeal of the immigration lines, and the trip overland by covered wagon, the Ozark hills did, indeed, look inviting. Elise loved the green grass and lush trees. Papa had built the two-story white frame house on the small fertile plot of farmland. He and ten-year-old Arnaud had worked dawn to dusk for days to clear the land of rocks so they could plow the sod. Warm memories of those years flooded over her.

She picked up a ball of dough and shaped it into a loaf. Papa's and Mama's deaths caused a constant ache of grief in her chest. Now they could lose the farm.

Justine spoke from the other side of the room where she was ironing. "Elise, August Perret asked Paul again last Sunday if he might court you."

Startled from her reverie, Elise spun around and scattered flour on the floor, the bread dough in her hands. "Why that man can't get it through his head that I'm not interested is beyond me!"

Justine placed the cooled flatiron on the cook stove and leaned against the ironing board. "You know, Elise, you should be thinking about finding a husband so you can settle down in a home of your own. You are nineteen."

Elise sighed. "You're right of course, but I'm not ready to get married." The dough exuded between her fingers as she squashed it out of shape.

Justine placed one of her husband's shirts on the ironing board and took the hot iron from the cook stove. "Maybe Arnaud's friend, Daniel, will come back." She grinned. "That wouldn't be so bad, would it?"

"Don't count on that." Elise reshaped the loaf and placed it into the bread pan. "He probably thinks of me as Arnaud's little sister." Actually, she hadn't been able to get Daniel out of her thoughts. His rugged masculinity combined with his sensitivity to the feelings of others had won her admiration.

Elise picked up another ball of dough and began shaping it. "What I want is to find a job, maybe move somewhere else." She hesitated. She hadn't mentioned the possibility of becoming a Harvey Girl to Justine. She needed more information first.

Justine frowned. "What kind of a job would you want? You could apply for a teaching position in one of the neighboring towns, but I didn't think you wanted to teach."

Marie came from the bedroom with an armful of bed sheets. Since it was Saturday, she was home for the weekend. "I couldn't help hearing you talk," she said with a smile. "Don't get so discouraged, Elise. God has a plan in all of this, even if we can't understand it. You know the Bible says all things work together for good to them that love God." She dropped the bedding beside the washtubs. "Somehow things will work out."

"That's easy for you to say. You have a job." Elise gave the loaf a pat and turned back to Marie. "Lately, it's been hard for me to believe anything could work out for good. I don't know if that verse includes me anyway. I'm not sure I even love God, anymore." She could hear the bitterness creep into her voice.

"Elise, you don't mean that. We've all been going through some hard times, but the Lord will see us through." Marie placed her hand on Elise's arm and spoke softly. "God loves us. He won't give us any more than we can bear. He promised that in the Bible."

Elise placed the dough into the remaining bread pans and set the loaves in the warmer above the cook stove. The turmoil inside her made her nauseated. If God loved them so much, why did he take Papa and Mama?

The sound of a horse galloping up the lane intruded on Elise's thoughts. Who would be coming this early in the morning? They weren't expecting anyone. Elise shuddered as she recalled the horse and rider who'd brought the telegram informing them of Papa's untimely death. What if something had happened to Arnaud? She closed her eyes, unable to face that possibility.

Marie hurried through the dining room and opened the front door. "It's our cousin, Jerome. I wonder what he wants." She stepped onto the front porch as the horse came to a stop by the hitching post. Elise and Justine followed her out.

Jerome held up three letters. "These came on the train this morning. I needed to see Paul so I brought them to you." He pulled off his hat and wiped his brow then looked at the letters. "There are two from Arnaud, one for you, Justine, and one for Elise. A waste of an envelope and stamp if you ask me." He frowned. "The other's from *Grand-mère* Dumond in France."

"Thanks, Jerome." Justine reached for the mail. She handed Elise the envelope addressed to her.

"Is Paul around somewhere?" Jerome swung down from his horse, wrapped the reins around the porch rail and walked up the steps.

"He and Jule are fixing fence in the east pasture. Maybe you could help them. The flood washed a section out down by the creek."

"I can't stay that long. Have to get back to town." Jerome settled on the porch swing.

Elise raised her eyebrows. Jerome wouldn't dirty his hands and help mend fence. He was a master at avoiding the very thought of work. All he wanted to do was carouse with his friends.

She touched Marie's arm. "I'm going for a walk to read Arnaud's letter. Tell Justine I'll be back in time to help with dinner."

Marie nodded. "I can help her. Take your time."

Elise hurried through the house and out the back door. She walked across the farmyard, past the barn and into a large stand of oak and hackberry trees which grew along the creek behind the pasture. Out of sight of the house, she slowed her pace and strolled along the bank, while her long skirt swished around her ankles. She loved the damp, cool air and the earthy fragrance of the new grass along the path.

She could hardly believe this gentle stream had overflowed its banks from the heavy rains just two weeks ago. It had almost flooded the small farmstead. She kicked at the debris left by the water. Paul and Jule had to replant the corn and oats.

Her shoulders drooped. How would they make it? It seemed impossible even with everyone working. Elise stopped and looked up through the new green leaves of a tall hackberry tree. "God, where are you when we need you? Why aren't you helping us?" She covered her face with her hands. If they lost the farm, there wouldn't be anything to hold the family together, no roots.

Several moments later, she swiped her tears away with the

back of her hand and walked around a curve into a small clearing. A fallen log near the water's edge was rammed against a tree and made a natural backrest. She spread her skirt and sat down facing the water, then pulled the letter from her pocket and studied Arnaud's bold handwriting. Always her favorite brother, he was her champion and co-conspirator in many adventures. When he left two years ago she'd felt lost and isolated.

She tore open the envelope and pulled out the enclosed pages. Her hands trembled as she unfolded them.

April 21, 1885

Dear Elise,

Sorry I didn't get this sent sooner. I had to leave on a run west as soon as I arrived in town last week so didn't have time to get the information about the Harvey Houses.

Daniel was on my train today. He'd come from his dad's ranch in Emporia. We had supper together at the Harvey House, and he asked about you. He gave his report to the Big Bosses. They were properly impressed if judged by their responses.

We checked with Millie, the head waitress in the dining room, and she gave me the enclosed application and list of rules. She said the salary would be $17.50 a month, plus room and board. You'll have to sign a contract for one year, during which time you must promise not to get married. That may be more difficult than it sounds. There are lots of eligible men out here (including Daniel Gilbertson)!

Elise, I've eaten in refreshment saloons along the railroad since I came out west; many were greasy, dreary places I don't ever want to see again. That's what makes the Harvey Houses so remarkable. You can't find better service or food anywhere west of the Mississippi. Men even have to wear coats to get in.

You'll need to fill out the application and return it to me before I can set up an appointment for you with Fred Harvey's office in Kansas City.

I hope you decide to come. Don't worry about the farm. We'll find a way to make that payment whether you take this job or not.

I hope things are going better since Justine and Paul moved back into the farmhouse. Give Justine and Marie a hug. I will be waiting for your decision.

Your brother,

Arnaud

Elise lifted the top sheet of the letter and scanned the application beneath, then lowered the letter to her lap. She stared across the stream at the tangled brush beyond. What would it be like to work in an eating-house? Could she do it? She had never been away from her family.

Daniel had asked about her? A thrill raced through her. Elise closed her eyes and pictured Daniel's deep golden tan accented by sandy hair, the cleft in his chin and the crinkly laugh lines around his deep blue eyes. It would be nice to see him again. Maybe, if she went as a Harvey Girl...

She opened her eyes. That was crazy. If she signed the contract for a year, there wouldn't be any time for a man. Well, friendship maybe, but nothing more.

Elise leafed through the pages to the list of rules. She studied them: Must live in a Harvey House dormitory; strict curfew hours; all must wear the same black and white uniform required by Fred Harvey; no makeup; no gum chewing; no jewelry.

Refolding the letter, she replaced it in the envelope and leaned against the tree trunk. What would Justine and Marie say? Her mother probably wouldn't have approved of her going west. It had not been considered a place for nice young women, but times were changing and besides, she had to have a job.

She picked up a twig and tossed it into the stream then watched it float away. She had always loved adventure. To move west and work in a Harvey House alongside the railroad stirred her desire for excitement.

Suddenly, Elise realized the morning had slipped away. She needed to help with dinner. She jumped up and headed back to the house.

As she walked across the pasture, she saw Jerome's horse still tied to the front porch. Jerome had probably smelled the fried chicken. He wouldn't pass up a free meal. She'd have to keep her news quiet. He wouldn't hesitate to spread the word, and she wanted to be certain of her decision before sharing it.

Jerome gave her a creepy feeling. She had learned long ago to keep her distance from him. When she was younger, he'd tried to touch her in inappropriate ways. The thought made her shudder.

Elise brushed a few pieces of dried grass from her skirt before she entered the kitchen. Justine was frying chicken, and Marie was setting the table.

"Sorry I'm late. I didn't realize what time it was."

"It's all right. We have everything under control." Justine turned a chicken leg in the skillet, making the grease sizzle. "What did your letter have to say? Arnaud sent us a banknote for $15." She laid down the chicken fork. "The other letter from *Grandme`re* and *Grandpe`re* will have to wait. It takes me a while to translate the French."

The aroma of apple pie and fresh bread drifted from the oven and made Elise's stomach grumble. She lifted the lid on the pot of new potatoes and poked one with a fork then pushed the pot to the back of the stove. "The potatoes are done." She gestured toward the front porch where Jerome sat on the swing, smoking a cigar. "I'll tell you about my letter after dinner."

Justine raised her eyebrows. "That good, huh? Must have something to do with Daniel." She placed the chicken pieces on a platter and added flour and milk to the grease in the pan for gravy. Voices outside caught their attention. "Here comes Paul and Jule. "Let's get these things taken up."

Justine poured the gravy into a bowl as Elise spooned the potatoes and green beans into serving dishes and Marie sliced the bread. They carried them into the dining room. Soon they were all seated at the table.

After Paul gave thanks for the meal, Elise dipped a serving of green beans onto her plate and passed the bowl. Her mind was occupied with the contents of Arnaud's letter. In a short time, she might be serving a meal such as this in a fancy Harvey House.

CHAPTER 5

Paul forked a chicken thigh and placed it on his plate then passed the platter. "Our neighbor, Charles Bigley, told me yesterday that the Baxters, north of town, are plannin' on movin' to Kansas to homestead." He took a large helping of potatoes. "They say there's free land to be had along the railroad. All a person has to do to homestead is build a house and live there a year. I guess there are several families thinkin' of movin' west, the Bigley's included."

Justine grabbed Paul's arm. "You're not thinking of moving, are you?"

Paul grinned at her. "Naw. We'll stay put. It would be an idea, though, if we can't get the money for the farm payment."

Elise drew in her breath. "Don't even think that. We have to get the money."

Paul turned to Jerome. "You been out west haven't you? You seen any homesteaders?"

Jerome nodded. "Sure. Folks are moving there in droves. The railroad is opening the way for lots of new towns, too." He smirked. "I'm setting up some businesses along the railroad, myself."

Marie frowned. "What kind of businesses?"

"Me and a couple of partners are going to open some saloons."

Elise laid her fork down and sat forward. "Saloons? You can't do that in Kansas, can you? Don't they have prohibition?"

Jerome chuckled. "Prohibition don't stop people if they want liquor." He took a bite of green beans and looked around at his stunned cousins, obviously enjoying the sensation his words had caused. "There's other places beside Kansas. Our saloons will be in New Mexico and Arizona. You girls could come work for me." He grinned. "A man named Fred Harvey is bringing girls from back East to work in his Harvey Houses. He thinks he can keep them locked away in dormitories. We'll see."

Heat climbed Elise's neck into her face. "I wouldn't work for you for a thousand dollars, Jerome, especially in a saloon!" She took a big breath. Why had Jerome brought up the Harvey Houses? Arnaud and Daniel said they were different.

Relief flooded through her when the conversation moved on to other topics. Her working in a Harvey House might be a wild idea. But her brother and Daniel wouldn't have suggested it if they were ill-reputed. They had both eaten in the Harvey eating houses.

Elise pushed her chair back, gathered the dirty plates and carried them to the kitchen. She set the dishes on the sideboard then felt for the letter in her pocket. She needed time to think before anything more was said.

After she'd served the pie, Elise poured hot water from the reservoir on the side of the cook stove into the dishpan and set it in the cast iron sink. Marie appeared. "I'll help with the dishes. I'm tired of Jerome's big talk."

"Thanks, Marie." Elise lowered the plates into the soapy water.

Marie took a clean towel from the cupboard. "What did your letter say, Elise?"

Elise spoke softly. "Have you heard anything about the Harvey Houses, besides what was just said?" She gestured toward the dining room as she placed a plate on the counter to drain.

Marie shook her head. "That's the first I'd heard of them. Why?"

"That's what Arnaud and Daniel suggested I might do; be a Harvey Girl." She touched her pocket. "Arnaud sent me an application."

Marie nodded her head. "What are you going to do?"

"I want to do it."

Marie raised her eyebrows as Justine walked into the kitchen carrying the dessert plates.

"Looks as if you girls have most of the dishes done." Justine set the plates on the counter. "I'll put things away and clean off the table while you finish." She grabbed a dishcloth and started back into the dining room, then paused. "I wish Paul hadn't agreed to loan Jerome the horse and wagon. I don't trust that man, even if he is our cousin. Imagine, him building saloons. I'll bet Aunt Victorine would find it scandalous, if she knew."

"Jerome can do no wrong in his mother's eyes. She made excuses for him when he stole money from McCandless' store. She blamed Arnaud." Elise swiped at the plate she was washing. "Jerome makes me so angry, I want to wring his neck. He doesn't care for anyone but himself."

Marie stacked the last of the clean plates on their proper shelf. "I guess we need to pray for him."

Elise emptied the dishwater out the back door and wiped out the dishpan. "I think that boy is beyond prayer."

"Nobody's beyond prayer." Marie hung up the dishtowel.

Elise turned and glared at Marie. "How can you say that? How can you be upbeat and spiritual all the time? Doesn't it even bother you that Mama and Daddy are gone?"

Marie's shoulders slumped and tears flooded her eyes. "Yes, it bothers me, a lot. I just try to stay positive... to keep from getting down."

"I'm sorry, Marie." Elise put her arms around her sister.

Justine sat at the table and pulled the letter from France out of her pocket. She tore open the envelope and read slowly, a frown of concentration on her face. "*Grand-mère* says they're fine. *Grand-papa* would like to come to America, but she says no." She chuckled. "I'm not surprised at that." She continued to read the letter.

"The authorities have decided to investigate Papa's robbery and murder, again." Justine sighed. "What can they find after all this time? I just wish we could forget it and get on with our lives. Papa's gone, and so is all our money. An investigation isn't going to help." Bitterness crept into her voice.

Marie touched her shoulder. "Papa meant well. He couldn't help it if he got robbed and killed. Maybe they'll find his killer."

"You know, I think we should write to our cousin, Julius Montague. He may have heard something about Papa's robbery since the money from the vineyard was supposed to be invested in his shipbuilding business." Elise leaned against the table.

Justine shook her head and placed the letter on the table. "It wouldn't do any good. It's all done and in the past." She set the ironing board back up. "Now, Elise, you can tell us about your letter from Arnaud. What did he have to say?" She shook out a skirt and placed it on the ironing board then picked up the hot iron from the stove.

Elise hesitated. She pulled the letter from her pocket.

"Arnaud and Daniel have both suggested a job possibility. I don't know how you'll feel about it, but I think I'd like to apply for it."

"What kind of a job possibility?" Justine stopped ironing and looked directly at her.

Elise took a deep breath. "Arnaud thinks maybe I could work in a Harvey House, be a Harvey girl."

Justine straightened to her full height, her eyes wide. "A Harvey House? Like Jerome talked about? What could Arnaud be thinking?" Her face turned red, and her voice nearly squeaked. "You're not going to work in one of those dirty eating houses on the railroad." She set the iron down on the ironing board then moved it before it could scorch the skirt. "You heard what Jerome said. Mama would never have allowed it, I know. You would be ostracized by the town women!"

"It can't be that bad. They aren't dirty eating houses, they're dining rooms and lunchrooms. Arnaud has been in the Harvey Houses to eat. In fact, he said he had eaten in several of them, and they are very clean and respectable. He has also talked to some of the girls who work in them. They like it."

"Yes, I bet he talked with them. Of course, they like it if all of the railroad men come in to talk to them." Justine turned back to the ironing board. "It's out of the question. There'll be something better for you, I'm sure."

"Justine, listen. I can't sit around and do nothing. You

know there isn't enough money. I need to help, but there isn't anything for me to do here in Pickens."

"I understand all that, but as your older sister, I can't let you do it. Something or someone better will turn up."

As Justine reached to exchange the now cold iron for a hot one from the cook stove, Elise grabbed her arm and spun her around. "I don't know what you think is going to turn up that will be better, but it's time I take some responsibility. Young women go west to be schoolteachers. This can't be any worse than that." She released Justine's arm. "I am going to send in the application. I don't care what you think."

Elise's heart pounded hard in her chest. Justine stood motionless, the cold iron in her hand.

"Maybe it won't work out, maybe it isn't the right thing to do, but I'll never know if I don't try." Elise turned on her heel and walked from the kitchen and up the stairs to her room. Her eyes ached with unshed tears and a sob pushed its way out.

The bed springs squeaked in protest as Elise flopped down on the patchwork quilt and gazed out the window at the large maple tree in the front yard. The anger drained as she stared at Arnaud's letter in her lap. She'd never spoken to Justine in such a tone, but why couldn't she understand? She hadn't even listened. Mama might not have agreed, but she would have listened.

Elise stood and walked to the window. The warm afternoon breeze blew in. She stared at the farmstead that had been her home since she was seven years old. It wouldn't be easy to leave; there were so many memories here of Papa and Mama, but this seemed to be the best choice.

She turned, walked to the wardrobe on the other side of the room, and took out her well-worn black cotton dress. Garden work usually helped clear her mind. She changed her clothes, grabbed her sunbonnet, pushed Arnaud's letter into her dress pocket then hurried down the stairs.

Justine looked up from the shirt she was ironing. "Where're you going?"

"Out to the garden. Paul and Jule worked it up yesterday morning. It should be about right to plant."

"I'm almost through ironing. I'll come out and help when I'm finished." Justine placed the flatiron on the cook stove and picked up the hot one.

"All right." Elise left the house and walked to the wash-house. She found the box of seeds they had saved from last year and grabbed the hoe that leaned against the wall. As she walked to the garden behind the chicken house, a cool breeze brushed her damp forehead and fluffed the curls that had escaped their pins,

She watched a robin hop along the ground. He stopped every few seconds to peck expectantly for a juicy morsel. Elise had the urge to be free, to run or fly like the robin. If she were a man, she could go work on the railroad; and no one would say no!

Elise leaned over to set the box of seeds on the ground as Marie walked up. "Can I help?"

"Sure. I can always use help." Elise attacked the dirt clods with the hoe.

Marie picked up a rock and threw it out of the garden. "Elise, don't be upset with Justine. Since she's older, she feels she's responsible for everyone. She forgets you are grown-up, too."

"I know. It's just aggravating at times. This morning she told me I was nineteen and should be getting a life of my own."

Marie smiled then gave her a questioning look. "May I read the letter from Arnaud? I'm curious to know more about the Harvey eating houses. Why haven't we heard anything about them before?"

"I don't know. There must be advertisements in a lot of newspapers and magazines. We just never noticed."

Marie took the letter Elise handed her. When she finished reading it, she looked up. There was a mischievous twinkle in her eyes. "I told you Daniel would remember you."

"Yeah, as Arnaud's little sister, who needs a job." Elise grimaced and wrinkled her nose.

Marie laughed. "I think he liked you a lot." She folded the letter and handed it back to Elise. "A job as a Harvey Girl isn't something I would want, but you have always been daring. You were the one to climb the tree when Mama told us not to." Marie squatted down to place the seeds in the furrow Elise made. "Me, I guess I'll stay here and teach and try to find a husband."

"I'm sure you won't have any trouble doing that. You could have your pick of the young men around here."

"Do you think so?" Marie hesitated and sat back on her heels. "Elise, are you sure you aren't interested in August? He's so handsome and caring."

"No, Marie, I'm not interested in August." Elise grinned. "If you want him for your beau, you can have him. That is, if he'll have you. If I'm accepted as a Harvey Girl, I won't be able to marry for a year anyway."

Marie nodded, a decided twinkle in her eyes as Justine arrived to help.

That evening, as they finished the supper dishes, Justine touched Elise's arm. "I'm sorry I talked to you the way I did this afternoon. I'm just concerned about your safety and reputation. I wish there were job opportunities closer."

Elise faced her. "I know. It's alright. I'm sorry I yelled at you, too, but I'm sending in the application. I need to get that job." At Justine's nod, Elise picked up the extra coal oil lamp, carried it up the stairs to her room and set it on her bedside table. She plumped up her pillow and sat against the headboard then reread the small crumpled newspaper ad Daniel had given her.

Wanted: Young women of good character, attractive and intelligent, ages 18 to 30, to work in Harvey Eating Houses on the Santa Fe railroad in the west. Generous salary plus room and board. Contact Fred Harvey, Kansas City, Missouri.

She was nineteen, so she qualified for the age. The generous salary sounded good. She looked across the room. Surely she qualified for the good character part. Her family had always attended church, and she tried to be as good as she could. She looked back at the ad. She was reasonably intelligent and hadn't made bad grades in school. As for being attractive, how could one tell? That depended on how others saw you.

Elise pulled Arnaud's letter from her pocket then picked up her mother's small portable writing desk from the floor beside her bed. She placed it on her lap and ran her hand over the smooth surface on the top. The warmth of remembrance flooded through her. This was one of the few articles Mama had brought with her when the family came to America. Tears sprang to Elise's eyes. "Mama, you would understand, wouldn't you? I have to help save the farm. This is the only way I know." She sat with her head bowed for several moments. Peace and certainty enveloped her. She straightened and pulled open the small drawer on the front of the desk and took out a sheet of paper, a pen and a bottle of ink.

She reread Arnaud's letter then scanned through the list of rules. Most of them were just common sense regulations. Justine hadn't even looked at them.

When she had the application filled out, Elise wrote a letter to Arnaud and requested that he make an interview appointment for her. She blew on the paper to dry the ink then proofread the letter. If only she could write to Daniel, but that presumed on a friendship that might not even exist. She folded the paper, placed it in an envelope with the application and wrote Arnaud's address on the front. Then she propped it against the lamp on her bedside table. Marie could take it to the post office on Monday.

Elise changed into her nightgown and grabbed her hairbrush. She sat on the side of her bed and brushed her waist length hair until it fell in shimmering waves around her shoulders then braided it into a single braid.

As she climbed into bed she realized with a start that she had forgotten to pray. Until recently, prayer was as natural as breathing. Since Papa and Mama died, though, it had become a struggle.

Elise pushed her legs from under the blankets and knelt by the bed. She tried to concentrate, but her prayer wouldn't crystallize. She rolled off her knees and sat on the floor, her head in her hands. Did God even care what happened to them? She'd cried out to Him down by the stream, but He hadn't answered, or had He? She had received the letter from Arnaud. Could that have been God's answer to their need? She shook her head in confusion. Why had He let Papa and Mama die after they were so faithful all those years? Maybe prayer didn't help at all. Wearily, she stood and crawled back into bed.

CHAPTER 6

Daniel frowned as the branding iron left the Lazy G mark on the right hindquarters of a young heifer. The stench of burned flesh filled his nostrils. He'd helped with the branding since he was nine years old, but he'd never gotten used to it. Daniel jumped from his sleek black quarter horse, and slipped the rope from the calf's legs. She bawled in protest as she scampered across the corral to join the other calves.

Slim, the ranch foreman, laid the branding iron down and stood to stretch his legs, before he walked to Daniel's side. "That was the last one." He slapped Daniel's back. "Be drivin' the yearlings to the stockyards in Emporia in the morning. Want ta' ride point with me?"

"I don't know. I'll have to see what Dad has planned."

"He won't care none. He may just ride along." Slim

removed his dirty Stetson and slapped it against his leg to dislodge some of the dust, then replaced it on his head. "It's been good havin' you here for spring round-up, Daniel. These last few weeks have gone by fast. How much longer you got before you go back to Texas on that railroad survey team?"

Daniel turned toward his friend. Slim had been ranch foreman as long as he could remember. Even at six-foot-two, Daniel had to look up to see Slim's eyes, shaded by a thick thatch of brown hair and his tattered Stetson. "I'll be here another week. I need to get my survey crew and equipment rounded up. I haven't heard when they want me to leave, but I want to be ready." Daniel shaded his eyes with his hand. "It's been good being back on the ranch, but working calves still irks me."

Slim nodded as he gestured toward the stallion that stood quietly to one side. "You and that quarter horse sure make a team cuttin' those dogies. You gonna take him with you?"

"I've thought about it." Daniel kicked his boot in the dust. "Slim, Dad wants me to run the ranch." He pushed his hat back and shoved his fingers through his blond hair. "I don't think I could ever come back. The railroad is in my blood. Thomas would do better. At sixteen, he knows more about the ranch than I ever want to know. He was born to be a rancher. I wasn't."

"Don't get in a big hurry makin' your decision. There's plenty of time."

Daniel glanced across the corral. The other cowhands were headed their way. Thomas rode up on a spirited, chestnut gelding. Daniel reached for his stallion's reins and prepared to mount. Slim was right. He didn't have to decide now, but he was pretty sure what his decision would be. Although, if he wanted to settle down and have a family, ranching would be better. Elise's face flashed into his thoughts. He would like to settle down and have a family.

A short time later, Daniel and Thomas trotted their horses into the farmyard. As he pulled to a halt at the barn door, Midnight pranced in a circle. Daniel dismounted and patted the stallion's side. "What's up, big fellow? Haven't you had enough for one day?" The brothers led their horses into the barn, rubbed them down and gave them a ration of grain. Appreciation filled Daniel for this time they could spend together.

He scratched his horse between the ears as Thomas went to hang the gear in the tack room. "You're a good fellow. Slim was right, you know. We make a good team." Midnight nodded his head and whinnied. Daniel laughed.

He sobered at the sound of heavy footsteps on the gravel at the door of the barn. "Daniel, Thomas, you here?"

"Yeah, Dad, we're back. We finished the branding. Slim said they'll start to Emporia with the yearlings in the morning." Daniel stopped and stared at his father in the half-light of the setting sun. "Dad, what's the matter? You look like you've seen a ghost." He hurried across the barn to his father's side.

"It's your sister, Mary." He sat down on a nearby bench and put his head in his hands.

"What about Mary? What's wrong?" Daniel thought back to his four-day visit with Mary and her family last March, before he went to the Dumond farm. He and Mary, who was two years older, were good friends as they grew up. She married George Tilman and moved with him to Columbia five years ago to open a law practice. They'd been back to the ranch only occasionally since then.

Apprehension clutched his mid-section. Daniel touched his father's shoulder as Thomas walked up. "Dad, what happened?"

"She...she's been killed...in a carriage accident." Daniel could just make out his father's muffled words as sobs racked his body.

He stood in stunned silence. Mary, beautiful Mary... How could she be dead? Surely there was some mistake. She was only twenty-four. "How do you know, Dad? Maybe you got the wrong information."

His father looked up, his face haggard. "No, it's true. We received a letter today from their minister. George was killed, too." He pulled out his handkerchief and blew his nose. "Elizabeth and her nanny are staying with the minister and his family."

Daniel pictured Elizabeth, George and Mary's daughter, as she was the last time he'd seen her. Her blonde curls had bounced as she danced. Now, she must be frightened and bewildered.

He was numb, unable to think clearly. What should they do? They couldn't leave Elizabeth with strangers.

His father rose to his feet. "We better get back to the house. Your mother's beside herself with grief."

Daniel followed his father and brother across the farmyard to the back door of the large, farmhouse. Cecelia met them. "I'm glad you're back. Esther is up in the sitting room. I tried to help her, but it's not as comforting as family."

"We'll go to her. Thanks for staying." Charles strode toward the staircase: Thomas on his heels.

Daniel pulled the door shut behind him. "Thanks, Cecelia. Why don't you bring up some tea and maybe those cookies you made for dinner? We're going to need something to sustain us."

"I'll be right up." Tears filled Cecelia's eyes as she pulled the teakettle to front of the stove. "I realize I'm just household help, but I loved Mary. She was my friend."

"I know. Everyone loved her. It's hard for all of us." Daniel touched her arm before he left the kitchen.

Pressure filled his chest and made it difficult to breathe as he headed toward the stairs. What would this do to his parents? Could his mother endure the grief with her weak heart?

When he walked into the room, his mother sat forward in her chair. Her eyes were red from crying, but she was all business. Daniel recognized the determined look. "I'm glad you're all here." She gave her husband a teary smile. "We know this is one of the hardest things we'll ever live through, but right now we need to think about little Elizabeth. She must be frightened out of her wits. She needs to be with family." Esther sniffed and dabbed at her eyes with a small white handkerchief. "At least she has the nanny who's been with her since birth."

She turned toward Daniel and took his hand. "You need to go to Columbia and bring her here. I realize you only have a few weeks before you leave for Texas, but you should be able to get to Columbia and back in plenty of time."

"Are you sure you're up to the care of a four year old, Esther?" Charles leaned in and kissed her forehead. "You know what the doctor said about your heart."

"Of course, I'm sure. What else can we do? She's our granddaughter." Wiping her eyes again, Esther stood and walked to the roll-top desk. "Now we'll need to make plans." She removed a pad of paper and pen from the desk.

Charles followed her then turned to Daniel. "You'll need to settle George and Mary's affairs while you're there. George's family live back East, in Massachusetts, I think. He never said much about them. We don't know how to get in touch with them unless you find more information."

Daniel watched as Cecelia brought the tea and a plate of cookies into the room and served them. He could use a cup. He felt as if the breath had been knocked out of him.

Daniel left early the next morning with Thomas, Slim and the other ranch hands. His mother's last minute instructions rang in his ears.

He rode point beside Thomas and Slim at the head of the herd. Cattle stretched behind them. A slight breeze ruffled the grass along the road as the sun rose in the east flinging hues of pink and orange across the sky. The clamor of bawling cattle and plodding hooves made conversation next to impossible, so Daniel settled into the saddle and let his thoughts roam.

Wildflowers bloomed profusely among the prairie grasses in every direction. Purple, white, pink, yellow and orange, they looked like a colorful carpet covering the rolling flint hills. The clear blue sky with its fleecy clouds made a fitting backdrop for the scene. Daniel's heart grew heavy as he contemplated the spring beauty. Mary had loved this time of year. She had always wanted to come back to Emporia when the wildflowers were in bloom.

Daniel scanned the open rangelands of the Lazy G. They spread as far as his eyes could see. Pride filled him. His father, Charles Gilbertson, and his young wife, Esther, had come to the Kansas prairie to homestead in 1860. They'd lived in a sod house for the first two years until they could haul in lumber to build a frame house. Mary was born in the soddie. Over the years the cattle trade flourished. His father had added to the original house and built it into a place of beauty; the envy of their ranch neighbors. All of this would be his if he stayed on the ranch. He closed his eyes and shook his head. Although he loved the freedom of the great outdoors, he had no interest in being a cattleman.

As a small boy he'd traveled into town with his parents to meet Grandpa and Grandma Gilbertson on one of their visits from back east. He'd been fascinated by the great puffing, smoking, ground-shaking monster as it pulled into the depot. And, he'd loved the sound of the lonesome whistle as the train disappeared down the tracks. The railroad had captured his heart.

His father had been disappointed when he left at the age of eighteen to work on the railroad. He still had fond hopes of Daniel's return to run the ranch, but Thomas was better suited for it. He loved the long hours fixing fences, working cattle and riding the range. Daniel hoped his father would eventually understand.

Around mid-morning, Daniel reined Midnight closer to Slim. "I'll go ahead. Don't want to miss that eleven-thirty train."

"Sure, we'll pick up your horse when we head home."

With a wave of his hat to Thomas, Daniel leaned forward

and let Midnight gallop up the road. The train pulled into the station as Daniel jogged the two blocks to the Harvey House from the livery where he'd left his stallion. He ordered a sandwich and cup of coffee at the lunch counter.

Fifteen minutes later, he stepped into the passenger car and dropped into the nearest seat. He heaved a sigh of relief as he pulled out his pocket watch. Five minutes to spare. He'd almost cut himself too short on time.

He relaxed as the train pulled out. His mind raced ahead to the next few days. What awaited him in Columbia? Would Elizabeth be frightened to come with him? After all, he wasn't much more than a stranger to her. His heart went out to the lonely little girl.

Daniel closed his eyes and let his mind wander to the brief visit at the Dumond farm in Pickens, Missouri. Had that been two months ago? He grinned as he thought of Elise's flying leap toward him across the yard. If he hadn't grabbed her she would have sprawled in the mud. He was glad he'd suggested Elise become a Harvey Girl. Arnaud said she was due in Kansas City for her interview soon. He planned to see her before he had to leave on the survey trip.

He sat up and looked out the window. What was happening to him? The thought of Elise made his heart beat faster. He was acting like an infatuated schoolboy. That would never do. Elise deserved much more than he could give her. He never knew when he'd have to leave and be gone for months on end.

At two-thirty, the Santa Fe pulled into the Topeka station. The area around the depot was nearly deserted except for passengers who had disembarked and who were boarding the train.

Daniel walked into the lobby and scanned the departure board. The train for Kansas City was due to leave at five after three; enough time for a piece of pie.

He sauntered up the stairs and into the lunchroom. Millie greeted him with her usual bright smile as he entered. "Hello, Daniel. Good to see you." She directed him to a seat near the door.

As he seated himself on the stool, he heard Arnaud's voice behind him and swiveled around.

Arnaud was standing at the entrance gazing at Millie. He took her hand. "Millie, you look wonderful."

Her face turned pink. "I'm glad you're back safely." She turned toward the lunch counter. "Would you like to sit with Daniel?"

Arnaud looked his direction, then walked to the adjacent seat and clasped his friend's outstretched hand. "Did you just get here? You must have been on my train again."

"Just arrived from Emporia."

Arnaud set down. "What brings you here? Is your leave up already? Or are they making you come back early?"

Daniel nodded his thanks to Millie as she turned their

cups over. "Neither." He waited while the Harvey Girl poured their coffee then leaned forward on the counter and sighed. "Wish I was headed to work. My sister, Mary, and her husband were killed this week in a carriage accident. I've got to go to Columbia and bring Elizabeth, my four-year-old niece, back to the Lazy G."

Arnaud set down the coffee cup he had just raised to his lips. "I'm sorry to hear that. You say they were killed in a carriage accident?"

"I don't know many details. My parents received a letter from George and Mary's pastor. Elizabeth and her nanny have been staying with him and his family. I've never been around kids, especially little girls. I don't know how we'll get along." He sat back as one of the Harvey Girls came to take his order. "I'll have a piece of cherry pie."

"Couldn't your mom go along?"

"Mom's health won't permit it. In fact, I don't know how she will manage a four-year-old, but she insisted I go after her. Elizabeth's nanny has been with her since she was a baby. I hope the nanny will come with us to the ranch. That would give Elizabeth a sense of stability and familiarity, and relieve Mom." Daniel braced himself with his hands on the counter. "All I can say, you better pray for me. I'm going to need it!" He thanked the girl, as she refilled his coffee cup. "By the way, when is Elise coming for her interview?"

68

"She's coming next weekend. Her interview is May eighteenth, a week from Monday."

"Hopefully, I'll see her again before I leave for Texas." Daniel took a drink of coffee as anticipation shot through him. He nodded his thanks as the Harvey Girl set his pie in front of him. He could easily imagine Elise, in the uniform. He tilted his head toward the door. "By the way, how well do you know that hostess? I noticed she called you by your first name. She even knew my first name and that I was your friend."

Arnaud half turned toward the entrance, while a flush crept up his neck. "We've become acquainted. In fact, she invited me to a dance the Harvey Girls are having tonight."

"Oh, just acquainted huh? Sounds like more than that to me." Daniel chuckled. "Never thought I'd see the day that ol' Arnaud would fall for a lady."

"We've been seeing each other the last few weekends. I hope it'll develop into something more."

"I'm happy for you."

Arnaud faced his friend. "How long will you be here?"

"I leave on the next train. There's a lot to do in a week. I need to settle my sister and brother-in-law's affairs and get back."

Arnaud clasped Daniel's shoulder. "I'll be praying for you."

"Thanks." Daniel pushed his plate back and finished his coffee as the train whistle beckoned.

CHAPTER 7

Elise looked around her bedroom. It seemed hollow with most of her things packed in the trunk that sat in the middle of the floor. She slid down to sit beside the open window, her chin on her crossed arms. The warm afternoon breeze caressed her face.

She stared across the farmyard. Star and Star Fire grazed in the pasture a short distance from the barn. The maple tree, fully leafed, cast its shadow across the yard, and a hen scratched in the drive as she kept close watch over her brood of chicks. Elise sighed. Tomorrow she would board the train for her Monday interview with Fred Harvey in Kansas City.

A mixture of excitement and sadness lodged in her chest. It was hard to leave her family and familiar surroundings; and yet, she was excited about the possibility of her acceptance as a Harvey Girl. She'd be able to contribute her share to save the farm.

Elise pushed herself up. She'd better get packed! She lifted the Bible from the bedside table, opened the front cover and scanned the names; family births, marriages, and deaths. It was Mama's Bible. Justine and Marie had insisted she have it. "It'll remind you of us when you're busy in Kansas," Marie had said. As if she'd need any reminders. She knelt by the trunk and slid the Bible under several layers of clothing.

She ran her fingers over the hand-crocheted lace on the camisoles and pantalets and placed the last of her neatly folded undergarments into the trunk. Justine and Marie had spent many long evenings helping her make them. She gave the clothing one final pat before she stood to look around the room that had been hers for the last twelve years. Insignificant things suddenly became important and precious. The colorful double wedding ring quilt her mother had made was on her bed. In the morning she'd fold it and lay it in her trunk, one of the last things to go in before she left to board the train to Kansas City.

Elise sat on the bed and picked up the doll from her pillow. She'd received Victoria for Christmas when she was nine-years-old and named her after an older girl in school. Elise looked into her doll's blue porcelain eyes and rubbed her black painted hair, then hugged the cloth body close. The long white dress spread out in graceful folds and the porcelain legs clinked together softly. She wished she had room to take her. But Victoria would have to wait here. Elise laid the doll back on the pillow as she heard footsteps on the stairs.

"Here are the sheets and blankets." Marie knelt to place them on top of the clothing. "It looks like you're almost packed." She stood and looked at Elise. "Are you excited?" She wrinkled her nose and grinned. "I'd be scared to death."

"I'm kind of nervous, but excited, too. It's only a little over a month since I first heard about the Harvey Girls. Tomorrow it'll be time to leave." Elise walked to the window then turned around. "Marie, what if I don't pass my interview? I couldn't bear to come back a failure."

"Oh, Elise, you'll make it. Arnaud and Daniel both said you would be perfect for the job."

"I hope so. I'll be glad when it's certain." Elise pushed the hair from her face as a trickle of sweat ran down her back. "Whew, it's hot. You wouldn't know it was only the fourteenth of May. It feels like summer."

"I know. I won't be surprised if we have a thunderstorm before the day's over." Marie sat on the bed.

Elise walked to her dresser and fingered her hairbrush. "I think I'll go for a walk. I can't settle down." She turned to face Marie. "I want to go down by the stream one last time. That always soothes me."

Marie glanced down at her hands. "I need to ask you something before you go."

Elise frowned, questioningly. "What's that?"

"Are you certain you aren't interested in August?"

Elise relaxed and chuckled. "No, Marie, I'm not interested in him. I've seen him talk to you. You're free to court him if you want."

Marie sighed. "Thank you. He's so strong, yet thoughtful. I don't know why you didn't want him, but I'm glad."

Elise gave her a hug. "*Merci, Cherie,* you're a wonderful sister." The two girls grinned at each other at the familiar endearment. Mama hadn't let them speak much French, reminding them they were Americans, but occasionally she would use some of her favorite French phrases.

The next morning, Elise awoke to a loud clap of thunder and a bright flash of lightning. She sat up in bed. Hail and rain pelted the window. Marie was right. The hot, humid weather had been the forerunner of a storm.

Elise lay back against the pillow and pulled the sheet around her. She put her arm behind her head and watched the flashes of lightning outside the window. She was awed by their majesty.

The intensity of the thunder and lightning slowly diminished, and the hypnotic pitter-pat of the rain on the window lulled her back to sleep. When she awoke again, it was fully light outside although it continued to rain from a gray sky. She threw off the sheet and looked toward the door as Marie walked in. "What time is it? I didn't intend to sleep so late."

"It's six o'clock. We're going to have to leave early because of the rain." Marie pulled the quilt from Elise's bed, folded it and added it to the trunk's content.

Elise washed her face, then walked to the wardrobe and took out her new navy blue dress. She slipped it over her head and smoothed down the front. The taffeta fabric was silky to her touch. "Do you think it's alright to wear something other than black? It's only two months since Mama died."

"Yes it's alright. Mama wouldn't want you to go to your interview in black. She's happy in Heaven, Elise. She wouldn't want us to continue to mourn for her."

Elise nodded solemnly.

At breakfast, Paul glanced out the window. "I hoped the rain would let up, but it doesn't look probable. I put the top up on the carriage and hung the curtains. Hopefully we won't get too wet."

As they drove down the lane a while later, Elise strained to get a farewell glimpse of the farm through the haze of falling rain. Her heart constricted as it faded from sight. When would she see her beloved home again? It reminded her of when they'd left France to come to America. She faced the front of the carriage. Marie sat beside her, and Justine and Jule sat across from them.

"Why did it have to rain today?" Jule pulled his coat tighter.

Elise frowned. "I've wondered that too."

Joe and Dobbin strained in their harness as they slogged through the mud. Elise shivered as a gust of wind blew rain in around the curtains and soaked her cloak. Suddenly the carriage lurched and swayed, nearly coming to a stop.

"What was that?" Marie leaned over to look out of the curtain.

Elise's heart leapt into her throat. What if they had an accident trying to get her to the train? She let out her breath in a rush as the carriage moved ahead slowly.

"Sorry." Paul's voice sounded from the driver's seat. "I didn't see that pothole."

Elise studied the brooch watch Papa and Mama had given her for high school graduation. The train was scheduled to leave in an hour. Normally, that would give them plenty of time. If they didn't make it to the train she might as well forget the interview. There wouldn't be another train to Columbia until Monday.

Marie grabbed her hand. "I'm sure we'll make it. I've been praying we would be on time."

Elise squeezed her hand. "I hope you're right."

The trip into town seemed to stretch on and on. Elise checked her watch as the minutes ticked away. Several times she was sure they were stuck, but the mules plodded on.

When they came in sight of the train station, she gave a sigh of relief. The huge engine sat beside the depot belching out great puffs of smoke. Paul pulled the carriage to the front door, jumped down and reached to help Elise. They both nearly slipped as he turned to set her on the station platform. Elise hurried across the depot lobby to the ticket window, her wet dress clinging to her ankles.

The stationmaster handed her a ticket. "Wasn't sure if you'd make it in this rainstorm, Miss Elise, but I told the engineer to wait a bit longer." He grinned a toothless smile. "You better git on out to that train. He's in a mighty hurry. Good thing you had your ticket paid for last Saturday." He patted her arm. "You should be in Columbia about eleven o'clock this mornin'. Then you'll need to git right on the train to Kansas City. It's supposed to leave at eleven-twenty-five. You can check in the station."

"Thanks, Hank." Elise picked up her carpetbag and hurried out of the depot. Paul carried her trunk to the baggage car. Justine, Marie and Jule waited for her beside the open door of the passenger car. She gave them all lingering hugs and laughed shakily as Jule ducked when she tried to kiss him. "I love you all. Please, don't forget to write." Quickly, she climbed the steps into the train.

She found a seat and looked out the window at the members of her family, who waved goodbyes. She returned their waves. Streams of water ran down the glass and nearly obscured her view. She felt a wild urge to rush off the train, to tell them she'd changed her mind. However, the wheels began to turn, the whistle blew and the engine steamed down the track.

Of course, she couldn't get off. She'd committed herself to apply as a Harvey Girl. She had to do her share to save the farm. Tears pricked her eyelids as she strained to watch her family grow smaller beside the track. She straightened her shoulders and swiped at her eyes. No more tears! She had a job to do, and she'd do it.

Elise surveyed the other passenger car occupants. It'd be nice if there were someone to talk to, but most of the other passengers were preoccupied with visiting, reading or looking out the windows. She turned back to the front, patted her wet hair into place and replaced some loose pins. Then she pulled her damp cloak around her shoulders and watched the countryside slide by. Lonely tears rolled down her cheeks as she listened to the clickety-clack of the wheels on the track.

Some time later, Elise opened her eyes and sat up. The train had slowed to a stop. It still rained outside, though not as hard. "Columbia", was written in large letters over the door of the depot.

Elise grabbed her carpetbag, hurried off the train and

headed across the platform to the depot door. She stopped short, awed by the elegance inside. The Pickens station was small and insignificant by comparison. Crystal chandeliers hung from the ceiling. The ticket desk was made of ornate, carved mahogany with a marble top. Two people stood behind it taking care of the lines of passengers. Sooner than she could believe, Elise had her ticket checked and was headed out the door on the opposite side of the depot. She hoped her trunk would also make the transfer.

She clutched her cloak about her as she looked up the track. Rain fell in a slow drizzle. The train seemed to go on forever in each direction; much longer than the one from Pickens.

Elise counted back to the fifth passenger car from the engine then headed toward it. As she approached, she saw the conductor at the door. "Is this car five?"

"It sure is, Miss." He offered her his hand.

The odor of damp leather assailed her as she climbed the steps. She stood in the rear of the passenger car and surveyed the interior. Rows of brown seats lined each side of the car. Several people were scattered throughout: a few laughed and visited, some looked out the window and one man was apparently reading. She spied an empty seat about halfway through on the right, made her way up the aisle and slid in pulling her bag behind her.

She leaned close to the window and peered out. Water

poured in rivulets down the outside. To make matters worse her breath caused fog on the inside. Elise sighed as she rummaged in her pocket for her handkerchief. She wiped the window and strained to watch the other travelers as they hurried by. Were they as anxious to reach their destination as she? Was it only this morning she had left home? It seemed an eternity.

The crowd outside thinned. Elise heard the conductor call, "All aboard." She started to turn from the window as two men moved across the station platform. She stared in consternation. One was her cousin Jerome. The other man walked with a definite limp, but his features were indistinguishable in the misty rain. The men hurried out of sight as the train began to move. A shudder slithered up Elise's spine. What was Jerome doing here? Was that his partner? They were bound to be up to no good!

CHAPTER 8

"We're almost late." Daniel lifted Elizabeth up the passenger car steps to Lucia. Then he stepped up and followed them down the aisle to one of the few empty seats. He frowned as he pushed the lunch hamper and Elizabeth's satchel under the leather covered bench seat. He should've thought to pay for an extra place. Space for his legs was non-existent. He'd be so stiff he wouldn't be able to walk by the time they reached Kansas City. The whistle blew and the train wheels started to roll. "Hurry, we need to get settled."

"I'm *trying* to hurry." Lucia glared at Daniel and scooted next to the window. She turned away as Daniel settled Elizabeth in between them.

Daniel let out an undignified snort as he sat down. *Women!* He couldn't believe how long it took to get around with a small child and a woman. He'd swear it was twice as long. He smoothed his hair back with his hand. He hoped he was all together. As much as he loved Elizabeth, it would be a relief to deliver her and her nanny to his mother.

As the train picked up speed, Elise relaxed and scrutinized the other passengers in the car. The conductor entered the train car from the front and made his way down the aisle as he checked tickets. When he reached Elise's seat, she handed him her ticket and then twisted sideways to scan the passengers behind her. Suddenly, her vision collided with a pair of intense azure eyes. Recognition flashed through her. She stared unbelievingly. Daniel? It couldn't be!

Elise ducked her head and closed her eyes. When she opened them again, his long, well shaped, Levi encased leg extended into the aisle between them. His other knee pushed against the back of the seat in front of him. Elise's eyes traveled back to his face, which was transformed by his captivating, breathtaking smile. His full lips parted over evenly spaced teeth, the dimple appeared in the cleft of his chin and laugh wrinkles extended from the corners of his eyes.

She caught her breath. It was Daniel! Elise looked away. In her peripheral vision, she observed the dark-haired young woman and blonde child in the seat beside him. Who were they? Were they traveling with him? Humiliation and anger swept through her. He must be married. She'd stared at him like a silly schoolgirl! She'd thought and dreamed about him almost every night since March. Why hadn't Arnaud told her? He'd indicated that Daniel was single. Maybe he didn't know. Surely he would.

Elise faced the front of the car. No empty seats. She'd have to stay where she was. She pulled the *Lippincott* magazine, borrowed from Aunt Victorine, out of her bag. How could she have been such a fool? What must his wife think? Angry at herself and Arnaud, Elise pretended to read the magazine. It wasn't Daniel's fault. She'd misread his actions and words. Arnaud should have told her.

Daniel stared in amazement at the back of the young lady on the other side of the aisle. *Elise!* Her hair, styled in a chignon at the nape of her neck had auburn highlights over soft, brunette hues. She was unmistakable. The object of his most frequent thoughts had materialized in front of him? He hadn't expected to see her until he returned from the ranch.

When Elise turned and stared directly at him, the intensity and surprise in her gaze had sent shock waves coursing through him. Before he could say anything, she'd spun away. Maybe she hadn't recognized him, or didn't want to see him. Daniel exhaled in frustration.

To his dismay, he'd seen a slight blush diffuse her face

when she glanced at Lucia and Elizabeth. Why hadn't he said something! He wasn't tongue-tied. He looked at Lucia and Elizabeth. What had she thought? Elizabeth leaned over Lucia and watched through the window as the train moved swiftly through the city and out into the countryside. He frowned as he realized how it must look.

Elise thumbed through the magazine. How could she occupy her time until they reached Kansas City? If only the seat would open up and swallow her.

She heard the animated chatter of the child. Elise held the magazine as if she were reading and sneaked a peek over her shoulder. Daniel had turned the other way. The little girl appeared to be about four-years-old with the most delightful golden curls. Of course, her hair would be blonde like her father's. Elise grimaced as she watched the child bounce in the seat, asking questions like a chattering squirrel.

Elise surreptitiously glanced at the young woman who shared Daniel's seat. She appeared to ignore the child as she sat close to the window and stared out at the passing landscape. *She was attractive though not exceptionally pretty. What did Daniel see in her?*

Elise gave herself a mental shake. That was a horrible thought! It was none of her business what kind of a woman he would pick. What had come over her? She'd never reacted this way to any man, especially a married one! A sudden troubled thought came unbidden. She bolted upright. *Maybe this was an indiscretion!* That would explain why Arnaud didn't know.

"Elizabeth, will you please sit still. You're going to bounce me off the seat." Daniel's masculine voice sent shivers up Elise's spine. The little girl's name was Elizabeth.

"I wan' a drink, Lucia. I'm thirsty," she stated loud and clear. "Take me to get a drink."

The young woman stirred and started to get up.

"What do you say, Elizabeth?" Daniel asked.

"Please?" Elizabeth's voice sounded angelic.

Elise peeked over her shoulder again as Daniel pulled his legs back under him and unfolded his tall, lanky frame. He ducked his head to keep from hitting it on the ceiling and moved to let them pass. He sat on the seat as Lucia and Elizabeth walked to the water bucket at the rear of the car.

A few minutes later, Elise heard Elizabeth run back up the aisle. "I love you, Uncle Daniel," she exclaimed as she scrambled onto Daniel's lap and threw her chubby arms around his neck. She gave him a kiss on the cheek.

Startled, Elise looked around. Uncle Daniel? Then he wasn't Elizabeth's father. Relief rushed through her, and she felt her face grow warm as she met his amused gaze. He was watching her.

Daniel sat up and let Lucia through, then settled Elizabeth on the seat beside him and extended his hand. "Miss Dumond, I'm Daniel Gilbertson, Arnaud's friend. Do you remember me?"

Elise felt foolish but nodded. "Yes, of course I remember you. I...wasn't sure...you'd remember me." Her hand trembled as she placed it in his larger one.

Daniel grinned. "Oh, no, I haven't forgotten you. Arnaud told me you'd be coming." He chuckled. "I just never expected to sit close to you on the train."

Elise shook her head. "Me either, but I'm glad." A friend of her brother's, especially Daniel, was almost as good as having Arnaud here. "When did you see him last?"

Daniel sat back. "Last week, just before I left for Columbia to rescue this little monkey. She's my niece." He ruffled Elizabeth's hair.

Elizabeth sat quietly and listened to their exchange then began to bounce up and down. "Do you know my Uncle Daniel?" she demanded.

"Yes, I know him." Elise smiled at her.

Elizabeth crawled down, crossed to Elise's seat and scrambled up beside her. "My name's 'Lisabeth, and that's my nanny, Lucia," she said, as she pointed across the aisle. "What's your name?"

"I'm Elise." She scooted back to make room then put her arm around the little girl and gave her a hug. She looked at

Lucia. Daniel wasn't married! Elise turned her head to hide a sudden smile. But where were Elizabeth's parents?

"My mommy and daddy got killed in a accin'dent so I have to go live with my gram'ma and gram'pa."

That answered her silent question. Elise placed her hand under Elizabeth's chin and raised her face. "You know what, Elizabeth?"

"What?"

"My mama and daddy have died too, so we are alike. I guess we'll have to be friends. How about it?"

Elizabeth threw her arms around Elise's neck. "I want to be your friend." She pointed to Lucia, who was slumped against the window asleep. "She's my friend, too."

Daniel glanced at his seatmate. "These last two weeks have been hard on Lucia. Even though they stayed with their pastor and his large family, she had full responsibility for Elizabeth after the accident. I'm glad she agreed to come along. I hope she'll decide to stay after we reach the ranch."

"Where is your father's ranch?"

"It's close to Emporia, Kansas." He looked at Elizabeth. "I have to take these two out there then come back to Topeka. I trust they'll get along alright on the ranch. It'll be hard for my mom to keep up with this ball of energy." He reached over and tousled her hair. "My survey team leaves in a few weeks."

Elizabeth shook Elise's arm. "I want my mama. Do you

want yours?" Tears gathered in her blue eyes, so like her Uncle Daniel's.

Elise gazed at the upturned face of the little girl. "I sure do, Elizabeth." She gathered the child into her arms. Why did God let their mothers die? She wasn't sure, but she knew she hadn't forgiven Him for it. How could she? Here was another little life ruined by sadness.

Daniel watched her with compassion and appreciation. Warmth enveloped her. She'd had many admirers, but never anyone as special as Daniel. He was the most attractive man she'd ever met; he was Arnaud's friend and he acted genuinely interested and concerned for her.

"Uncle Daniel, I'm hungry." Elizabeth bounced on the seat.

Daniel pulled out his pocket watch. "It's after noon. We better eat." He gently awoke Lucia then lifted the lunch hamper from under the seat. "Care to join us, Elise? We have plenty. The minister's wife packed enough for an army."

"Justine sent me a lunch. Maybe we can share." Elise pulled the lunch packet from her carpetbag. There were several pieces of the delicious chicken from the night before, biscuits with homemade butter and jam and new radishes from the garden, the first of the season.

Thirty minutes later, after everything had been put away, Elizabeth curled up in the curve of Elise's arm and fell asleep.

Lucia had settled back by the window and closed her eyes.

Elise scooted back into her seat to make room for Elizabeth's legs and looked at Daniel. "Tell me more about your family. What happened with Elizabeth's parents?"

Daniel's shoulders sagged, and he sighed. "They were both killed in a carriage accident two weeks ago. Their horse got spooked and had a runaway. Their carriage crashed into a tree, turned over and threw them out."

"I'm so sorry to hear that." Elise shook her head. "Do you have other brothers or sisters?"

"Yes, I have a younger brother, Timothy. He's sixteen."

Elise was amazed at how easily and naturally their conversation flowed. She moved her arm and shifted Elizabeth to lie on her lap. "You said you have to leave on a survey trip soon?"

"I'm going to lead the survey team into the Oklahoma lands to map the new route into Texas."

"When will you leave?"

He ran his fingers through his hair. "I don't know for sure; probably, sometime around the end of June. I'll deliver Elizabeth and Lucia to the Lazy G then return to Topeka to gather the supplies and get my crew together."

Disappointment raced through Elise. Even if she got hired they wouldn't have much time to get acquainted.

"I hope we can get together when I return from the ranch."

"I'd like that..." Elise wrinkled her nose. "But I'm not sure

I'll be accepted as a Harvey Girl. I may not be there."

Daniel grinned. "You will. I don't have any doubts about that."

"I hope so. I would hate to be a failure."

Sooner than Elise could believe, the conductor entered the railroad coach. "Kansas City; next stop. Prepare to disembark."

Elise gently shook Elizabeth. "Wake up, honey, we're almost to Kansas City?"

"We should come into the station in a few minutes." Daniel handed Lucia a doll blanket that had slid to the floor.

The rain had stopped and the sun was shining. A sign read "Kansas City" on the siding as they rolled by. Excitement welled up in Elise. In a few minutes she'd see Arnaud, and on Monday she'd have her interview. She would make it. She had to.

The train whistled then slowed beside the depot platform. Elise studied the huge building. The size of it nearly took her breath away. It was much larger than the Columbia station with intricate towers of varying heights, arched windows framed in stone and rows of dormers projecting from the steeply pitched roof. There was a clock tower above the main entrance.

After the train stopped, Elise grabbed her carpetbag and followed Elizabeth and Lucia down the aisle to the exit. Daniel carried the other bags.

As they stepped onto the platform, Elise scanned the crowd and tried to see Arnaud through the throngs of people.

"There he is." Daniel grabbed her elbow and pointed. "There. See he's barely out the door."

Elise looked in the direction he pointed. Arnaud had spotted them and was making his way toward them. Elise grabbed Elizabeth's hand and headed through the crowd as Daniel and Lucia followed.

Chapter 9

May 18, 1885

It was Monday morning and Elise was alone. The weekend had flown by. Daniel, Elizabeth and Lucia left on Saturday for Emporia. Now Arnaud was on this train to Topeka. She watched as the railroad cars rushed past, gradually picking up speed.

Elise wiped her eyes with a trembling hand as the caboose pulled out of sight. She straightened her shoulders and took a deep breath. She must pull herself together. Soon it would be time for her interview.

Her interview! A cold chill ran up her spine. What time was it? Was she late?

She craned her neck to see the huge clock tower. Twenty minutes before ten. Her knees weakened with relief. She'd have enough time to check her hair. She brushed some soot from the front of her skirt and headed inside to the ladies' lounge.

Elise grinned as she emerged a few minutes later. Her family in Pickens would be amazed at the luxury of an indoor water closet. No trips to the outhouse! She'd have to write and describe it.

She checked the time once more. Arnaud said Fred Harvey's office was on the second floor of the depot. She took a deep breath and slowly exhaled, then skirted the growing line of people who waited to board the next train, and strode up the stairs.

Elise walked down the carpeted, dimly lit, hallway to a door with *"Meals by Fred Harvey, Fred Harvey Corporation"* written in black letters across the clouded glass window.

An immaculately groomed woman in a dark suit with white blouse sat at a desk in the small waiting room. She looked up and smiled. "May I help you?"

"My name is Elise Dumond. I'm here for an interview with Mr. Harvey about working in a Harvey House." She felt relieved her voice hadn't quivered.

The young woman scanned a list on her desk. "Yes, here's your name. Miss McGuire will see you shortly. She does the hiring when Mr. Harvey isn't here." She motioned to some chairs across the room by a window. "Have a seat. It shouldn't be long."

Another applicant sat in one of the chairs. She looked up as Elise walked over and sat down. "Hello, my name's Elise Dumond. Are you here for an interview, too?"

A brief smile lit the other girl's face as she nodded and nervously twisted a handkerchief in her lap. "I'm Tessa Gillespie." She smoothed the handkerchief then twisted it again. "Where are you from?"

"Pickens, Missouri. What about you?" Elise moved in the seat so she could observe her new acquaintance. Tessa had blonde hair drawn into a bun, rosy cheeks and lively brown eyes. In spite of her nervousness, she appeared likable.

"I'm from Little Rock, Arkansas." Tessa's voice dropped to a whisper. "I've never been away from home, and I'm scared to death." Tears gathered in her eyes, and she wiped them away with the handkerchief.

Elise reached over and gave her hand a squeeze. "Me too. We'll just have to stick together."

Tessa nodded. She straightened in her chair, lifted her chin and smiled, a full, pretty smile that lit her face. "Thanks. I needed that."

A slight breeze blew in the window beside Elise, but it did little to alleviate the warm heaviness in the air. Butterflies had taken up permanent residence in her stomach. How would she be able to talk around the lump in her throat?

She glanced up as a door to her right opened. A girl, about

their age, stormed out and slammed it behind her. She stomped across the floor and muttered, "I didn't want that old job anyway." Then she turned toward Elise and Tessa and sneered. "Don't get your hopes up." As she swept out the door Elise noticed her low-cut red dress, elaborate hairdo and excessive make-up.

"Oh, dear," Tessa breathed with a quiver in her voice. "I'm next. What if they send me off like that?"

Elise shook her head. "Don't worry. Didn't you see how she was dressed? You're dressed modestly, not nearly as flamboyant as her."

Tessa smiled a shaky smile as the door opened again, and an older, well-dressed woman announced her name. Elise took several slow deep breaths. She leaned her head against the back of the seat and closed her eyes. If only her interview were over. Even if she didn't get hired, it'd be better than this uncertainty.

Suddenly Daniel's handsome face floated before her eyes. Before he left for Emporia on Saturday morning he'd taken her hands and smiled that wonderful, breath-catching smile. His words came back with clarity now. "I'm looking forward to seeing you in a Harvey Girl uniform. I'll be praying for you next Monday morning."

Elise opened her eyes and sat forward. Daniel was praying for her. She wasn't sure what good it would do. God hadn't answered her prayers lately! Even so, she was glad Daniel had confidence in her. He wanted to see as a Harvey Girl. She smiled.

Elise picked up a magazine from the table beside her, just as Tessa opened the door. She had a huge grin and her eyes shone. "I made it. You can, too."

When Elise's name was called, she took a steadying breath and rose to her feet. Miss McGuire was tall and thin, about the age of Elise's mother. She held the door open and gave Elise a friendly appraisal. "Hello, Elise. My name is Grace McGuire." She indicated the red cushioned chair in front of her desk. "I trust you have had a good weekend."

Elise sat on the edge of the chair. "Yes, thank you, it was very nice."

Grace chuckled as she walked to the chair behind the desk and sat down. "I daresay it would have been better if you had not had to think about this interview."

"Yes, ma'am." Elise looked up in surprise.

Grace's eyes twinkled as she picked up several papers from her desk. "Elise, I was impressed by your answers on the application. What are your feelings? Do you still want to be a Harvey Girl?" She handed Elise a sheet of paper. "We have strict rules and regulations. Mr. Harvey will not put up with anyone who will not abide by them."

Elise scanned the list. She knew them by memory. She lifted her chin and looked Grace in the eyes. "Yes, ma'am, I want to be a Harvey Girl; and I'm willing to abide by the rules."

"You will sign a year contract. You must promise not to

marry in that year. There is a strict curfew in the dormitories, and every Harvey Girl is expected to wear the uniform and hairstyle outlined in detail by Fred Harvey."

"Yes, ma'am. I've thought a lot about this, and I'm prepared to follow the regulations."

Grace smiled. "I felt certain you would." She laid the prepared contract on the desk indicating the line for Elise's signature. "You may visit with your family today, but you will be expected in Topeka tomorrow morning on the seven-thirty train to settle into the dormitory and get fitted for your uniform. Training starts Wednesday morning. The first month will be without pay. Thereafter, you will earn $17.50 each month plus any tips you receive. You should always refer to yourself as a Harvey Girl."

Elise glanced up from the contract. "The first month is without pay?"

Grace nodded. "That will be your training period. Your first paycheck will be at the end of July."

Two months! Two months before she would have money to send home. Dismay filled Elise as she stared at the contract. She hadn't counted on that, but there wasn't any other choice. She signed her name on the line.

"If it's alright, I'll go on to Topeka today. I don't have any family here."

"Of course, you may go. The next train leaves at one-thirty-five." Grace gave Elise a kind, motherly look. "That will give you time to check your bags and eat dinner. Tell the ticket agent you have been hired. Harvey Girls always ride free on the Santa Fe."

"Thank you very much." Elise stood and walked to the door.

In the hallway, she looked both ways to make sure no one was around then gave a little skip causing her skirt to swing around her ankles. She'd made it! She'd been hired. She wouldn't go home a failure. It'd be better if she was paid sooner, but she had a job.

She composed herself as she walked down the stairway.

Tessa waited at the bottom. "Your eyes are shining. You made it, didn't you?" She clasped her hands. "I'm so glad. I was afraid I'd have to go by myself. I feel like I know someone now. Do you think they'll let us be roommates?"

Elise laughed at Tessa's exuberance. "I hope so. At any rate I'm sure we'll be friends."

"We sure will." Tessa turned to walk toward the depot door. "Come on, let's get our baggage checked and get some dinner."

Elise felt ravenous. Her stomach had been too queasy to eat breakfast.

～～

Elise clenched her hands in her lap and pressed her nose against the passenger car window as the train passed the first few houses on the outskirts of Topeka. A thrill of excitement rushed over her. She was finally a Harvey Girl. When the conductor passed through earlier taking orders for the Topeka Harvey House, she and Tessa proudly told him they'd be working there.

The train slowed and rolled closer to the depot. A large sign, which hung over the main door of the building, read TOPEKA. For a month, at least, she'd be living and working in this red frame, two-story building.

"What does it look like? Is it as big as the Kansas City station?" Tessa leaned over Elise to look out the window.

"No. It's not that big, but it looks pretty busy."

Tessa settled back as the train came to a halt with a long blast from the whistle and a screech of brakes. Elise glanced at the sun still high in the western sky. "We can move in this evening then we won't be rushed in the morning." She picked up her carpetbag and followed Tessa to the exit. "My brother, Arnaud, should be here somewhere. I want you to meet him."

"I'm looking forward to it."

"From the way he was talking over the weekend, he has a new girlfriend; the head waitress in the Harvey House dining room. She must be special for Arnaud to care for her." She grinned. "It's hard to picture him with a girl. He's never shown much interest in women."

Tessa gave an exaggerated sigh as they stepped off the train and walked across the tracks toward the building. "Just my luck. The good ones are already taken."

Elise chuckled and gave Tessa a friendly shove on the arm. "Oh, not necessarily. I hear the prairies are full of them if you're interested. I'm not." She wrinkled her nose at the pungent smell of horse droppings mingled with the smoke from the locomotive.

"Oh yeah, what about this Daniel you've been talking about? Not interested, huh?" Tessa grinned. "Do you think I believe that?"

"That's why I'm not interested in the ones on the prairie."

A loud, metallic, clanging sound caught their attention. A bellboy on the platform beat repeated strikes on a large gong. "Right this way to the Harvey House dining and lunchroom." His voice boomed across the train yard.

The girls joined the stream of passengers headed for the main depot. "Do we go to the dining room now?" Tessa hesitated when they reached the steps to the platform. She moved aside for a group of elegantly dressed ladies and gentlemen that descended to board the train.

"Let's go to the main desk. Maybe Arnaud will be there. If not, the ticket agent can direct us."

Tessa brushed Elise's arm as they started up the steps. "Look at that bay window, and there's a balcony over the door. This is a fancy building."

Elise nodded and looked in the direction Tessa pointed as they reached the top step. Consternation spread through her as her gaze met her cousin Jerome's surprised expression. He was standing next to the bay window in earnest conversation with two well-dressed gentlemen. She stopped abruptly, which caused the man behind her to bump her forward. Apprehension shivered up Elise's spine as Jerome gave her a pleased smirk. What was he doing?

Elise apologized to the man behind her, then grabbed Tessa's arm and hurried into the depot. She looked over her shoulder to make certain Jerome hadn't followed them.

The girls strode across the depot lobby and took a place in the line at the ticket counter behind an older couple. Someone touched Elise's arm. Startled, she swung her bag and smacked Arnaud on the shin.

"Hey, watch what you're doing with that thing. You could hurt someone." He grinned as he took it from her.

"Oh, Arnaud, I'm glad to see you." Elise gave him a hug. "We weren't sure where we were supposed to go."

Arnaud turned her to face the lady beside him. "Here's someone who can tell you. Elise, this is Millie Petersen."

Millie stepped forward. Her sapphire eyes shone with life. "Hello, Elise, Arnaud has talked about you so much, I feel I already know you." Her soft voice and friendly manner seemed to enfold Elise in a blanket of acceptance.

"Hello, Millie. I've wanted to meet you, too." Elise reached to take Millie's outstretched hand. Although dressed in the black and white uniform of the Harvey girl, Millie was elegant. Her golden hair framed classic facial features and the uniform enhanced her figure.

Elise turned to her friend. "Tessa, this is my brother, Arnaud, and this is Millie, the head Harvey Girl for this house." Elise almost giggled at Tessa's wide-eyed, awestruck expression.

"Arnaud and Millie, this is Tessa Gillespie. She's my new friend and a new Harvey Girl. We met this morning while we waited for our interviews."

Millie smiled and shook Tessa's hand. "Come along. I'll show you to your room." She motioned them to follow her across the lobby. "Arnaud, would you get another man to help you carry these ladies' trunks? We'll meet you upstairs."

The two girls followed Millie up the elegant wooden staircase at the opposite end of the lobby. The crystal chandeliers sparkled. Elise ran her hand along the smooth surface of the banister as they ascended the stairs. The unmistakable aroma of fresh baked bread wafted through the air. It reminded her of home.

The entrance to the dining room was on the other side of the foyer at the top of the stairs, but Millie led them through a door on the left. "This is our living quarters. Tomorrow I'll show you more."

They walked through a tastefully decorated parlor and down a corridor with doors on each side to a room near the end. "You'll have to share this room for now. I hope that's alright."

Both girls nodded.

"It sure is alright. We wanted to be together." Tessa gave a little bounce.

The cabbage roses in the carpet pattern appeared to come alive in the swathe of sunlight that flooded through the west window. Elise and Tessa entered the room. Elise stared around stunned by the beauty. A bed and dresser were situated on each side of the room and a double-sided wardrobe sat left of the doorway.

"Oh, it's beautiful." Elise dropped her bag on the bed and twirled to give Tessa a hug. "Isn't it wonderful?"

Tessa stood transfixed. "I've never seen anything like it."

Millie sat on the other bed. "You'll find that Fred Harvey takes care of his Harvey Girls. As long as you do your work, he'll provide your needs."

Elise ran her hand over the polished surface of the dresser and fingered the intricate flower pattern on the pitcher and bowl of the dresser set. "Someone needs to pinch me so I know this isn't a dream."

"Oh, it's not a dream. You'll find out when you start work. You'll earn your keep." Millie stood and walked to the door. "I heard Arnaud's voice. I'll go direct them here." A few minutes later, she motioned the two men into the room.

"What do you have in this thing, Elise? It must weigh a ton."

Elise giggled. "Just about everything I own."

Arnaud scanned the room. "Where do you want it?"

Elise gestured toward the right. "Put it here at the foot of the bed. Is that alright, Tessa?"

At her nod, Arnaud lugged the trunk over and set it down. The other young man placed Tessa's trunk by the other bed.

Millie shooed the fellows from the room then faced Elise and Tessa. "You girls will be on your own. The evening train arrives at five-twenty, so I have to be on duty at five." She smiled. "When you get unpacked and freshened up a bit, come over to the lunchroom for supper." She looked in the mirror over the dresser and re-pinned a wayward curl. "Tomorrow, four more new girls will arrive. We'll go over the rules, issue uniforms and show you around then." She gave them both a cheerful smile and headed toward the door. "I better go."

After the door was shut, Elise sat on the bed and rummaged in her bag. "Now where did I put that trunk key? Oh, yes, I put it in my hand bag." She pulled it out and knelt beside her trunk.

Tessa walked across the room and sat on the other bed. "Elise, I've never had a room like this. I've always shared a bed with my four sisters."

Elise sat back on her heels. "You shared a bed with your four sisters? How did you all fit in one bed?"

Tessa grinned. "We slept across the bed sideways. I don't know if I'll like sleeping by myself. I was lonely last night."

Elise laughed. "Well, stay out of my bed."

"All right." Tessa chuckled timidly. "I'll stay in my own bed." She jumped up, opened her trunk and began to put her things away. She kept her back to Elise but it didn't disguise her sniffs or the tears that she wiped away.

Elise sorted and put away her own clothes. She was close to tears.

Chapter 10

The next morning, Elise awoke and rolled over to stare at the unfamiliar room. There it was again. The sound of the train whistle blasted through the morning air. The smell of coal smoke drifted through the open window. She sat up and threw off her blanket. The shadows outside indicated that the sun was up. What time was it? Were the other girls on that train?

Elise looked at Tessa. Curled in a ball, hugging her pillow, she was still sound asleep. Elise leaned over and shook her. "Tessa, get up. I just heard a train whistle. The other girls may be here."

Tessa rolled over with a groan. She still clutched her pillow. "Um...wha'd you say?" She opened her eyes a crack then closed them again.

"I said we better get up. The other girls may be here."

Tessa's eyes flew open, and she sat up in bed. "Oh, I forgot where we were. I was dreaming about my family. I didn't think I'd be able to sleep a wink last night, but I did." She jumped up and began to dress. "I need to hurry. We don't want to be late on our first day."

"I know, me too." Elise brushed her hair and twisted it into a soft bun at the nape of her neck in the same fashion Millie wore.

Thirty minutes later, the girls made their way down the hall toward the dining room. "What do you think the other girls will be like? I hope we all get along." Tessa pulled her handkerchief from her pocket and wiped her forehead.

Elise patted her on the back. "We'll do fine, I'm sure."

They waited as Millie greeted a couple and took them to a table. The dining room hummed with the conversations of the early morning train passengers, and the delectable aroma of bacon and eggs filled the air. Elise's stomach growled, and Tessa giggled.

Millie walked toward them. "Hi, Tessa, Elise, I see you made it up alright. The other girls just arrived on the train." She motioned with her hand toward the smaller room on the left. "Why don't you go into the lunchroom and get breakfast. We'll start orientation after morning rush."

Elise looked around. "Millie, is Arnaud still here?"

Millie shook her head. "No, he said to tell you good-bye.

He had to leave this morning on the New Mexico run. He won't be back for a week."

Elise and Tessa walked into the lunchroom. The large circular counter nearly filled the middle of the room. Elise stopped for a moment and watched the Harvey Girls as they served customers. She followed Tessa toward two empty stools nearest them. As they walked closer Elise drew in her breath. The man who sat next to the empty seat had sandy, blond hair, the same color as Daniel's. He turned, and she looked into his wonderful azure eyes.

Excitement bubbled up in Elise. "Daniel, I didn't expect you back so soon. Is everything okay?"

Daniel stood. He took her elbow and assisted her into the seat next to him. "Yes. Everything's fine." He sat back down. "I hoped I'd see you this morning. I talked to Arnaud last night. He said you'd arrived." He grinned, boyishly. "I knew you'd be hired. I've been praying for you."

"Oh, Daniel, have you?" Elise's heart was pounding so hard she thought he would hear it. "How are Elizabeth and Lucia? Did they get settled in at the ranch?"

"They're okay. I just hope Mom can handle Elizabeth." Daniel frowned and took a drink of coffee. "Lucia decided to stay for now. I pray she'll continue on. Mom needs her help."

Tessa cleared her throat and punched Elise in the ribs with her elbow. "You going to introduce me?"

Elise felt her face grow warm as she turned to her friend. "I'm sorry, Tessa. This is Daniel. You remember, I told you, he's Arnaud's friend. He came out to our farm with Arnaud after Mama died. I also met him on the train to Kansas City from Columbia."

"I remember." Tessa reached around Elise to shake hands with Daniel. "Glad to meet you. I'm Tessa Gillespie. I'm also a new Harvey Girl. Elise and I met at the interview, and now we're roommates."

Daniel smiled. "I'm glad to meet you, Tessa."

"May I help you?" One of the Harvey Girls had laid menus in front of Elise and Tessa and waited to take their orders.

"Yes. I'll have the ham and egg special and a cup of coffee." Elise smiled up at her.

Tessa nodded. "I'll have the same."

When she left, Tessa leaned over. "That's what we'll be doing tomorrow, Elise."

"I know." Elise watched the Harvey Girl as she delivered their order.

Daniel placed his knife and fork on his plate, pushed it back, then picked up his coffee cup. "I'm not concerned about you. You'll do great."

Elise wrinkled her nose at him. "Oh, sure. I'll probably pour coffee in someone's lap."

Tessa shuddered. "Don't even mention it."

Daniel laughed. "You girls will be alright." He set his coffee cup on his plate and swiveled his stool toward Elise, his expression serious. "Elise, I hoped we could spend some time together, but I need to go to Kansas City today. I have to contact one of the fellows on my survey team. I'll be back by Friday afternoon to meet with William Strong. Do you think we could have supper together Friday evening?"

A thrill of pleasure shot through Elise. "I...I don't know, I'll have to ask to be sure, but I'd like to."

Daniel let out his breath. "Would six thirty be okay?"

"I'll check. How can I let you know?"

He captured her gaze with his for a brief moment. "Leave a message at the Windsor Hotel. I have a room there." At her nod, he stood. "I better go now. I have a train to catch. I'll look forward to Friday evening."

As Daniel walked toward the door, Tessa grabbed Elise's arm. "Wow! And you thought he wouldn't remember you? I don't think you have to worry about that. But I would suggest you come back to earth. Your breakfast is here, and the other girls just walked in."

Elise glanced around. Millie waved the other four girls toward empty stools at the counter.

Later, Millie directed them all into the parlor. Elise looked around with interest. The morning sun streamed through the east window of the large room highlighting the fashionable rosewood and mahogany sofas and wing chairs. The olive and buff brocade upholstery looked soft and inviting. An oval marble-top table sat in front of the sofa. Ornate gaslights flanked a large Currier and Ives print that depicted a train crossing the vast prairie, a pioneer village, covered wagons and Indians.

Millie read the house rules then asked the girls to introduce themselves. Elise listened carefully as she tried to remember each name: Carolyn, Abigail, Dorothea and Isabel. When the girls had introduced themselves, Millie spoke again. "You'll observe proper procedure in the dining room for a few days to get familiar with the Harvey House routine. But you will start your training at the lunch counter." She scanned the room. "You'll not work in the dining room, except to serve drinks, until you've served the manager a meal and he feels you can do it right. We have a definite standard to uphold. It can take up to two months or more to work in the dining room." She paused dramatically, a twinkle in her eye. "Now, it's time for you to get your uniforms." An audible ripple of excitement pervaded the room as Millie continued. "You will each be issued two. After you receive them, you will go to your rooms, put one on then gather in the dining room to meet the other girls."

Later, Elise stood in front of the mirror in her room. Pride and anticipation rushed through her as she slipped on the black skirt and blouse. "We've finally made it, Tessa. We look like Harvey Girls." She fitted the white collar around her neck.

"I know. I have to pinch myself to make sure it's true." Tessa sat on her bed to put on the black stockings and shoes.

Elise tied her white apron strings then looked at her feet. "Is the skirt the right length?"

"It looks alright to me. We'll know when they measure them." Tessa raised her chin at an imperious angle and repeated in a monotone, "The skirts must be exactly eight inches from the floor, and the aprons must be kept spotless white. If you get a blemish on your uniform, you must change immediately."

Elise burst into laughter. Tessa joined in. It was several moments before they could catch their breath. "Oh, Tessa... you're perfect. You'd make a perfect head waitress." She checked her hair in the mirror. "We'd better go. We don't want to be late."

Each of the new girls was assigned to an experienced Harvey Girl for the training period. Elise was excited when paired with Kate, a friendly, petite blonde. During the lunch rush, Elise was amazed at the efficiency of the Harvey Girls as they moved from patron to patron quickly filling their orders. In less time than seemed possible, the train crowd was fed and on their way to the next destination. Apprehension gripped her midsection. Could she learn the routine? Would she make a horrible mistake, perhaps dump food on someone? She held the back of a chair as Kate explained the fine points of cleaning the tables. Kate was efficient and conscientious.

When Tessa and Elise returned to their room, they hung

their uniforms in the wardrobe and sat on their beds. Elise pulled her legs under her and rested her elbows on her knees. "What did you think of the first day?"

Tessa made a comical face. "It was alright. But I'm afraid I'll make a terrible blunder, get lost, or forget something I'm supposed to do."

"I know, like stumble with a tray full of dishes." Elise grimaced.

Tessa shuddered. "Let's not talk about it or I'll be certain to do it." She walked to the dresser, picked up the white china pitcher and poured a glass of water. "Here's to our new job."

The next morning, Elise awoke to Tessa patting her shoulder. "You better get up. We have to be at work in thirty minutes."

Elise rolled over and groaned. It was still dark outside. She dragged herself from bed and splashed water on her face. "I'm glad we are observing today. I'm not ready to be on my own yet." Her spirits lifted as she dressed in her new uniform and put her hair up. This was what she had looked forward to.

After a hurried breakfast, the girls scattered to their assigned stations. Elise followed Kate to the dining room. "These are our tables." Kate pointed to two tables with eight chairs each toward the back of the room near the kitchen. "According to the telegraphed order, all the places will be full."

Kate arranged the silverware, cup and saucer, water glass and perfectly folded linen napkin. "Each piece has to be placed just so. Many things must be done the Harvey way so they'll be consistent in all Harvey Houses." Kate grinned as she gave a mock shudder. "You'll find it very unpleasant if Fred Harvey shows up and finds anything out of place: a chipped plate, a spotted water glass or a soiled napkin. He's been known to pull the whole setting off onto the floor, tablecloth and all, and make you do it again."

She chuckled at Elise's horrified expression. "Don't worry. You'll soon learn everything. I didn't think I could when I first started, but I have."

As Kate set the tables Elise quickly picked up the pattern. Soon every place in their section was set with the folded napkin in place and an attractive fruit plate in the center.

"There's a different menu each day. They're sent out by headquarters every four days." Kate handed the current one to Elise. "The aim is to ensure that a traveler will not see the same choices during their travel."

"One more thing you need to know: the drink code." Kate picked up a coffee cup. "When Millie seats the customers she'll ask each one what they want to drink, then she'll place their cup in position. A cup right side up in the saucer means coffee; upside down, hot tea; upside down and tilted against the saucer, iced tea; upside down and off the saucer, milk." She demonstrated as she talked.

"Whoa, wait a minute." Elise waved her hand in the air.

"How am I supposed to remember all that?"

"You'll pick it up." Kate spoke, confidently. "It's fun to watch people's expressions when they try to figure out how you know what they want to drink." She smiled at Elise's worried look. "Rebecca will be assigned to drinks today, watch her. You'll soon understand."

The gong sounded, and people streamed into the dining room. Elise watched as Kate took the food orders. Mentally rehearsing the drink code, she smiled at the bewildered expressions on the customer's' faces as Rebecca filled their glasses and cups without asking their preferences.

The manager entered the dining room with a large tray balanced on one hand high above his head. He lowered it to a small stand beside the table and Kate distributed the orders to the diners. A common order consisted of steak and eggs with a large serving of hash brown potatoes. Another was a stack of pancakes with fresh butter melting on top and maple syrup spilling down the sides. Some people, with hearty appetites, even had apple pie with coffee for dessert.

As the first group finished their meals, Kate removed the dishes and reset the places. The local townspeople, who had waited until after the train rush for a more leisurely meal, filled their emptied places. Elise was amazed at how smoothly the morning went, but she knew it would be a lot harder to actually work than to observe.

Soon only a few stragglers remained to drink coffee and visit. Kate cleaned everything from the morning and prepared the tables for the noon meal.

Millie walked into the dining room. "Well, what do you think after observing your first train rush?"

Elise shook her head. "I don't think I'll ever be able to do all that."

"Sure you will." Millie put her hand on Kate's shoulder. "Before long you'll be as efficient as Kate." She smiled at Elise. "Now let's go into the lunchroom. We're going to work on table settings for a while."

So it went the rest of the day. There was little time for resting. After Kate cleared the tables following the evening meal Elise sat wearily on one of the chairs. "I don't think I can do this." She rubbed her aching neck muscles. "How do you keep going? I'm beat and I just observed. There is so much to remember."

Kate sat across from her. "I felt the same way my first day, but I promise you'll survive, and you'll be a great Harvey Girl. Get some rest. Tomorrow will be better."

Too tired to argue, Elise met Tessa and they trudged to their room together. Elise couldn't remember being so exhausted. Her bed would feel wonderful.

The week passed quickly. They worked morning to night, observing and learning. Elise soon felt more at ease with the

Harvey House routines. She was convinced she would never catch up on her sleep. Her new shoes rubbed blisters on her feet, and the kitchen crew delighted in teasing her and the other new girls.

CHAPTER 11

Friday afternoon, Daniel stood in William Strong's office and studied the map on the table. "When do you want us to start the survey?"

Strong leaned against the map table and watched Daniel trace his finger across the Indian Territory south of Arkansas City, Kansas. "Can you be ready by June fifteenth?" He looked at the calendar. "That's about three weeks."

Daniel hesitated. "I should be able to get everything together by then." That was two weeks earlier than he'd planned. "I do need to find someone to replace Baxter. He signed with the Missouri Pacific. I spent most of this week trying to locate a replacement."

Strong pounded his fist on the map table. "That yellow-bellied, two-timer. We'll find you someone better." His eyes snapped with anger. "Schroeder still available?"

Daniel nodded. "Abe's as dependable as the sun."

"Good. You take care of getting your supplies and equipment together. I'll have you a man." William slapped Daniel on the back as they walked toward the door. "Keep me informed."

Daniel sighed as he left the office. Only three weeks to spend with Elise before he had to leave. As he hurried past the dining room he glanced in, but didn't see any sign of her. He pulled his watch from his pocket, flipped it open and checked the time. Five-thirty. He was supposed to meet her for dinner at six-thirty. That is, if she'd left a message that she could see him.

His long legged stride carried him rapidly along the brick sidewalk toward the hotel. He'd arrived in Topeka barely in time for his interview with Strong. Now he'd have to hurry.

Daniel grinned ruefully as he broke into a jog. It was just his luck to meet the sweetest, prettiest girl west of the Mississippi and have to leave for the wilderness. Heaviness settled around his heart. How would he tell her he'd have to leave so soon?

With a nimble leap, he took the two steps of the hotel porch in one bound and walked into the lobby. "Leroy, any messages?"

"Hi, Mr. Gilbertson. Good to have you back." Leroy nodded. "As a matter of fact, you do have a message." The desk clerk grinned as he pulled his handkerchief out of his back pocket. He mopped the sweat from his brow before he turned to retrieve an envelope from the pigeonhole box behind him. "That was a right pretty little number brought it in." He handed it over the counter. "Hope it's good news."

"I hope so too." Daniel took the note. "Would you send some water to my room? I need to freshen up."

Leroy straightened from leaning on the registration desk. "Sure thing. I'll send one of the boys."

"Thanks." Daniel tore open the envelope as he climbed the steps to his room. The short message made him light-headed with relief.

Friday

Daniel,

I wanted to let you know that I will be able to have supper with you this evening. I don't get off work until six o'clock so I may be a little late getting ready. I hope you don't mind. I can meet you in the Harvey House parlor.

Your friend,

Elise

"Must'a been a good message." Daniel turned. Leroy was watching him, a grin nearly splitting his thin face.

"Yes, as a matter of fact, it was." Daniel couldn't help smiling back.

"One of them Harvey Girls? I hear there's some new ones come in this week. Dumond's sister is one of 'em."

Daniel glared at him. "Don't you get any wrong ideas about those girls."

"Ah, I know. I'd never have a chance with any of 'em. You have to wear a coat to even get in the door." Leroy moved from behind the desk and headed for the back room. "I'll send your water up."

Daniel sprinted to the second floor two steps at a time. One of the Harvey Girls was Arnaud Dumond's sister, and Leroy better keep his hands off. He opened the door to his room, walked in and stared at himself in the mirror over the bureau.

"You fool, you know there's no future in this. What can you expect to offer a lady like Elise?" Months on end away from home with no way to let her know where he was. She deserved the best of everything, and he was in no position to give her that. He ran his fingers through his hair. Why had he let himself get so emotionally involved?

He shrugged as his mind shifted to his meeting with Elise on the train. He hadn't had any choice. When she looked into his eyes, his heart started pounding and he couldn't turn away. Those beautiful golden, hazel eyes, as fresh and innocent as a summer day, had captivated him.

Aware of her confusion and look of vulnerability, he had focused his attention on Elizabeth. But he knew in those few fleeting moments that he wanted to become much better acquainted with Elise Dumond.

A knock on the door pulled Daniel's attention back to the present. A young boy delivered the water he had ordered.

Excitement filled Elise as she glanced at her watch. "Hurry, Tessa, it's already twenty minutes 'til seven." Tessa pushed the last pins into Elise's hair.

"Relax, he'll wait. You told him you'd be a little late." Tessa surveyed the light blue dress Elise wore and straightened a ruffle. "You need to be perfect for this evening."

Elise looked in the mirror over the vanity. Tessa had brought her hair up in the back leaving some of the long dark curls to hang over her right shoulder. "Thank you, Tessa. it's beautifully done. Where did you learn to fix hair?"

"I have five sisters, you know." Tessa grinned and pushed her toward the bed. "Now get your shoes on and you'll be ready."

Elise grimaced as she pulled on her dress shoes and buttoned them. Aching blisters were reminders of long hours spent on her feet during the first week. She giggled. "I hope I can walk without hobbling like an old lady."

Millie stepped in as Elise moved toward the door. "Are you ready? Daniel's waiting in the parlor." She had a twinkle in her eyes. "I noticed he got a lot of interested looks from some of the other girls."

"They better stay away." Elise hugged Millie. "Thanks for letting me be with him this evening."

Millie nodded. "Spend your off hours as you wish; just don't forget ten o'clock curfew."

"I won't." Elise hurried out the door and down the hall toward the parlor. She hadn't been able to concentrate all day. She'd wondered what Daniel was doing and if he would make it back in time.

Elise paused in the doorway and scanned the parlor. The gaslights highlighted the Currier and Ives pictures on the walls. Another couple sat on one of the brocade upholstered sofas situated around the room.

Her heart skipped a beat when she located Daniel. He stood in front of a window and conversed with another man. The afternoon sunlight highlighted his neatly groomed hair and tanned skin. He looked handsome in a crisp white shirt, with the sleeves rolled to his mid-forearm, and brown slacks.

As Elise walked into the room, Daniel glanced her direction and stopped mid-sentence. Elise's pulses quickened at the expression of admiration that crossed his face.

Daniel found it hard to breathe. He excused himself, grabbed his coat from a nearby chair and strode across the parlor toward Elise. Each time he saw her, she was more beautiful than the last. What was happening to him? He rolled down his sleeves and reached for her hand. "You look wonderful. Working a week as a Harvey Girl must not have been too hard on you."

A small giggle escaped Elise. "You can't see my sore muscles and the blisters on my feet."

A concerned look crossed Daniel's face. "Has it been bad?"

"No." Elise placed her hand in his. "I like the work. I just need to get used to it. I'm not accustomed to standing on my feet for twelve hours at a time."

Daniel frowned. "I can understand that. I hope you're not sorry I suggested that you come." He slipped on his coat and offered her his elbow as they walked to the door.

Elise laughed lightly. "Oh no. I'm glad you did."

After Millie escorted them to a table, Daniel gazed at Elise. The urge to touch her dark curls was almost irresistible. "You know, I still haven't seen you in uniform."

Elise looked at the menu then glanced up. "There will be plenty of time for that. You'll probably get tired of seeing me in it."

Daniel shook his head and studied his menu as another Harvey Girl came to pour their coffee. If only there was more time.

That evening, after they ate a delicious meal of baked ham and yams with strawberry pie, Elise and Daniel walked to the park across from the depot. The sun was still in the western sky, and the scent of honeysuckle wafted on a soft breeze. In the middle of the park, a small fountain merrily spouted water into the air.

Daniel brushed some leaves off a nearby bench and then sat beside Elise. He turned to face her and smiled gently. "Elise, I'm glad I came to your farm in March. If I hadn't, I might never have met you. I wouldn't have seen your magnificent leap across the yard."

~~~

Elise pursed her lips and felt her face grow warm. "I'd like to forget that. I don't know why you'd ever want to see me again after the way I acted that day, but I'm glad you did."

Daniel sobered. "You had a lot on your mind. I respect how you handled everything as well as you did."

Elise touched his hand. "It helped to have you there."

Daniel rotated his hand to capture hers. "By the way, how is Star Fire?"

Elise curled her fingers through his. It felt so right to have her hand nestled in Daniel's large warm one. "Star Fire is doing fine. She'll soon be as big as her mother."

Elise considered Daniel's face, suddenly aware of his closeness and the intense light in his azure eyes. Her breath caught in her throat and her heart pounded. She pulled her hand away, surprised at her reaction. "I...I wish you could see her."

"I do too, but there's not much chance for a while." Daniel hesitated, his gaze holding hers. "I found out today that I leave on June fifteenth for the survey trip. I hoped it would be the end of the month."

June fifteenth was just three weeks away. Elise clasped her hands in her lap. He would be gone before they even got to know each other. She cleared the lump in her throat and turned away. Maybe it was best. Her initial attraction had begun to develop into deeper feelings. It would hurt to see him leave if they spent a lot of time together. She noticed how his shoulders slumped. "Don't you want to go? I thought you enjoyed your work."

Daniel nodded as he sat up and looked at her. "I do like my work. I'm just not ready to leave this time. I've just begun to get acquainted with you." He grinned. "I'm going to have to thrash Arnaud because he didn't introduce us sooner."

The setting sun silhouetted Daniel's head and turned his sandy blond hair into a halo. Elise gazed at him. He was so strong and caring. She wanted to know him better, a lot better.

She reached out and touched his arm. "I know it's not very long, but we do still have a little time." She tried to laugh, but it came out more as a strangled cough.

"You're right. We need to make the most of what we have." He covered her hand with his. Raising it to his lips, he kissed her fingertips. Elise smiled as a delicious shiver ran down her arm. "I hate to tell you this, but I have to go in." She looked at her watch. "It's nine-forty-five. Ten o'clock curfew, you know." She wrinkled her nose, making him laugh.

Daniel stood and pulled her up beside him. He held her hand as they walked back to the Harvey House.

The next morning Elise glanced at the door as she finished refilling a cup of coffee for a customer. Millie was directing Daniel toward her section of the lunchroom counter.

As Daniel slipped onto the stool, his gaze captured Elise's. Her heart did a fast two-step at the sight of his freshly groomed, good looks. The scent of his shaving soap mingled with the fresh coffee aroma. "Good morning. I finally get to see you in uniform." He smiled appreciatively. "You look great. But then I knew you would."

"Thank you. I'm glad you approve." She lifted the coffee pot. "Would you like a cup of coffee?" At his nod, she turned his cup over and filled it.

Later after Daniel had eaten his meal, Elise returned to pour a refill.

"Thank you." He picked up the cup. "I guess I'll go back out to the ranch today to tell my parents when I'm leaving. Since Mary died, Mom's been pretty upset." He took a sip of coffee. "I should be back on Monday to get supplies together for the trip. Would you like to do something Monday evening, or can you on weekday nights?"

"My evenings are free after the evening meal as long as I'm in by curfew." A lightness filled her. "I'd be delighted to see you on Monday evening." She hesitated. "Millie is planning a picnic at the river next Saturday night for the Harvey Girls and their friends. Would you like to go?"

"Yes. I'd like that." Elise was amazed at the intensity of emotion in his deep blue eyes.

Daniel swallowed the last of his coffee and rose to leave, Elise leaned against the counter. "I'll be thinking about you, Daniel. I know it'll be hard on your parents to see you go and hard on you to leave them."

Daniel covered her hand with his. "Thanks, Elise. I appreciate that." The train whistle blew. "See you Monday."

Elise watched as he walked from the room. A painful lump lodged midway between her heart and her throat.

Sunday morning Elise awoke with a start, threw back the sheet and sat up on the side of the bed. It was growing lighter outside. If she and Tessa didn't hurry, they would be late to work.

Moments later, she sagged with relief. *This was her day off!* With a sigh she rolled back onto the bed and pulled up the sheet. She turned on her side, wadded her pillow under her head and stared out the window. Events of the week flooded her mind. From her interview on Monday to the moment she had fallen into bed last night, the week had been incredibly full and exhausting. It had been hard to concentrate on her work after she'd talked to Daniel in the lunchroom Saturday morning. How could her feelings for him be so intense in such a short time? The thought of his departure made her despondent.

Elise punched her pillow. She needed to concentrate on her new job. She'd signed a contract for a year. That would be an eternity.

The next thing Elise knew, Tessa shook her awake. "Get up. It's time for breakfast. Are you going to church?" She walked to the window. "I saw the prettiest little church building down the street. It'd do us good to go after this wild week."

Elise opened her eyes and shook her head. "You go on. I'm going to sleep this morning." She rolled over and buried her head in the pillow. "I'll go next Sunday."

"Are you sure? It's a beautiful day. I think you'll regret it if you miss out."

Elise lay still. She pretended to sleep as Tessa dressed. Guilt stabbed her. Of course, she should go. She'd never missed a Sunday in her life that she could remember. Mama would be sad to know she didn't want to go. Besides, she was already wide-awake.

She threw back the sheet and sat up with a groan. "Oh, all right. I suppose I better go." She dressed and brushed her hair.

"Come on. We can finish primping when we get back from breakfast." Tessa walked toward the door as Elise placed the last pins in her hair. "Millie said we could walk to church with her. She's off work this morning."

An hour later, the three girls left the depot. The warm morning sunshine greeted them as they stepped outside. A slight cooling breeze blew from the north and the fresh scent of dew on new mown grass filled the air.

"Aren't you glad you decided to come?" Tessa bumped Elise with her elbow.

"Yes, I'm glad." Elise nodded as she watched the fleecy clouds floating in the azure sky. The color made her think of Daniel's eyes.

The small white church reminded Elise of the one in Pickens with its bell tower and stained glass windows. Sadness enveloped her as she glanced at the tree-shaded cemetery behind the church. It awakened memories of Papa and Mama's deaths. She was glad they were together in heaven, even if God had forsaken their children.

The three friends entered the cool foyer and shook hands with the pastor. Tessa and Elise followed Millie to a pew near the front where some other girls from the Harvey House were already sitting. Warm air wafted in the open windows and sunlight streamed through the beautiful stained glass. One at the front of the church depicted Jesus as the Good Shepherd.

Elise had given her life to Jesus Christ in a church much like this at the age of eleven. Somehow, she'd lost the joy of that relationship since her parents' deaths.

Everyone stood to sing the first hymn. Elise looked up the page number in her hymnal, "*Savior Like a Shepherd Lead Us*". Was the Savior leading her? Ha! Hardly.

As the pastor stood to give the Bible reading for the day, Elise listened to the words of Psalm 23. *"The Lord is my Shepherd; I shall not want. He maketh me to lie down in green pastures: He leadeth me beside the still waters. He restoreth my soul: ...*

Elise's thoughts lingered on verse five. *Thou preparest a table before me in the presence of mine enemies: thou anointest my head with oil; my cup runneth over...* She smiled to herself. A table in the presence of her enemies. Could that be a Harvey House in Kansas? Elise shook her head at her own thoughts. Daniel and Arnaud had been the ones to suggest she become a Harvey Girl. Not likely that God had anything to do with it!

CHAPTER 12

Under Kate's supervision, Elise worked her own area of the lunch counter on Monday. She watched the door for Daniel's return as she served her customers. In the noon train rush, he walked into the lunchroom with the other passengers and seated himself in her section.

Elise felt a thrill of pleasure when their eyes met. She smiled as she approached. "May I help you, sir?"

"Yes, as a matter of fact, I could use a garden salad, a turkey sandwich and a cup of coffee. I'm famished." The smile lines crinkled at the corners of his eyes. He lowered his voice. "You look beautiful in that uniform."

"Thank you." Elise's heart skipped a beat, and she felt her face grow warm as she turned to take the order from the next customer. The room seemed brighter since he'd walked in.

Elise returned a few minutes later with his sandwich and salad. "How was everything on the ranch? Are Elizabeth and Lucia getting along alright?"

"Elizabeth and Lucia are fine. In fact, they seem to be thriving in the country air." A shadow crossed Daniel's face as he spooned some dressing onto his salad. "Mom's heart is weaker. The doctor told her to avoid too much excitement." He grimaced. "She shouldn't have Elizabeth there, but she won't hear of anything else."

"I'm sorry about your mother's poor health. I imagine that makes it harder to leave."

Daniel gazed at her and grinned. "That's not the only thing that makes it hard to leave." He watched as she refilled his coffee cup. "You free this evening?"

Elise nodded. She nearly overfilled his cup as she glanced up. "I have to work until seven."

"Would you care to go for a walk in the park after you get off?"

Elise set the coffee pot on the counter. "I'd like that."

"Good. I'll meet you about seven-fifteen in the parlor if that's agreeable."

"I'll be there as soon as I can."

Daniel finished his sandwich. "Could you get me a piece of that raisin pie? Then I'd better be going. I have to get to work, or I'll never get done."

Daniel strode into the parlor that evening a few minutes after seven and dropped into a chair near the window. It felt good to relax after his harrowing afternoon.

When he'd taken the surveying equipment out of storage, the canvas covers were ruined by mildew. The local mercantile was out of the waterproof material needed to make new coverings, and it would take several days for them to get more. He'd have to go to Kansas City to purchase the material and have the covers made. He could also buy many of the other supplies and have them shipped while there.

He sat up and stared at Elise as she walked in. She wore a light green dress that enhanced the soft gold in her hazel eyes. Her hair was still styled in the Harvey Girl fashion.

Daniel walked toward her and held out his hand. "Good evening. How was work?"

"It was alright. I think I've adapted to the routine."

"Are you too tired for a walk? Would you rather stay here and talk?" Daniel felt intoxicated with the scent of roses floating around her.

"Oh, no. I've looked forward to getting out into the evening air. A walk will invigorate me." Elise placed her hand on Daniel's arm as they started toward the door. "How was your afternoon? Did you get a lot accomplished?"

Daniel grimaced and shook his head. "Not the way I'd

planned. The instruments weren't stored correctly, and the covers mildewed. Now I have to make a trip to Kansas City and get new ones made."

"Oh, no, Daniel. That'll put you behind, won't it?"

They'd descended the stairs and Daniel opened the depot door for her. "I can buy supplies and ship from there." He escorted her across the street to the park. "But I'd hoped to spend more time with you this week. I may be gone most of it." Regret filled his voice.

Daniel took her hand from his arm and held it in his. He entwined his fingers through hers, as they moved through the park. The evening warmth enveloped them as they strolled under the maple trees, content to be together. A cardinal perched above them chirped her sweet song before flying off to join her mate, and a mockingbird launched into his repertoire of music in a nearby Rose-of-Sharon bush.

Elise relaxed her shoulders. Her hand felt so right in Daniel's strong, capable grip. She didn't want him to let go. The clean scent of Daniel's shaving soap wafted toward her. Mingled with the earthy smell of sun-drenched grass and the sweet aroma of flowers from a nearby garden, it seemed the perfect complement to the evening.

As they approached the fountain, Daniel removed his handkerchief from his pocket with a flourish and placed it on the stone bench. "There you are, my lady." He bowed as he motioned for her to sit.

With an impish smile, Elise gave a mock curtsy before sitting on the handkerchief. "Thank you, most kind sir."

Daniel chuckled as he sat beside her. "Guess I have too much country in me to make a very good knight in shining armor."

Elise joined in his laughter. "Oh, I don't know. You do a pretty good job." She swiveled on the bench to face him as he stretched his legs and pushed the Levi's over his boot tops. "Daniel, tell me what you'll do when you go on the survey trip. I know you'll survey the new railroad line, but what all does that include?"

Daniel leaned forward, his hands clasped between his knees, and stared at the fountain. "It's hard to explain. We locate the straightest, most level route so the railroad tracks won't go up and down a lot of hills or around a lot of curves." He faced her. "We'll also lay out town sites every ten miles or so once we reach the Oklahoma Territory. When the territory is opened to settlers, they'll be ready. There's not much there now but rolling hills, jack rabbits, a few illegal settlers, Indians and outlaws. No telegraph, no towns, nothing." He shifted on the bench and sat up.

"Is it dangerous to go across the Indian lands?"

"It can be, but there are Cherokee ranchers who are happy

to have the railroad so they can ship their cattle. Hopefully, we can make contact with some of them."

"How long will you be gone?"

"I don't know, maybe two, three months, if the weather cooperates."

Elise's heart pounded, and she clasped her hands in her lap. Two or three months seemed like forever.

Twisting to face the fountain, Daniel placed his hands on the bench on either side of him. "It's never bothered me to go before. I like the solitude, spending months in the big outdoors." He glanced at her, his eyes dark with emotion. Elise's heart skipped a beat. "But now, since I've met you, I don't want to leave." He took her hand and caressed her fingertips. "Elise..."

She held her breath as he touched her face. Would he kiss her? Here in the park? She knew she wouldn't mind if he did.

He dropped his hand and sat up with a slight laugh. "There, I shouldn't have said all that. I don't want to spoil our evening." He laid her hand back in her lap. "I enjoy being with you, but I don't want you to feel you have to wait for me while I'm gone."

Elise's heart plummeted. She'd wait, if only he'd ask.

Daniel gave her a strained smile. "All right, enough about me. Tell me about your day. I noticed you have your own section of the lunch counter and doing a very nice job of it. You'll be head waitress before you know it."

Elise shook her head. "Not much chance of that for quite a while, I'm afraid. There are too many ahead of me. I enjoy the work and I'm glad I got hired. I love being around the railroad."

"Gets in your blood, doesn't it? I've been fascinated with the railroad since I was a little boy." He chuckled. "Someday I'd like to be in the railroad management. President or vice president would be nice."

"You're a diligent worker. You'll make it."

Daniel shook his head. "No. That's a dream. You have to be somebody to get into those positions. I don't have the right connections." He looked back at the fountain.

The air began to cool and another couple entered the park. A train whistle sounded on the other side of the depot, and a nearby cricket choir began a serenade.

Daniel looked at his pocket watch. "Would you like to go for a stroll up the street before you have to go in?" At her nod, he stood and offered his arm.

Elise rose and folded the handkerchief. She gave it to him before she placed her hand on his arm. "It's delightful out here. I hate to go back inside."

They walked in comfortable silence past the Windsor Hotel and toward the main part of town. The sun made its way toward the western horizon and the birds sang their evening songs. Daniel took her hand and held it as they walked.

When they returned to the parlor, Daniel touched Elise's

elbow and swung her to face him. "I'm sorry I have to leave again. It seems that's all I do."

Elise gazed into his eyes. "It can't be helped. I'll look forward to seeing you when you get back."

Daniel reached up and followed the contours of her jaw with his fingertip, ending with her lips. "I'll be looking forward to that, too." His voice was rough with emotion. "If all goes well, I plan to be back on Friday. I plan to go with you to the picnic Saturday." He clasped her hand "I'll let you know when I get back into town."

Elise nodded as the awareness of his touch tingled up her arm. She couldn't think of anything to say as he squeezed her hand and walked from the room. How would she cope with his absence for two or three months?

The next week was a flurry of busy days. Friday evening, Elise sighed as she carried a tray of dirty dishes to the kitchen. She wiggled her toes in her shoes. Her feet hurt, and a lump of disappointment lodged behind her breastbone. She had watched for Daniel all day, but he never appeared. Served her right for getting so involved.

She returned to the lunchroom and wiped the counter, then picked up a menu and scanned it. The variety of foods offered by the Harvey House was amazing: blue points on shell, fillet of whitefish with Madeira sauce, young capon with hollandaise sauce. She had never heard of most of them, let alone eaten them, but she knew the ingredients had come from all over the country in cooled railroad cars and were expertly prepared.

Elise replaced the menu in its rack and walked to the large silver coffee urns. It was her turn to polish them so they would be ready for the next day. She glanced around the lunchroom. There were only a few other girls left to finish the cleaning.

As she rubbed hard to remove a stubborn fingerprint on the polished surface of the urn, Elise saw the reflection of a man sneaking up behind her. When he reached to put his hands over her eyes, she recognized him and spun around before he could touch her.

"Jerome, what are you doing here? How did you get in?" Elise backed away from him and looked toward the lunchroom entrance.

"Walked in. That gal out front told me you were here." Jerome smirked. "Couldn't pass up the chance to see my loving cousin."

Elise frowned. "What do you want? I know you didn't come in just to be sociable."

"Elise, how could you say such a thing?" Jerome pretended to look hurt. "Mom said you had come for an interview. You look pretty good in that uniform. Think it'll protect you from all the men who come in here?"

"I'll be fine as long as you stay away." Elise folded her arms across her chest. She could feel her anger rising. Jerome had teased and tormented her since they were children. He'd caused her to get in trouble more times than she could count. Aunt Victorine wouldn't believe her perfect little boy could do anything bad, so Elise had been punished when he started the fights.

Jerome scanned the room. "Why don't you come work for me? I can pay you more than you make here. Help you pay off your farm debt quicker."

Elise gritted her teeth. "Get out, Jerome. I wouldn't work for you if it was the last job in the world, especially not in a saloon."

Jerome wrinkled his forehead and pursed his lips into a maddening expression. "You wouldn't, huh?" He nodded smugly. "We'll see."

"Leave, Jerome. And don't come back." Elise grabbed his arm and pushed him toward the door.

"All right, all right, I'm leaving, but I'll see you around."

Elise watched until he walked out the lunchroom door then closed her eyes tight and leaned against the nearest table. *Oh, that man!* Of all the people in the world, Jerome Dumond could get her temper riled quicker than anyone. The trouble was, he knew it.

She turned and attacked the coffee urn with a vengeance.

Ten minutes later, Elise walked into the parlor. She stopped short. Arnaud and Millie were on the sofa talking with Daniel. Her breath caught in her throat as instant relief and excitement flooded through her. "Daniel, Arnaud, you're both here." She put her hand over her heart. "Millie, why didn't you tell me?"

Millie laughed as Daniel scooted over to make room for Elise. "Arnaud wanted to surprise you, and Daniel just arrived. He missed his earlier train." Her eyes sparkled with amusement. "Besides, I wouldn't have got any work out of you if you'd known."

Elise sat beside Daniel. "I'm so glad you're here. I was afraid something bad had happened." An unbelievable thrill shot through her as he put his arm around her shoulders and pulled her close. She leaned into the curve of his arm, feeling his body warmth.

Daniel grimaced. "I intended to come earlier, but I got detained at the shipping office. The shipping labels were printed wrong. We had to redo them. " He shook his head. "Seems that's the way everything's been."

Elise gave him a mischievous grin. "Maybe that means you aren't supposed to go."

"I wish." Daniel gave her shoulder a squeeze.

Elise had a wild urge to push the stray strands of hair off his forehead, but turned to her brother instead. "When did you get in, Arnaud? Did you have a good trip?"

Arnaud chuckled. "I thought you'd forgotten all about me." He leaned back, his arm around Millie, and stretched his legs out straight. "I got in on the evening train. Nothing exciting." He glanced at Daniel. "By the way, when do you leave for the wild?"

Elise frowned. "He has to leave on the fifteenth."

"The time is coming up fast, isn't it?" Arnaud shook his head. "When did you find out?"

Daniel crossed his leg. "Strong told me last Friday. I wasn't expecting it until the end of the month."

Millie sat forward. "Did Elise invite you to the picnic tomorrow evening?"

Daniel nodded. "Oh, yes, I wouldn't miss it."

Arnaud moved his shoulders around to stretch the muscles. "Well, I think I'll go hit the sack. I've been riding the rails all day."

As he started to get up, Elise touched his arm. "Arnaud, Jerome came into the lunchroom when I was cleaning up." She scowled. "He said he wanted me to work for him. I wish he would leave me alone."

Millie leaned forward. "Who is Jerome? He came into the lunchroom after everyone had gone?"

Arnaud faced her. "He's our cousin. Sort of the black sheep of the family."

Elise shuddered. "He said someone told him he could come in. He's nothing but trouble."

Millie shook her head. "I'm sorry, I'll make sure that doesn't happen again. I don't know who would've let him in."

Elise shook her head. "Maybe no one did. He might've just come in without asking. He would do that." She sighed. "Hopefully, he will stay away."

"I hope so too." Millie checked her watch. "It's time for you men to go. It's nearly ten o'clock."

Arnaud stood and pulled Millie up beside him then turned to Daniel and Elise. "Don't stay too long, you two."

Daniel took his arm from Elise's shoulders and sat forward as Arnaud and Millie left the room. "Are you alright? You looked upset when you talked about your cousin."

Elise shrugged. "I'll be okay if he stays away. I don't think he's dangerous. He just makes me angry." She couldn't take her eyes away from Daniel's ruggedly, handsome face. He had a day's growth of beard, and his blond hair brushed his collar. When she was with him it was easy to forget Jerome and his veiled threats.

"Well, I better go." Daniel stood, took her hands and lifted her up beside him. "I'll see you in the morning." He gave her hand a squeeze.

Elise squeezed his hand in return then watched him walk down the stairs with Arnaud.

The next morning, Daniel and Arnaud met in the lobby of the hotel on their way to breakfast. The sun had risen in the eastern sky, and the air was beginning to warm as they stepped outside.

Arnaud clapped Daniel on the back. "Glad you made it in."

"If I hadn't made that late train, I would've hired a carriage. I was determined to get here last night. Elise and I have such a short time before I leave. I don't want to waste a minute of it." At the depot, Daniel stepped back and held the door as a crowd of people walked out.

They walked into the depot together. "I think she understands." Arnaud motioned toward one of the lobby lounge chairs. "What are your intentions toward my sister? I know she likes you a lot."

Daniel sat across from his friend. "She's the most wonderful woman I've ever met. I thought ladies like her only existed in dreams."

Arnaud smiled. "That's the way I feel about Millie."

Daniel swatted Arnaud on the knee. "By the way, why didn't you introduce me to Elise sooner."

Arnaud shrugged. "Never thought about it."

Daniel sobered. "I want Elise to be happy above everything else. I'm not sure I can provide that for her with my job. Being gone weeks and months at a time is not very conducive to a lasting relationship."

"I'm confident she'd wait for you."

Daniel shook his head. "I don't want to tie her down. If it's God's will for us to be together, He'll keep her for me and work out the details."

Arnaud clasped him on the shoulder. His voice was husky. "All right, friend. I'll be praying for God's will." He stood. "We better get breakfast. The girls will be waiting."

Daniel hesitated in the lunchroom doorway and watched as Elise served her customers. He wanted more than anything to ask her to wait for him.

His heart skipped a beat then raced at the happiness in her face when she saw him.

CHAPTER 13

That afternoon, Elise hurried to clean her station before the last train stop of the day. Tessa and Dorothea worked next to her. "I'm so excited about the picnic this evening. I haven't been to a picnic in a long time." She smiled at Tessa. "Who was that fellow you talked to at lunchtime? He was good looking."

Tessa grinned as her face grew pink. "His name is Edward. He's a signalman for the railroad. I asked him to go to the picnic with me, and he said he would."

"Good. I'm happy you'll have someone to go with." She turned to Dorothea. "I'm glad Millie planned the outing. It will give us more time to get acquainted."

Dorothea smiled shyly. "Me too. Isabel and I are going together."

The gong sounded to signal the arrival of the train crowd.

An hour later, as the last of the local customers left, Daniel walked in the door. Excitement flooded through Elise as he sauntered to the counter. He wore the cowboy boots, jeans and casual shirt that he'd worn the day of their surprise encounter on the train.

"Hi, Daniel." She wiped the salt and pepper shakers and placed them in their rack. "I need to finish cleaning then I'll go to my room and change. Are the others gathered in the lobby?"

Daniel settled on a stool. "Millie's out there with a few others. Arnaud had to make a run to Kansas City."

"Oh. I wish he could've stayed."

"Millie said we could ride in the carriages she ordered, or we can walk. It's not far up Kansas Street, across the river bridge. Which would you rather do?"

"Oh, let's walk." Elise faced Tessa. "Would you and Edward like to walk with us?"

"I'll ask him. It's such a beautiful day, I think it would be delightful to walk." Tessa put away her cleaning cloth. "Are you ready, Dorothea? Let's get changed. I want to have some fun."

Daniel escorted them to the door then descended the stairs while they went to their rooms.

Elise changed into her blue dress and some comfortable shoes then hung her uniform in the wardrobe. "Can you believe we've been here two weeks? We've already learned so much it somehow seems longer. And yet the time has gone by so fast

Daniel will have to leave soon." She took her straw hat from the shelf and fluffed the ribbon.

Tessa nodded. "It's hard to believe that my life could change so drastically in such a short time, but I'm glad it has. Except for homesickness for my family, I love it here."

Elise put a handkerchief in her handbag and followed Tessa out the door. "Especially since you met Edward, right?"

Tessa laughed. "That certainly doesn't hurt."

Elise and Tessa walked down the stairs and looked around the lobby. Tessa pointed across the room. "Look, Daniel is talking to Edward over by the window. I wonder how he knows Edward?"

"Maybe they're acquainted from their work. Railroad men seem to know each other pretty well."

As the girls made their way across the lobby, Daniel and Edward stood up. Daniel held out his hand to Elise. "You ready to go?"

Edward stepped toward Tessa. "Would you like to walk?"

Tessa nodded. "It's such a beautiful evening. It'd be a shame to ride."

Daniel held Elise's hand as they headed out the door. Houses, which lined the street on each side, gave way to a row of trees. Beyond them the large bridge, with huge wooden trestles, spanned the Kansas River. The sun lowered in the western sky, and a warm breeze blew from the South. The girl's skirts swirled around their ankles as they walked onto the wooden planks. Daniel pulled Elise to the railing. "Look at all that water."

She stared at the large flowing river. "It's beautiful."

"It's amazing. I've never seen a river this big. And it's so close to us." Tessa exclaimed.

They walked slowly across the bridge with other Harvey girls and their escorts. The carriages, loaded with more girls, passed them. Elise, Daniel, Tessa and Edward arrived at the park on the opposite bank. Millie supervised as several girls laid out blankets, and kitchen workers arranged the food on tables.

Elise pulled Daniel across the grass. "Let's find a place to sit." The girls laid their handbags on a blanket, then walked to the food tables filled with several kinds of sandwiches; platters of fresh vegetables and fruits; and incredible desserts. "Look at all that food. I was too busy to eat much lunch."

"Me too." Tessa giggled as her stomach rumbled. "I think my stomach anticipates this picnic, too. The food isn't quite ready. Let's go over and see what Dorothea and Isabel are doing."

The two girls worked with Caroline and Abigail to set up wickets for a game. Caroline looked up as the four approached. "Would you like to join us for a game of croquet?" She picked up a mallet. "You hit your ball through the series of wickets. The object of the game is to be the first back to the starting point. If you've never played, we'll show you how. My family plays this back home."

Soon they were having fun. They took turns with the mallets to smack their balls around the course. The challenge was to hit an opponent's ball and knock it away from the wickets so he or she would need more moves. In the end Daniel was victorious, hitting the final stake.

"Yay! I won!" He held his mallet high.

Elise laughed. "I wasn't far behind." She pivoted toward the tables where the others were filling their plates. "Right now I want something to eat. I'm famished."

The evening zipped by. The sun had set and twilight streaked the western sky when they walked across the bridge toward the Harvey House.

Daniel gently squeezed Elise's hand as they stepped into the depot. "That was fun. Thank you for inviting me."

Elise looked into his face. "I'm so glad you came. It was a wonderful evening."

"It's close to ten so I won't walk you upstairs, but I wondered if you're going to church tomorrow."

Elise nodded. "Yes, I plan to go."

"Good, I'll see you then." Daniel smiled and carressed her hand again before he left.

The next morning, Elise and Tessa met Millie in the lunchroom for breakfast. "I think Dorothea and Isabel are going to church with us," Elise said. "They asked what time we leave."

"Good, the more the merrier." Millie smiled as she finished her meal. "I'm glad you girls are getting better acquainted."

Dorothea and Isabel walked in with Caroline and Abigail. "We brought more girls. Is that okay?" Isabel asked.

"Definitely." Millie smiled at them. "Glad you are all going. Get your breakfast first then we'll leave."

A short time later, Elise and Tessa walked with the other girls toward the little white church. The sun shone brightly in the morning sky and a slight breeze cooled the air. Elise took a deep breath and watched as a robin hopped across the grass and grabbed a fat worm. She laughed softly.

Tessa touched her arm. "Is Daniel coming to church? Edward said he might if he didn't have to work."

"He said he'd be there." Elise looked around as they entered the foyer, but didn't see Daniel or Edward. She and Tessa followed Millie and the others to the front of the church. As they approached the pew, Elise slowed. "Tessa and I can sit in this next pew. I don't think there's room for all of us to sit together."

As Millie nodded agreement, Elise gestured for Tessa to enter the pew behind the others. Purposely, she sat at the end next to the middle aisle hoping Daniel and Edward would sit by them.

Tessa elbowed her side and whispered. "Don't look around, but guess who just walked in."

Excitement spiraled through Elise as Daniel walked up. "Is there room in this pew for a couple of railroad men?"

Elise smiled. "I'm sure we can find room."

"Yes, I think we can." Tessa giggled as she scooted back so Edward could get past her.

Daniel took Elise's hand as he moved in beside her. Elise glanced at him. He looked handsome in his dark suit. She sighed as the service started. Though she was struggling with her faith, she was glad to know Daniel went to church. The morning sun, which shown through the stained glass window, seemed brighter than before.

The next week whizzed by. Daniel's days were full as he assembled and prepared the supplies he and his survey team would need. He saw Elise in the Harvey House lunchroom at each meal, but they had little time beyond brief greetings and a few words. He looked forward to spending more time with her on the weekend.

On Friday afternoon, Daniel met with William Strong one last time before his departure. His boss was sitting at the huge desk as Daniel walked into his office. He looked up as Daniel entered. "So, how's it going? Everything ready?"

"We have most of the supplies ready. Abe Schroeder has been an invaluable help." He hesitated. "Have you found another man for our team?"

Strong pushed his chair back. "Yes, I have. His name is Carlos Devina. He'll be a good replacement. He's been on our California team and is on his way. He'll be here by the fifteenth."

Daniel nodded. "I'll look forward to his arrival."

Mr. Strong stood and walked to the corner where the maps were stored. He selected one and slid it into a leather case. "Here's the map you can use to record your coordinates. Any other questions?"

Daniel took the map. "Not now. I think I've thought of everything."

Mr. Strong shook his hand. "I'm sure you'll do a good job. See you when you get back." He ran his hand over his beard. "I'm leaving for California to see that that job is finished on time."

"Thank you, sir. I'll do my best." Daniel let his shoulders relax as he walked from the railroad president's office. Now he was free to spend some time with Elise. He walked to the door of the dining room where Millie was greeting incoming train passengers. He leaned the map case against the wall and stood back to wait. He swung around as he felt a hand on his shoulder.

"Hey, Daniel, what's going on?" Arnaud was standing behind him. He indicated the map case. "Everything ready to go?"

Daniel nodded. "I'm getting closer. Only have one more week. I just met with William Strong." He smiled wryly. "The responsibility has begun to set in."

"You'll do okay." Arnaud cupped Daniel's shoulder.

Millie motioned to them. "Do you men want to eat in the dining room this evening? You can use our dinner jackets." She indicated the row of jackets hanging on a rack by the door.

"Yes. I'm famished." Arnaud grabbed a jacket then turned to Millie as Daniel selected one. "How has your week been?"

"Good. I'm glad you're back." She smiled. "We can talk later, okay? I'm really busy right now."

Arnaud nodded. "That's fine."

Millie led them across the dining room to a table. She turned their cups over. "Would you like to play a board game in the parlor after Elise and I get off work?"

Daniel picked up a menu. "Sounds like fun."

"Okay, I'll tell Elise you're here."

Elise cleaned her station as the last of her diners left. Finally, she would get to spend time with Daniel. The days were slipping away. One more week: Daniel would leave in one more week.

Millie walked into the lunchroom as she finished. "Are you ready to go? I told the guys to meet us in the parlor. We can play that new game of "Eckha". One of the girls bought it for us to share."

Soon they were sitting across from the men at a game table in the parlor. "How do you play this?" Daniel took the playing pieces from the box and laid the board between them.

Arnaud read the instructions. "Each person has ten tokens that they place on squares on their side of the board. You have to take turns and move your tokens across the board, jumping your own or other player's tokens when possible. The object is to be the first to get all your tokens to your opponent's starting squares on the other side of the board."

Elise counted out the different colored playing pieces. "I haven't played a parlor game for a long time." She glanced at Arnaud. "Our family used to play board games together when we were all younger. Mama was very competitive." She smiled.

"Have you heard from your family?" Millie placed her red playing pieces on the board as she looked across the table at Elise.

"No, I haven't heard a word. I'm ready for a letter. You haven't either, have you, Arnaud?"

Arnaud shook his head. "I imagine they are just getting settled with all the changes. This is a busy time of year with planting and gardening. We'll hear soon."

Elise chose the yellow tokens and pushed the blue toward Daniel. "Here these match your eyes." She laughed.

Their hands touched as Daniel took the game pieces. He winked. "There isn't a color that matches your unusual eyes." He turned back to the board. "You're first, Millie, you have red." He looked at Arnaud. "Are you here for the weekend or do you have to leave in the morning?"

"I have to work this weekend, but I'll be off next weekend."

"Oh, that reminds me." Millie moved her playing piece. "We're going to have a dance in the parlor next weekend. That'd be a good send off for you, Daniel."

"Don't say send off. I'm not ready for that." Elise made a face. "The time has passed too fast, but a dance does sound festive." She watched as Arnaud moved his green piece then moved her yellow one.

They continued to play until Millie won.

"Way to go, Millie." Elise clapped her hands. "That was enjoyable." She looked at the other girls who had watched them. "I think there are some others who want to play,"

As he prepared to leave, Daniel took Elise's hand. "Would you like to take a carriage ride tomorrow evening? We could drive around the State Capitol Building and see the main part of the city."

"That would be wonderful."

The next evening, Daniel rented a carriage and drove to the depot. He met Elise in the lobby. She looked beautiful as she walked toward him. He could hardly breathe. How had he allowed this to happen? How could he leave and not know if she would wait for him. They had known each other such a short time he couldn't ask her to wait.

They drove up Kansas Avenue, over the river bridge and

into the main part of town. The street was lined with small stores and large buildings. Horses and carriages were parked along the street and people walked along the boardwalks.

"It's Saturday evening. Looks like everyone is in town doing their weekly shopping and having a night out." Daniel slowed as a group of people crossed the street toward a building with a sign that read "Opera House" on the front. "Maybe we should've gone to the opera. It looks like a popular place."

Elise shook her head. "I'd rather just ride and enjoy the beautiful evening. I have to be inside so much at work."

Daniel cocked his head at her and smiled. He took her hand. "I'd rather ride too."

They drove on down the street past more stores and a bank building to Eighth street then turned right toward the Capitol Building.

"Oh, that's a beautiful building." Elise leaned forward as they approached the Capitol Square. "It looks like they're still working on it."

"They've finished the East and West wings and are about to finish the middle section. It's built with native Kansas limestone." Daniel stopped at the end of the walkway. "It should be impressive when it's done."

Elise nodded. "It's already impressive, I'd say."

They turned right and headed back toward the river. The street was lined with beautiful, stately homes with wide porches and white columns. The warm evening air was redolent with the scent of flowers, which bloomed in flower boxes and gardens.

Elise sighed happily. "I'd love to live in a house like these someday. They look so welcoming."

Daniel took her hand and smiled. "Hopefully you will."

Elise smiled back. "Maybe, but right now I have to concentrate on making money so I can help save the farm."

As they drove back to the depot and Harvey House, the sun set in the West.

Daniel jumped down and helped Elise to the edge of the street. "Do you mind going in alone? I need to get this rig back to the livery. I'm sorry I brought you home late."

Elise smiled. "No, of course not. I'm fine. Will I see you at church in the morning?"

"I'll be there." He took her hand, lifted it to his lips and kissed her fingertips. "I plan to go to the ranch next week to tell my parents goodbye. I'll be back by the weekend and be here for the dance."

Chapter 14

Elise couldn't keep her eyes off the wall clock at the back of the lunchroom as six o'clock approached. Anticipation bubbled through her. She'd never been this excited to spend time with other young men in her past. She tried to ignore the thought that Daniel would leave on Monday.

He was back in town from the visit with his parents. Wednesday evening they'd gone for a walk. Otherwise, she'd only seen him in the lunchroom at mealtime. He'd been busy with last minute preparations for the survey trip.

Tessa walked over from her section of the lunch counter. "Come on, Elise. Helen and Alma are here to relieve us for the last train rush." She straightened the salt and pepper shakers. "Guess what. Edward came in for lunch. He asked me to supper, and I invited him to the dance."

"Oh, Tessa, that's wonderful. He seems friendly and considerate." Elise touched her arm. "Let's go get ready."

When they reached their room, Elise slipped off her uniform and pulled on her robe. I'm going to take a bath. I won't be long. She gathered her clothes and toiletries. She locked the bathroom door and turned on the faucet of the heated reservoir to fill the bathtub. She sighed. What a luxury to soak in a tub of warm water. Her family would never believe it.

Back in the room, Elise splashed rose water on her wrists. "Which dress should I wear tonight?"

"Your green brocade. It complements the color of your eyes." Tessa hung her uniform in the wardrobe and pulled out a light blue dress. "I think I'll wear this. It'll feel strange to wear a bustle. I'm glad we don't wear one with our uniforms."

"Me too. Can you imagine how that would look?" She laughed as she laid her dress on the bed. "Will you help me get into this?"

"If you'll help me." Tessa gathered the dress, slipped it over Elise's head and down over the bustle then fastened the buttons in the back.

"Thank you." Elise lifted Tessa's dress and assisted her.

Elise looked in the mirror. "I wish I could use Caroline's curling iron, but there isn't time to heat it in the lamp." She ran her brush a dozen strokes through her long hair.

"Don't worry. Your hair will look beautiful. Put it in a

chignon with ringlets down the back. It has enough curl." Tessa rummaged in her drawer. "Here's a white silk rose. That will look elegant with your green dress."

It took a second attempt for Elise to fix her hair in the fashion Tessa suggested. She smiled with satisfaction as she slipped the white rose under the pins. "How does this look?" She pirouetted so Tessa could see the back.

"Perfect."

"Will you need more help dressing or with your hair?" Elise watched Tessa. "That dress looks heavenly on you."

"Thanks." Tessa smiled. "No I don't need anything else. You go on. I'll see you in a few minutes."

Elise paused at the parlor door and scanned the room. The chairs and sofas were pushed against the walls to make room for dancing and a table was set for refreshments. Daniel sat on one of the sofas in earnest conversation with another young man. She watched his animated features as he talked. It felt natural to have him here. What would she do after he left?

Daniel glanced up, excused himself and grabbed his coat from the seat beside him. As he walked toward her he shook his head. A small smile played around his lips. "How is it possible that you're more beautiful every time I see you?"

Elise felt her face grow warm. She couldn't help but smile. The musky scent of his shaving soap teased her senses.

"Let's eat, shall we? I'm hungry." Daniel offered her his

arm. "Maybe you'd rather eat somewhere else since you work here all the time."

"Oh, no. This is the best food in town. I wouldn't know where else to go."

They waited while Millie seated two groups of locals, then followed her across the room. Elise acknowledged the two couples already seated at the table. They were Harvey Girls and their escorts.

Elise glanced at Millie as Daniel seated her. "I didn't know you had to work tonight. Will Arnaud come to eat?"

"Yes. He'll be here soon. I've watched for him." She smiled. "I get off at seven-thirty, so I'll have time to get ready."

"Bring Arnaud over when he comes in. He can sit with us."

Daniel sat beside Elise and picked up the menu. "Let's order something different, something we've never had. Do you like fish?" He chuckled as she wrinkled her nose. "No, I guess not."

Elise studied the menu. "Let's try the Salmi of Duck with queen olives. I've been serving a lot of that, and it looks wonderful."

"Sounds good to me. How about chocolate eclairs for dessert?"

"It's enjoyable to order for a change instead of serve. I see these tantalizing meals, but seldom get to eat them."

Arnaud joined them as the Harvey Girl arrived to take their order.

Later, as Elise, Daniel and Arnaud walked into the parlor, the stringed quartet, in the corner of the room, were tuning their instruments. Millie walked to meet them. "What do you think of the live music? I was able to bring in the Topeka Orchestral Group."

Elise stopped and listened as they ran the bows over the strings then broke into a song she hadn't heard before. There were two women with violins and two men, one with a viola and one with a cello. "Very impressive. Better than a piano."

Millie held out the sheet music she was holding. "This is a new song they brought. They just received it."

Elise looked at the title. 'Oh, My Darling Clementine', is that what they're playing? I like it."

Arnaud flipped through the pile of sheet music Millie had chosen. "Here, have them play 'Oh! Susanna', first. It's a peppy one; a good selection to get everyone started."

Daniel and Elise sauntered to the refreshment table while Millie and Arnaud discussed the order of the dance songs. The table was cheerful with yellow and green streamers and a centerpiece of Kansas sunflowers. One of the Harvey Girls served punch. They each took a cup and sat down on one of the sofas that had been moved to the edge of the room. Elise felt Daniel's presence beside her. If only this night would last forever.

Other couples milled about. Some drank punch and ate cookies while they waited for the dance to begin.

Daniel stretched his arm across the back of the sofa and gently nudged Elise closer. She sighed with contentment as she settled into the curve of his body. His warmth flowed through her. She wanted to soak it in.

Millie welcomed everyone and introduced the first song. Elise didn't want to move, but Daniel stood and offered his hand. "Come on, Elise, let's make the most of this evening." He led her onto the floor to join Arnaud and Millie in a fast two-step.

Elise and Daniel danced the next slow dance together before another young man claimed her hand. Elise noticed that Daniel danced with various other girls when she danced with someone else, but he always sought her out with a smile at the end of the dance. One time, as he took her in his arms, he leaned down and whispered in her ear. "I'll remember this night for a long time. Will you?"

Tears sprang to her eyes as she nodded. "Yes, I will."

Toward the end of the evening, Arnaud touched her arm for a slow waltz. He looked at her as he led her onto the floor. "Have you and Daniel talked?"

Elise shook her head. "Nothing but small talk. We've avoided any serious conversation. I guess it's best." She looked away and blinked to keep the tears away.

"Sorry I brought it up. I just don't want you to be hurt."

"I'm afraid it's too late for that. You should have warned me back in March."

Arnaud gave her a squeeze of understanding. "I'll be praying for you."

"Thanks, big brother."

Millie took her place beside the stringed quartet. "Good Night, Ladies" will be our last dance. You'll have thirty minutes before the gentlemen are dismissed and you have to go to your rooms."

Arnaud walked Elise back to the chairs. Daniel appeared at her side and touched her hand. "Do you want to go outside for a bit of fresh air?"

Elise nodded. "Yes, I'd like that. It's awfully hot and stuffy in here."

Daniel took her hand and led her through the lobby and outside to the dimly lit station platform. Benches were situated at intervals under gaslights lit earlier by the stationmaster. Streaks of light still illuminated the western sky and a cool breeze felt refreshing against Elise's flushed skin. Crickets chirped merrily and fireflies flashed in the darkness.

They chose a bench halfway down the deck, Daniel indicated for Elise to have a seat then sat beside her. For several moments neither spoke.

Elise could feel her heart flutter in her throat, nearly suffocating her, as Daniel took her hand. "Elise, I knew this time would have to come. I've been avoiding it all day."

She closed her eyes. "I know."

He enclosed her hand in both of his. "I don't know what to say. Maybe there isn't anything to say." He hesitated. "You're so sweet and beautiful." Elise glanced at him as he sighed. "Now when I find you, I have to leave." He squeezed her hand. "I won't ask you to wait for me. That wouldn't be fair since we've barely got acquainted. But I will ask the Lord to keep you in His care."

"Oh, Daniel." Elise could barely breathe. *I'll wait. Oh, please, Daniel. Just ask.* Her heart cried out. She wanted to make him listen, but the words wouldn't come. *What about your Harvey House Contract?* The thought intruded. She couldn't promise anything either.

Daniel lifted her hand and kissed the back of it with a slow, gentle kiss. "Goodbye for now, Elise. I leave in the morning. I meet my crew in Arkansas City." He touched her face and let his eyes skim over her features as if to memorize them. "I'll be back."

She stared at him. How could he just leave?

He stood and pulled her up beside him. "I'll walk you back to the parlor." His voice sounded strange, rough and gravelly.

Elise shook her head and pulled her hand away. "I want to stay out here a while. I can make it back." The words came out in a shaky whisper. A tear rolled down her cheek.

"Are you sure?"

She nodded as she wiped away the tear.

Daniel stood transfixed then pulled her toward him. His lips found hers tenderly, softly. Elise moved into his arms. Her heart palpitated as she returned his kiss, awe and delight burst through her.

He pulled away. His gaze held hers. "I...I'm sorry. I shouldn't have done that." His voice was a mere whisper. He reached up and wiped her tears then dropped his hand and, with one last lingering look, turned and strode off the platform.

Elise watched as he walked out of the circle of lamplight. Was he truly sorry? Her heart ached with uncertainty.

Unable to stand on her shaky legs, Elise sat on the bench and stared at the spot where Daniel had disappeared into the darkness. She raised her hand and touched her lips. Surely he cared, or he couldn't have kissed her that way. Could he?

She'd had time to prepare for Daniel's departure; he'd warned her. But preparation didn't make the hurt and loss any less painful.

Elise stood and walked back into the depot. In the parlor she helped clean up from the dance. She pretended not to notice that the other girls looked with concern at her tear-reddened eyes.

~~~

Daniel stepped from the train in Arkansas City, Kansas, the next afternoon and strode into the depot. He scanned the small lobby as he approached the agent's window.

The agent was checking baggage in the adjacent room. After several minutes, he turned toward Daniel. "Can I help you?"

"My name's Daniel Gilbertson. I'm with the ATSF survey team. Have my supplies arrived from Kansas City?"

"Yep." The agent gave an unintelligible grunt as he pointed to a pile of crates at the back of the room. "They 'bout took over my storage area. Glad you're here to get 'em." He gestured over his shoulder. "There's a stallion at the livery, came in Friday."

Daniel let out a sigh of relief. "Good! Do you know if the other two members of the crew have arrived?"

"Yep. Got here yestiday. They're roomin' at Melinda Dickerson's boarding house up the street." He waved toward the city side door before he turned back to the assortment of baggage. "Is one of these yours?"

"Yes. The one at the bottom of the pile." Daniel pointed to the medium sized brown bag. "Did you locate a covered wagon?"

The agent pulled the bag from under the stack of boxes and bundles and slid it toward Daniel through the opening in the wall. "Yep. A family, just arrived in town, was wantin' to git rid of theirs so I picked it up fer ya'. Got the mules too. The telegram said the railroad would pay back the money."

"Thanks. I appreciate it." Daniel nodded. "Telegraph the amount to headquarters. They'll reimburse you."

"The wagon's sittin' behind the livery. You say you're surveyin' for the railroad line? You headed into the Cherokee territory? I hear tell those Indians ain't too happy about white men comin' into their reservations. You'd best be careful."

"We will. We'll stay close to the cattle trails. Do the cowboys drive the cattle here to ship them east?"

The agent squinted. "Yep. We get a herd in ever' now and again."

Daniel picked up his bag. "Thanks for your help. The guys and I'll come get the crates and boxes out of your way." He moved aside to let the other passengers claim their baggage then walked to the door opposite the track. He stepped out onto a wooden boardwalk and gazed across the dirt road and up the street before him. He still hadn't met the third member of the team.

Large, two-story houses lined each side. As he crossed the road, he saw someone on the porch steps of the house to his right. The man was hunched over, his hands between his knees.

"Hello. Can you tell me where Melinda Dickerson's boarding house is?"

The man looked up then bobbed his head toward the door. "Thes' is the boarding house." He watched as Daniel stepped into the yard. "You Daniel Gilbertson?"

"Yes." He walked toward the porch and held out his hand. "Are you Carlos?"

"Sí." Carlos stood and grasped Daniel's hand. "Et's good to meet you. Señor Abe and I got here yesterday. He's waitin' in hes room."

Daniel nodded and followed Carlos across the porch. "I'll put this bag in my room then we can get Abe and load the wagon."

The sun peeked over the horizon, the next morning, as Daniel made his way to the livery stable. He and Abe had spent the previous evening in a discussion about their plans and the route they would take. Carlos had sought out female companionship at the local saloon.

Before bed, Daniel wrote a letter to Elise. It would be his last contact for some time. He was heavy hearted at the thought of leaving her. He shouldn't have kissed her, but it had been impossible to resist the urge when he saw her cry. Actually, he was glad he had.

The letter in Daniel's pocket made a slight crackling sound as he led Midnight from his stall and threw the saddle blanket across his back. Daniel patted the stallion's neck then placed the saddle on and cinched it tight. Midnight danced sideways and snorted when Daniel grabbed the reins. "It's going to be a long trek, old man. You might as well get used to it." He looked his horse in the eyes. "We're in this together, buddy." Daniel was glad he had arranged for his dad to send Midnight here on the train.

Carlos and Abe walked into the livery. Abe glanced around. "Looks like ever'ting's in fine shape. Good job gettin' it together, Daniel." He spoke with a strong German accent. He walked into the stall and led the two mules out. "Ve better get these ladies harnessed up and be on our vay before it gets too hot."

Daniel laughed. "That's as close to ladies as we're going to get for quite some time."

Carlos gave an undignified snort as he took the halter rope of the mule named Dolly and led her from the building.

"Don't t'ink Carlos is used to being vithout his vomen."

Daniel nodded. "You're probably right."

They soon had the mules hitched to the wagon.

"Mrs. Dickerson, at the boarding house, said she'd have breakfast ready for us. I'm going to mail this letter then meet you there." Daniel glanced at the brilliant streaks of sunlight in the eastern sky. Already the air felt hot. The day was going to be a scorcher.

After eating a large country breakfast of biscuits and gravy with eggs and ham, the three headed south. Farmsteads dotted the countryside for a short time. Then, they rode into the rolling red hills of the sparsely inhabited Cherokee Strip.

CHAPTER 15

The next Saturday afternoon, Elise swiped the counter with her cleaning cloth and set the flower vase down harder than necessary. Homesickness invaded her thoughts. She'd waited for the mail each day, hopeful that Daniel had sent a letter before he left Arkansas City. To make matters worse, she hadn't heard from anyone at home since she left, almost five weeks ago.

Millie walked into the lunchroom. "Elise, look what came in the mail; two letters for you. One from your sister, and one from guess who."

"Daniel?" At Millie's nod, Elise clapped her hands and then reached for the letters. "They must have read my mind. I was scolding them for not writing."

Millie smiled. "Take a short break before the train arrives."

"All right." Elise hurried to her room. She dropped to the bed, ripped open the envelope to Daniel's letter and pulled out the single sheet. She unfolded the paper and held it to the afternoon sunlight shining in the window.

Dear Elise,

I had to write and let you know how much I enjoyed our time together in the last four weeks. I wish it could've been longer. You're the most amazing girl I've ever known. I can't believe I had to leave for the wilderness so soon after meeting you.

I know it's not fair to ask you to wait for me. After all, you hardly know me, and I don't have any idea when I'll be back. But please remember our evenings together. I'll never forget them.

You'll make a great Harvey Girl. I'm glad I had a part in suggesting it.

This will be the last letter I can send as we leave tomorrow, but I'll look forward to seeing you when I get back.

Your friend,

Daniel

Elise refolded the letter and held it to her chest. She closed her eyes and pictured Daniel outside their barn as she saw him back in March—Broad shouldered and full of vital masculinity. She had been attracted to him from that moment.

She picked up the other letter. Marie's beautiful handwriting embellished the front of the envelope. Elise tore it open and held it to the light.

June 15, 1885

Dear Elise,

We've enjoyed your letters. I'm sorry I haven't written sooner. We've worked hard to get the wheat shocked. The flood destroyed about half of the crop, but there should be enough to reseed and some to sell. Paul and Jule will haul the shocks over to Paul's father's farm to be threshed. We don't have enough grain for the threshers to come here.

Hope you enjoy your new job. Justine, Paul and Jule all say "Hello". The garden is starting to produce. Most things aren't ready to harvest, of course. The canning will begin in July.

August Perret has come out several times and we're beginning to court. He is so thoughtful and romantic. I don't know why you didn't want him, but I'm glad you didn't.

Elise smiled at that.

Have you heard anything from Daniel? Yes, yes she had.

I'll close this now. Tell Arnaud I'll write a letter to him soon. Are he and Millie getting serious? I'm glad for him. We miss you and hope to hear from you soon.

Your little sister,

Marie

Elise lowered the letter and stared out the window. She had a close-knit family. Surely things would work out for them if they all pulled together. She refolded the letter and stuffed both of them in her apron pocket then hurried back to work.

She could make it through the day now.

Monday morning Elise awoke and looked out the open window. The room was already warm at sunrise, and the scent of roses and honeysuckle pervaded the air. The clock on the dresser showed five o'clock. Thirty minutes before she had to be up.

She rolled onto her back and put her arms behind her head. Could it be possible that five weeks had passed since she and Tessa had come to work in Topeka? She glanced at the calendar. Sure enough, it was June 22th. Another month before she'd receive her first paycheck to send home.

Elise looked across the room. Tessa was wrapped in her sheet, snoring softly. Elise watched her friend sleep. This might be their last few days together. A month ago they hadn't even met. Now it seemed like they'd known each other forever. They'd grown as close as sisters.

Today they'd receive their permanent placements. They had asked to be together, but Millie said new girls were often placed where needed. The more experienced could choose to move if they wanted to.

She sat up and pulled her knees under her chin. This last month was a learning experience for her. The job of Harvey Girl required responsibility for her actions every minute. Fred Harvey, or one of his representatives, could arrive at any time to observe and inspect.

Elise stood and padded barefoot to the dresser for a drink. She made a face after the first swallow. The water was lukewarm. Another hot day and it wasn't even July. She poured water into her bowl and splashed her face then combed her hair.

She returned to her bed, reached under the pillow and pulled out two envelopes. She smiled as she looked at the bold handwriting on the top one. The envelope was dog-eared and wrinkled from her pocket, but Elise didn't care. The contents were memorized. She pulled the sheet of paper out and read the well-worn lines. Warmth filled her. Daniel enjoyed her company and wanted to see her when he got back. Maybe, just maybe, their relationship would develop into deeper feelings for each other. She missed the way he'd sauntered into the lunchroom at mealtime, and the time they'd spent together on the weekends.

Tessa rolled over and threw back the sheet. "What time is it?"

Elise looked at the clock. "Goodness, it's five-thirty. We better get ready."

Thirty minutes later, Elise slid onto the lunch counter stool between Tessa and Abigail. "Umm. Breakfast smells good. I'll have a stack of pancakes and bacon."

"Me, too." Tessa leaned forward on the counter. "Today we find out where we'll be moved."

"Any place will be better than this," Carolyn stated between bites. "It's dull around here. I'm ready for adventure."

"Maybe you'll get to go out West, New Mexico or someplace like that." Abigail chuckled. "I hear there are Indians out there."

"That's exactly where I want to go, New Mexico or maybe Arizona."

"We'll know soon. Millie wants us to meet her in the parlor after breakfast." Elise drizzled hot syrup over her pancakes and took a big bite. "Umm, these are as tasty as they smell. I love Harvey House food."

A short time later, the girls took seats around the parlor as Millie handed each of them an envelope. "These are your permanent assignments. You'll leave on the train Wednesday morning, so you need to pack." From the edge of the chair by the door, she looked around the room, her eyes suspiciously damp. "You've all been enjoyable to work with. I know you'll do well wherever you go."

She stood and walked to the door. "After you've checked your new assignments, you need to go back to work."

Carolyn gave a whoop. "I go to Las Vegas, New Mexico."

"You ought to have some adventure there." Abigail held up her paper. "I'm going to La Junta, Colorado. Maybe I'll get to see the mountains."

"I've heard Colorado is beautiful." Dorothea pulled the paper from her envelope. "I'm going to Newton, Kansas."

Isabel gave a happy squeak. "I'm going to Florence, Kansas.

I have an aunt and uncle who live there. I hoped I'd be placed there."

Elise stared at the name on her assignment sheet. Emporia, Kansas. A small thrill ran through her. Daniel's family ranch was near Emporia. Maybe she would see him when he came home.

"Where'd you get?" Tessa held her paper for Elise to see. "I'm going to Hutchinson, Kansas. Do you know where that is?"

Elise wrinkled her brow. "I think Hutchinson is near the center of Kansas." She showed her assignment to Tessa. "I'm going to Emporia, Kansas."

"Where's Emporia? Oh, that's where Daniel's family lives, isn't it?"

"Yes. I'm excited to go there."

The next evening, after work, Elise sat on her bed, her writing desk balanced on her lap. She watched Tessa kneel to pack clothes in her trunk. It was hard to believe she and Tessa would work in different cities after tomorrow.

Tessa stood and wiped her forehead with the back of her hand. "My it's hot. There isn't any breeze." She walked to the window and opened it wider. "Even with the sun going down, it's stifling. I doubt it'll be any better in Hutchinson."

Elise set her desk aside and scooted to the edge of the bed. "I don't know. We're going where there are fewer trees. It's mostly grass." She slipped her feet out of her shoes. "At least, that's what Arnaud said."

"That's just great! Edward said Hutchinson is a small town on the prairie. I'm used to big cities." Tessa plopped down on her bed.

"Oh, Tessa, you'll be alright. The towns they send us to are small railroad towns, but we'll be safe in the Harvey Houses."

"I know. I wish we could go to the same place." Tessa grabbed her pillow and threw it across the room.

"Me, too. But we'll always be friends. We just need to write and keep in touch." Elise waved the envelope and walked toward the door. "I wrote to inform my family where I'll be after the move. I need to take this to Millie so she can mail it tomorrow."

Tessa sat on her bed. "I need to do that too. Can I borrow your writing desk?"

The next morning, the scene out the window had changed dramatically. Dark clouds billowed in the west, and a cool breeze blew in the window. Tessa had already folded her blanket. Elise threw back the sheet. "Looks like we're in for a thunderstorm."

"It's all right with me if it rains as long as it cools the air. I'm tired of this heat." Tessa stuffed her quilt into her trunk. "Why is it so hard to get everything in? I didn't have this much trouble when I packed at home. Surely I haven't accumulated that much more stuff." She tried to shut the lid then opened it and refolded the quilt.

Elise laughed as Tessa sat on the lid to fasten it. "You'd better be careful when you open that. Everything will fly out."

After their trunks were taken to the baggage room, Elise and Tessa walked to the parlor where Millie waited. Elise looked around at the other four girls, who had all come to work a month earlier. It seemed a lifetime, and yet it had gone by rapidly. They'd become good friends, but soon they would be scattered. Would they ever be together again? She felt a bitter-sweet mixture of excitement and sadness. It would be interesting to get to her new Harvey House and meet her new co-workers.

Elise hugged Millie on the platform as they all said good-bye, then hurried through the drizzling rain to the waiting train. She leaned out the door of the passenger car and waved before making her way down the aisle. The smell of damp leather reminded her of the day she'd met Daniel on the way to Kansas City. She'd remember that every time she rode in a train for the rest of her life. She suddenly felt a sharp pang of loneliness. Where was Daniel? Was he safe?

"Here's where we sit." Tessa indicated a seat toward the front of the car with a window toward the depot.

Elise scooted in beside her. "Just so I can see. I want to watch as long as possible. It's like leaving home again. So much has happened this last month."

"I know. I feel I've grown to womanhood while being here." Tessa heaved a huge sigh.

Elise laughed. "My, you're being dramatic."

"Well, don't you feel you've matured, become more responsible since you've been here?" Tessa leaned over and rubbed the steam from the rain-streaked window.

Nodding, Elise looked through the rivulets of water. "Yes, I do." She chuckled. "What do you think we'll be like after we've worked a year for Fred Harvey?"

"Heavens, I don't know." Tessa grinned at her. "However, I wish we could do it together."

"Me, too." Elise leaned back against the brown leather seat. The other girls had been given places near them. The whistle blew and the train slowly began to move forward. The depot passed out of sight. Next they passed the small white church where they had attended services on Sunday mornings. Soon the last houses and buildings of the city were behind them.

She gazed at the passing landscape through the steam-fogged window for a while, then lay her head against the seat. The train would take her farther from the family she loved in Missouri but closer to Daniel's hometown. What would she do if she met his parents? When would she see him again? She closed her eyes.

Elise awoke abruptly as Tessa shook her arm. "Hey sleepy head, we're almost to Emporia."

She sat up and rubbed her eyes. Her neck cramped from the awkward position it had been in. "We're almost to Emporia already?" Reaching across Tessa, she wiped the steam from the window and looked out at the rolling countryside.

"That's what the conductor said when he came through a few minutes ago. We just stopped at a small town called Reading and Emporia is next."

Elise pushed her hair back from her face and felt to make sure her hair pins were all in place. She wrinkled her nose and tried to prevent a sneeze as the cool dampness in the air made her shiver. "Who would have thought we could feel chilly after the heat yesterday."

"I know. Isn't it wonderful?"

"Well it's nice to be cool." Elise looked out the window again as the train began to pass the first houses and buildings of Emporia. "Look, Tessa, there's the city limits. I'm almost there."

"I wish this was my destination."

Elise watched in amazement as the train rolled through the city and stopped under a train shed in front of a brick building. A sign that read, "Harvey Dining House," was over the door.

Elise turned to Tessa and threw her arms around her. "I know you're going in to eat, but I'm not sure I'll be able to tell you goodbye." She leaned back. "I'm gonna miss you so much. I'm so glad we met at our interview. You've been a wonderful friend and roommate. Don't forget to write."

Tears sprang to Tessa's eyes. "I don't know what I would have done without you. You've been a special friend to me. I'll never forget you."

They hugged again then Elise grabbed her carpetbag and followed the others down the aisle. The air smelled fresh and earthy as she stepped from the train. The bellboy clanged a gong and led the way into the Harvey House.

The lobby of the building was large and spacious with chairs and couches arranged to encourage patrons to visit. The manager stood in front of a registration desk and welcomed the noisy, chattering passengers. He directed them to the lunchroom or dining room.

As Elise and the other girls approached him, he smiled a welcome and held out his hand. "I'll bet you're the Harvey Girls. We've been expecting you." He scrutinized each of them. "Which of you will be staying here with us?"

Elise raised her hand. "I will. I'm Elise Dumond."

He smiled at her. "My name's Charles Ramsey. I'm the manager here. I can tell you we're delighted to have you." He gestured toward the lunchroom. "Go on in. You other girls need to eat so you can be on your way." He glanced at Elise. "Our head Harvey Girl will show you to your room after dinner."

The aroma of fried chicken wafted in the air as the girls approached the lunchroom door.

Twenty minutes later, Elise stood under the roof of the depot platform and waved as the train, which carried her friends, moved out of sight down the track. Rain poured off the eaves in sheets. Loneliness and homesickness nearly over-whelmed her. She crossed her arms and hugged herself. She didn't know another soul in this Harvey House. How would she make friends?

Someone appeared at her elbow. "Hi. My name's Della Ross. You must be the new Harvey Girl."

Elise jumped and spun around. She stared at the pretty, dark-haired, young woman beside her. "Oh, I didn't hear you." She felt the heat climb into her face under the other girl's friendly appraisal. "My name's Elise Dumond. I...I was just watching my friends leave. Saying goodbye is difficult."

Della nodded. "Kind of scary, isn't it? I remember how I felt when I first came." She smiled. "It won't take you long to make friends, though. We have a lot of great girls here."

Elise relaxed her tense shoulders and sighed in relief.

Della pulled her toward the door. "Come on, let's get inside. Mr. Ramsey and Florence will want to show you to your room."

Charles Ramsey and a woman, who appeared to be in her mid-twenties, met them inside the door. "Elise? Is that right?" At her nod, Mr. Ramsey continued, "This is Florence Baitey, our head waitress and house mother. She will take you to your room and introduce you to your roommate. Your baggage should be there."

Elise waved to Della as she followed Florence up the ornate

staircase to the second floor. They walked through a spacious sitting room and into a hallway, with rooms on either side, similar to the ones in Topeka. Florence stopped at the second door on the left.

"This will be your room, Elise." She stepped in and frowned. "Rosa, I told you to get this room cleaned."

"I've been working on it. I have that side clean." Rosa, a petite, blue-eyed beauty, with strawberry-blonde hair hanging around her shoulders, walked to the door and held out her hand to Elise. "I'm glad to know you, Elise. My name's Rosa Bauer." She indicated the messy room. "I've had the room to myself for a while, so I kind of spread out. I'll get it picked up. Come on in."

Rosa walked to the bed on the left. She moved a pile of clothes and sat down. "There's your trunk. They brought it up a while ago. I hope you don't mind that side of the room."

Elise was glad to see her familiar trunk at the foot of the bed. "That's all right. You have your choice since you were here first."

Rosa flipped her hair over her shoulder. "Did you have a good trip?"

Elise sat on the empty bed. "The trip was uneventful. It rained all the way."

"It's been raining all day here, too. It's so dreary. I don't like it." Rosa looked out the window then stood. "Listen, I have to go to work soon, so I need to go down to the laundry and iron my uniform. Why don't you make yourself comfortable and get unpacked? I think Florence will come back and take you on a tour."

"That sounds good." Elise breathed a sigh of relief as Rosa gathered up her wrinkled uniform and left the room.

She looked around and shook her head. She wasn't terribly organized herself, but this clutter was beyond any she'd ever seen. She'd have to keep her side of the room as clean as possible.

She opened her trunk, took out her bedding and soon had the bed made. Her mother's cheery double wedding ring quilt brightened the room. She opened the window a crack so she could smell the fresh summer rain as she hung her clothes in the wardrobe. Other things went in the dresser.

As Elise finished, Rosa swept into the room, her freshly pressed uniform over her arm. "Wow, you've done wonders with your side of the room. Want to do mine?" She grinned as she picked up a bright colored dress and then dropped it back on the pile. "I don't know what I'll do with all these clothes. My wardrobe is already full." Expertly, she flipped her hair up in a bun on the back of her head, then touched some light color to her cheeks.

"You aren't supposed to wear makeup, are you?" Elise asked in consternation.

"Oh, a little bit doesn't hurt. Nobody ever says anything."

Rosa slipped on her uniform and put on her black hose and shoes. "My skin is so light. If I don't wear something, I look pale as a ghost."

Elise watched as she adjusted her collar and apron. Rosa was stunning, even in the black and white uniform.

Rosa waved her fingers. "Toodles. I have to go to work. I'll see you tonight. Enjoy your free evening."

After Rosa left, Elise scooted back on her bed and leaned against the wall. She was exhausted.

Florence peeked in. "It looks like you've brought order to your side of the room, at least." She shook her head. "I'm afraid I let Rosa get away with more than I should. She does wonderful work as a Harvey Girl, keeps her station straight and clean, but her room is a completely different story!"

Elise slid to the edge of the bed. "She has so much stuff there's not room to put it all."

"You're right." Florence waved toward the hall. "You ready for a tour?"

CHAPTER 16

The next day, Elise awoke to rain drumming against the windowpane. She rolled over and looked out at the gray, overcast sky. She couldn't tell what time it was, but Rosa was still asleep. She'd moved the pile of clothes from her bed to the floor.

Elise sat up and squinted at the clock on her dresser. Five fifty seven. The alarm would go off in three minutes. She pushed her legs out from under the blanket and sat up. It was her first day in a new house. What would it be like?

She curled her toes and walked across the carpet. Tessa had realized her wish for cooler weather. Homesickness shot through Elise as she thought of her friend. Had the other girls arrived at their destinations safely? Elise reached the dresser just as the alarm went off. She pushed the button down then went to the washbasin and splashed water on her face to wake up.

Rosa sat up then lay back down. "Was that the alarm clock? It can't be time to get up, already."

Elise wiped her face dry on a towel. "I'm sorry. I need time to get ready."

Rosa rolled on her side. "Sorry I got in late. Joe and I met after work, and you were sound asleep when I came up." She tucked her hand under her head as if she intended to stay there all day. "Did you sleep well?"

"Yes. I did, and I had a pleasant evening. I met several of the other girls: Betsy, Mabel, and Della." Elise braided her hair and wrapped it around her head, then put on her hair net. "You see this Joe a lot?"

"As much as I can. He's on a train crew, so he's out of town more than I like. He'll be here for the Fourth of July celebration, though." She sat up with a bounce. "Hey, I have an idea. You can go with us to the Randolph's. They have a fabulous dance floor, and they'll have a big dance and fireworks. I'll have Joe ask one of his friends to escort you."

Elise smiled. "Sounds like fun. I love fireworks. I don't need an escort, though. I already have a beau. His name is Daniel. He heads a railroad survey crew." She shrugged. "Besides, I may be scheduled to work."

"Aw, come on, Elise. You can't dance without a partner. It'd only be for *one* evening. What's wrong with that? We'd all be together." Rosa shrugged her shoulders. "As for work, I'll talk to Florence. She can give us Saturday evening off. They try to manage some time off for everyone that day, anyway."

Elise watched as Rosa began to dress. It would be fun to go to the dance and fireworks display, but she didn't want to go with another man. Daniel hadn't asked her to wait for him, but she would.

When they arrived in the lunchroom several customers were already seated at the lunch counter. Betsy motioned Elise over to the window. "Have you looked out? Looks like a river running down the street."

Elise couldn't believe her eyes. "Where did all that water come from? I didn't know it rained that hard."

"You must have slept like the dead." They walked back to the lunch counter. "It poured rain all night. It's a mess. Streets and houses down by the river are flooded."

Elise picked up the coffee pot and filled the cups of the early diners. "Will the trains be on schedule?"

"As far as we know now, everything's on schedule." Betsy gathered the dirty dishes and wiped off the counter where a customer had just left. "You better go ahead and eat, so we'll be ready when the train gets in."

Elise ate quickly then kept busy pouring drinks and cleaning up after departing diners. Train passengers and the local town folk tracked in mud and water. Harvey standards would not allow messy floors, even on such a day.

Mid-morning the rain stopped, but reports of more flooding continued. The Cottonwood River was over its banks and threatened to spill over the dam. Elise didn't know how close that was, but knew it was serious.

At noon, Elise overheard the engineer of the eastbound Santa Fe train talk with Mr. Ramsey. "All the streams we passed were swollen and we heard that a section of track was completely washed away west of Dodge City. We skimmed through about an hour before it happened."

"Will that delay the Cannonball Express?"

"If reports are correct, a crew is at work to repair the track, but the Cannonball will be delayed. It may be tomorrow before it gets through Emporia."

Elise's hand shook as she poured their coffee. Her heart felt as if it were lodged in her throat. Arnaud had taken a train west. Daniel might be in danger. Tessa and the other Harvey Girls were on their way west. As she turned to the next customer, Elise offered a silent prayer for the safety of all her friends.

It was July 4th, a week after her arrival. Elise rolled out of bed and knelt at the open window. The warm, humid breeze caressed her face, and the air smelled fresh and clean. The floodwater had receded, but mud lingered in the streets. She took a deep breath of the morning air then rose and prepared for the day's work.

True to her word, Rosa had spoken to Florence about the evening off. Elise glanced at Rosa, still curled up in bed. She seemed to get whatever she wanted. Maybe that wasn't a good thing. Even so, Elise looked forward to the dance and fireworks.

At four o'clock, Rosa appeared at her elbow as she cleaned the pie case. "Come on, Elise. We're off duty."

Elise gave a final swipe to the shelf and replaced the pie. "All right, I'm ready. I'm finished here." She followed Rosa to their room.

She sat down to remove her working shoes then laid out her light green dress. "Since Daniel left I haven't had many occasions to dress up." *Since Daniel left.* Her heart gave a lurch at the thought.

"Then it's time you get out and have some fun." Rosa slipped into a bright pink dress lavishly trimmed with ruffles. It fit her slim figure perfectly, with a daringly low neckline. Rosa pulled her hair up into a chignon on top of her head. Some locks cascaded down her back in full curls. She finished the style with a pink silk rose pinned in the mass of curls.

Elise felt older and more mature next to Rosa. Although her dress was decorated with lace and fell gracefully over her bustle, she felt dowdy beside Rosa's radiant appearance. Arranging her hair into a chignon, she tucked a matching piece of lace around the knot.

"Come on." Rosa grabbed a small matching handbag. "The men will be waiting."

Elise grabbed her arm. "Rosa, I told you I didn't want an escort."

Rosa pulled her arm away. "Now how would that look if you tagged along with Joe and me? Come on, it's just one evening."

Elise reluctantly followed her to the parlor. As they entered, Rosa hurried across the room to the taller of the two men. He had dark hair and a rather dark complexion. "Joe, this is Elise Dumond, my new roommate."

He smiled and acknowledged the introduction then turned to his companion. "Miss Dumond, this is Richard Humbard. We work on the same train crew."

Richard was a shorter man with a stocky build. His brown hair was combed back in a jaunty, shoulder-length style. A shiver of apprehension raced through Elise as he gave her an appraising look. His brown-eyed gaze never quite reached her face.

Rosa and Joe left the parlor before Elise could protest. Richard took her arm and escorted her outside. As he assisted her into the back seat of a stylish carriage behind Joe and Rosa, Elise noticed that several of the other Harvey Girls were prepared to leave. Joe guided the team of horses out of the parking lot and onto a country road, which led to the Randolph's ranch.

Elise was uncomfortable beside Richard but didn't want to be rude or disappoint Rosa.

As soon as they arrived at the ranch, Rosa jumped from the carriage, grabbed Joe's hand, and nearly dragged him across the muddy ground. Richard helped Elise alight so she wouldn't get her dress soiled against the mud-encased wheel.

A large white gazebo enclosed the dance floor. The pillars and elaborate gingerbread trim under the eaves cast shadows across the floor. Musicians were set up along one side, and several couples were already dancing. Elise and Richard joined the others in a cotillion. Elise began to relax and enjoy the festivities as she recognized some of the other girls on the dance floor.

As the evening progressed she danced with several partners. Lanterns were lit and hung on the pillars around the gazebo as the sun sank below the horizon.

The Skater's Waltz drifted softly from the musicians and filled the air. "Care to dance this one?" Richard held out his hand.

Elise looked at the watch brooch pinned on the lapel of her dress. "I need to find Rosa. It's after nine o'clock. Our curfew is ten. I don't want to be late."

"Aw, come on. We've only danced three times. One more won't make you late." Richard grabbed her hand and pulled her toward the dance floor. He swung her into the waltz; his arm firmly encircled her waist.

She pushed back and turned her head away, but he wouldn't release her. "Don't hold me so tight."

"Come on, Elise. Relax and have some fun. You don't have to be Miss Prim and Proper Harvey Girl now." Elise could feel his breath brush her cheek and she smelled alcohol. Drinking was illegal. Where could he have obtained liquor?

"My name's Miss Dumond, and I'd appreciate it if you'd let me go." She tried to push away, again without making a scene.

"No, *Miss Dumond.*" His rough voice mocked her. "You'll dance this dance with me then we'll watch the fireworks together."

Panic rose in Elise. "We have to leave." She struggled to work herself free.

When the music ended, Richard's grip tightened on her wrist. "We're gonna find a dark, shadowed spot to watch the fireworks." His voice grated in her ear.

Elise looked about for Rosa, or anyone else she could recognize who would help her. Though there were couples on the dance floor, she couldn't see any of the other Harvey Girls. They must be gathering to head back into town.

Richard pulled her from the gazebo into the darkness away from the lanterns. Elise twisted her body and yanked her arm free. She slapped him hard across the face. "You leave me alone." The words escaped through clenched teeth.

Before she could get away, he grabbed her again and, with

a growl, pulled her close. The smell of his breath nauseated her. Revulsion and fear spiraled through her. Elise looked up and whispered, "God, help me." With strength she didn't know she possessed, she pushed him away and ran back to the gazebo. *Where was Rosa?*

A group of women visited near the refreshment table. Elise hurried to stand with them.

"Where've you been?" Rosa spoke behind her. "Where's Richard?"

Elise whirled around. "I've looked everywhere for you." She scanned the dance floor. "I don't know where he is, and I don't care. We have to go, or we'll be late getting back."

"Oh, calm down, Elise, we have time. They haven't even started the fireworks, yet."

Elise followed Rosa and Joe to the chairs set up for viewing the fireworks display. She couldn't see any of the other Harvey Girls. Panic gripped her again. What would happen if she missed curfew her first week at this new Harvey House?

Unable to enjoy the spectacular fireworks, Elise stood as soon as they finished. She could see her watch in the light of a nearby lantern. Twenty minutes before ten. They would have to hurry to make it back on time. Her stomach tied in knots. "Rosa, we have to go."

"We're coming." Rosa and Joe ran behind her across the dance floor.

As they approached the carriage, Elise felt cold fear race through her again. Richard lounged against its side.

He pushed himself up, a smirk on his face. "Well, li'l bird. I knew you'd...have to come sometime. Did ya' think ya' could get away so easy?" His words slurred as he lunged toward her.

Instinctively, Elise threw her hands up to shield herself. She stepped back but not before he had grabbed her wrist.

"Richard, let her go." Joe gripped his friend by the shoulders, which caused him to drop Elise's arm. "What's the matter with you? Where did you get liquor?" Anger was evident in his voice. "Get in the carriage. You need to sober up before the boss sees you or you'll lose your job." He heaved and pushed Richard into the front seat then turned to help Rosa and Elise. "I'm sorry, Miss Dumond. He's really a decent fellow. He gets crazy when he drinks, but I didn't think there was any chance out here. "

Joe untied the horse's reins and vaulted up into the carriage beside Richard. In a few minutes, they left the farmyard and traveled down the muddy, rutted road.

Elise released her breath. She felt miserable as she looked at the dark, night sky. "God, I need your help. I shouldn't have come. Please help us get back on time." She clutched the seat as the carriage lurched over a deep rut. Mud on the wheels slowed them more than normal. Tears of frustration sprang to her eyes.

As they drove past the first houses on the edge of town,

Elise squinted at her watch in the moonlight. She could just make out the numbers on the dial. Her heart sank. Ten minutes after ten!

Joe pulled the carriage to a stop in front of the Harvey House and Elise scrambled down before he could get to her. While Joe helped Rosa out of the carriage and gave her a quick kiss, Elise stared at the dark, forbidding building; the door obviously locked! Despair flooded through her. If she lost her job she didn't have a clue what she would do. She didn't want to go back home.

"Come on, Elise. We've got to get in." Rosa took her arm and pulled her toward the side of the building.

"Where are you going? Don't we have to sign in?"

"Shhhh! Just follow me. I can't sign in again or I'll be fired. I've been late too many times." A carriage rumbled by, and Rosa pulled Elise into the shadows.

"But I can sign in."

"If you do, they'll wonder why I haven't. Relax, we'll make it."

When they rounded the back of the building, Rosa picked up a small stone from the driveway and tossed it at a window beside the kitchen door then pushed Elise over to the building. Elise held her breath. What was Rosa doing?

After a few moments, Rosa picked up another pebble and tossed it at the window. It made a soft clicking sound as it fell to the ground. A light went on inside the room then the window opened a few inches.

"Who's there?" A soft, masculine voice spoke from inside.

Rosa leaned close to the window and whispered. "Hans, it's Rosa. We need to get in. We got stuck in the mud and it made us late."

"Not again, Ro-sa. Vhat am I going to do vith you?"

The window closed and a few moments later a key rattled in the kitchen door. As the door opened, Rosa grabbed Elise's hand, and pulled her inside.

It took a few seconds for Elise's eyes to adjust to the darkness. The yeasty aroma of rising bread assailed her. Hans, the head chef, stood inside the door. He was a short, round man with a pleasant smile.

"Ro-sa, you say you not do this again. You make me lose my job."

"Hans, it wasn't on purpose. We got stuck in the mud on the way back into town from the dance."

Hans shook his head. "It's never on purpose is it, missy? Go, be on your vay." He pushed them toward the back stairs. "Next time I not be so ready to help."

Rosa slipped off her shoes and motioned for Elise to follow. Elise held her breath as they crept up one step at a time. If she got out of this mess, she'd never do it again.

When they reached the top, Rosa peered into the hallway

then nodded. "No one in sight. Come on." She sprinted down the hall with Elise close behind.

Elise darted into their room on Rosa's heels, closed the door behind her then slumped onto her bed. She took a long, deep breath. She'd never expected to make it without getting caught. Hopefully they hadn't been seen.

Rosa undressed. "Don't collapse yet. Get your clothes off and your nightgown on. In case anyone asks, we've been here for thirty minutes."

Elise changed into her nightclothes then sat on her bed. Her hands trembled. "Rosa, if you ever get me into a fix like this again, I will...will... Oh, I don't know what I'll do. I've never been so scared."

"I'm sorry, Elise. I never expected trouble like that. It won't happen again."

"No, it won't!" Elise walked on shaky legs to the dressing table and splashed cold water into her face. Sleep would be long coming tonight.

Elise checked the clock on her dresser. Dawn had begun to lighten the sky and she could barely see the hands in the half-light from the window. It must be about five o'clock. She heaved a sigh, settled back and covered her head with her pillow. She'd rolled and tossed the biggest share of the night and now her body felt like she'd been trampled by a herd of wild horses. A shudder coursed through her at the memory of Richard's unwelcome advances. His attempt to kiss her made her feel sick. She groaned. What would Daniel think of her behavior? He probably wouldn't want anything to do with her.

And what should she do about coming in late? She couldn't afford to lose her job, and Rosa had threatened her life if she told. What if someone saw them come in and reported it? Elise threw off the pillow and sat up on the side of the bed. She had to get up.

She walked to the window and watched as the morning sky lightened. She slid down and rested her arms on the window-sill. The day's warmth could already be felt in the slight breeze that wafted in. Elise laid her head on her arms and continued to watch as morning took over the sky. Finally she rose and walked to the dresser to wash her face. Her head felt about as thick and fluffy as her pillow.

Elise knelt beside her trunk, opened the lid, and rummaged through her things until she came to Mama's Bible. She lifted it out and held it to her chest. She needed to go to church this morning.

At nine-thirty, Elise met Della, Mabel and Betsy in the Harvey House lobby. They had told her at breakfast that she could accompany them to church.

The bright morning sun warmed their backs as they walked the five blocks to a small white church building. A multi-voiced, feathered choir serenaded them from the trees along the board sidewalk and roses filled the air with a delicate scent.

"Weren't the fireworks spectacular last night?" Della glanced at her companions. "Even from the edge of town they looked wonderful. Did any of you go out to the dance?"

"I did." Mabel raised a finger, and smiled. "I went with several of the other girls who worked the morning shift. We had to leave before the fireworks to get back to town in time, though." She slowed her step to match Elise's. "We watched the fireworks from the carriage. You went, too, didn't you, Elise?"

Elise nodded. "I wish I'd gone with you." She clutched Mama's Bible to her chest.

"Oh, you went with Rosa, didn't you?" Della nodded, causing her bonnet brim to flop. "We should have warned you about her and her friends. She does like to party."

"Um-hm. You could say that." Elise kicked a rock lying on the boardwalk. "I'll never do that again."

"Rosa would have been fired long ago if Florence hadn't covered for her." Betsy shaded her eyes from the sun.

"Why does Florence do that? Doesn't she know she is putting her own job in danger?" Elise wrinkled her brow.

"Florence and Hans, the chef, have been seeing each other, which is against the rules. Rosa knows that and holds it over their heads."

"Oh, I see." Elise nodded.

At the church door, the tall, middle-aged pastor and his wife greeted them. The girls entered the cool sanctuary, and Elise followed Mabel into a pew towards the front. She sat and stared at the cross behind the pulpit. She felt so far away from God. How could she get back into fellowship with Him? Her heart cried out, but it seemed her prayers reached no higher than the vaulted ceiling of the church.

CHAPTER 17

Daniel sat cross-legged on his saddle, with a woven wool, Indian blanket wrapped around his shoulders, and watched the embers glow in the campfire. The fire hissed and sputtered as light rain fell into it. He'd decided to give up on sleep after he'd listened to the night sounds and stared at the gray clouds for an hour. Abe and Carlos snored a few feet away.

It was July fifteenth. They'd been on the trail a month and only covered a third of the prescribed distance. Since they'd entered the Cherokee Strip, they'd been besieged with problems. The continual clouds and sporadic rain had inhibited their survey. It was difficult to set up the transits and see the elevations. One of the level scopes broke after a week. Thankfully he'd brought a backup. The threat of outlaws who hid in these hills, and ambushes by hostile Indians compounded their troubles.

He smiled. He shouldn't be discouraged. God had provided for them. On their seventh day out, they'd met Running Bear, a friendly Cherokee rancher who befriended them. He was glad to have the railroad come through so he could ship his cattle. He'd gone to the Counsel to request protection for them. Although there were differences of opinion, the chief had declared safe passage.

Daniel slid off the saddle and rested against it. Coyotes howled in the distance, a small animal scurried through the grass beside him, and the horses and mules stomped and moved about nearby. Daniel pounded his fist against the ground. He'd always enjoyed the outdoors and his job as surveyor for the railroad, but this time it was wearing on him. To make matters worse, Carlos was frustrated with the delays and had threatened to turn back. Daniel understood his discontent. Carlos had left his home and family in New Mexico to work on the survey crew in Arizona and California. He hadn't had an opportunity to return home before this job assignment.

Daniel looked at the cloud-shrouded sky and ran his hand over his bewhiskered jaw. "Father. What is it You have to teach me? Have You brought me into the wilderness like You did Moses?" He buried his face in his hands. "Please, Father, keep Elise safe and let her know I think of her, even if I can't get word to her." His heart ached with loneliness. She had probably been transferred to another Harvey House and he had no idea where.

He dragged his pack closer and pulled out his Bible then turned to his favorite verses, Proverbs, three, five and six. Holding it close to the fire, he read the verses aloud. *"Trust in the Lord with all thine heart; and lean not unto thine own understanding. In all thy ways acknowledge Him, and He shall direct thy paths."*

"Thank You, Lord." He stared into the fire again. "I'm glad You know the way through this wilderness. I'll keep trusting You." He pushed the Bible back into his pack and lay down on his blanket. Peace flooded through him. They should soon be to the unclaimed Oklahoma territory.

Elise looked at the calendar on the wall. *Thursday, July sixteenth.* She'd been in Emporia two weeks. In spite of the July heat, she enjoyed the small town and its citizens. If Daniel were here, it would be perfect.

She glanced around and realized that most of the diners had left. Her section was empty. The other three girls on duty had only one or two customers each.

She walked to a small enclosure at the back of the lunch-room, took out her handkerchief and wiped the beads of per-spiration from her forehead. She pushed an escaping strand of hair beneath her hair net and pinned it in place then washed her hands. The heat made work difficult. Even with the win-dows open, there wasn't enough of a breeze to move the air.

She dropped a piece of ice from the icebox into a glass and filled it from the spigot on the water tank.

Betsy carried a tray of dishes to the kitchen. "This has been some morning, hasn't it? I've been busy since I came on duty."

"I have too." Elise sighed.

"Have you heard? Florence resigned as Harvey Girl. She and Hans are getting married." Betsy poured a glass of water.

Elise frowned. "Where did you hear that?"

"Della told me at breakfast this morning. Florence has three months left on her contract, so she'll have to pay back some of her wages. If they get married, they can't both work at the Harvey House. I imagine Hans was afraid he'd lose his job since they were together so much. Almost everyone knew."

"That means Della will be the new head waitress, doesn't it? Isn't she next in line?"

"She doesn't know if she'll get the job. It'll be several days before anyone knows."

Elise shook her head. "That will change things around here." She grabbed a dust cloth. "I think I'll dust over the door and windows and clean the window sills since no one's here. The dust collects so quickly with the windows open."

A few minutes later some local customers sauntered in. Elise hurried to replace her dust cloth and wash her hands. She glanced at her apron. "Oh no. Betsy, I have dirt on my apron. Can you cover for me while I run up to the room and change?"

"Sure. Hurry back, though. The eleven-thirty train is due shortly."

"I know. I'll hurry."

When Elise returned with a clean apron, the lunchroom had become a busy place. Betsy rushed past with a pitcher of ice water and a menu. "The train got in early."

As Elise served a tray of food orders to her customers, she glanced up to see a tall, dark haired man standing with Mr. Ramsey in the doorway.

Alma brushed past her. "That's Mr. Harvey."

In spite of the mid-morning heat, a shiver ran down Elise's spine. Thank goodness she'd dusted and changed her apron. She glanced around her area. Everything was in order. The diners ate and visited unaware that the boss had arrived.

As Elise took orders and served meals she tried hard not to watch the two men as they proceeded through the room. She held her breath as Mr. Harvey whipped out his white handkerchief and wiped it above the window, then released it with a soft sigh. He was satisfied with the result!

Elise shared a relieved look with Alma and Betsy when the men walked into the kitchen. At least Fred Harvey hadn't seen anything, yet to draw his sudden wrath.

A sound resembling a deep growl drifted from the dining room. The girls stopped in their tracks and listened. "Is that makeup on your face? What's your name?"

Elise put a trembling hand over her mouth. Rosa?

The whole house was filled with Mr. Harvey's enraged voice. "You know that's strictly against the rules. You're released from your duties right now!"

A few moments later, Rosa ran from the dining room.

Mr. Harvey and Mr. Ramsey walked into the foyer. Their voices carried back. "Where's the head waitress? She should've been knowledgeable of this."

"Yes, Sir. I know, Sir. She has quit to get married. She hasn't been replaced yet."

Betsy looked at Elise, her neck tense and her eyes large. "Lucky for Florence and for Della," she said quietly.

Elise leaned against the counter. She was afraid her knees would buckle. She'd never break another rule!

As the train passengers left the lunchroom, several locals walked in to fill the stools. Elise gathered the dirty dishes in her section and hurried to the kitchen then returned to clean the counter. She glanced up, stopped in mid-swipe and did a doubletake. One of the men who sat in her section was an older version of Daniel. His hair, a few shades darker blond, was tinged with grey at the temples, but the resemblance in his face was unmistakable. This had to be Mr. Gilbertson, Daniel's father. He had the same azure eyes and square chin. A teen-age boy who appeared to be a couple of years older than Jule accompanied him. There wasn't much doubt he was Daniel's younger brother. A tall, lanky cowboy followed them. Another young cowhand sat in Becky's section. They all wore boots, Levi's, work shirts and their cowboy hats.

Elise felt her pulse rate increase and her hand shook as she quickly finished cleaning the counter. She'd wondered if she would know Daniel's family if they came in. Now here they were in front of her. But they didn't know who she was.

It was hard not to stare as she approached with water and menus. "What can I get you to drink?" She smiled at Daniel's brother.

He glanced up. "I'll take a large glass of milk." His eyes were also the same deep blue as Daniel's. He scanned the menu. "I'll take one of those Monte Cristo Sandwiches." He turned to the older man. "You ought to try one of those, Dad. They're incredible. Daniel recommended it when I came into town with him before he left."

Mr. Gilbertson flipped his cup over. "I'll take coffee." He pointed to the menu. "I'll just have a ham and cheese then I'll get a piece of pie to finish off."

The younger man grinned. "I want pie, too. We need to celebrate when we get into town."

Elise faced the tall cowboy. "And what can I get you?"

"Wa'll now, Miss, Ah'll have coffee and one of them there Monte Cristo sandwiches, like Thomas. Ah'll have some pie to finish up, too."

Elise smiled as she turned to enter their orders then continued to her other customers. She didn't mean to eavesdrop but couldn't help overhearing their conversation as she worked.

Mr. Gilbertson swiveled on his stool toward the tall cowboy. "Slim, will you and William go to the stockyard and make sure the paperwork is complete for the shipment of the steers? Thomas and I need to go to the Mercantile and get some supplies for the womenfolk."

"Sure thing, boss. Did I hear the auctioneer say those beeves brought ten cents a pound? That's a right fancy price."

"Yes, it is. There's a lucrative market back east for beef cattle right now. Good time to sell. I may look into buying more stock."

"Ah'm glad things are lookin' up. It's been a hard coup'la months with losin' Mary and then Daniel havin' to go on thet surveyin' team."

Mr. Gilbertson sighed. "I was hoping Daniel would come back and take over the ranch, but I'm afraid he's been lured away by the railroad."

Slim peered over his boss's shoulder. "I think ya' have your rancher right here."

"I think you're right." The father turned back to his son as Elise served their sandwiches.

The conversation slowed to a stop as the men ate their lunch. When they finished their pie Mr. Gilbertson waited as

Elise refilled his coffee cup. "Slim, Thomas and I'll meet you and William back at the livery in a couple of hours. Take time to finish any business you have while we're here." The four of them rose and departed.

Becky hurried to Elise's side as the last customers left. "Did you see that handsome cowboy in my section? His name is William. He said he's a hand at the Lazy G ranch. That was his boss and son with their ranch foreman in your area. I hope William comes in again. I'd love to get better acquainted with him."

"Slow down." Elise paused on her way to the kitchen with the dirty dishes. "Yes, I saw him, and he is quite handsome. But do you know who the Lazy G's owner is? The boss, as you put it? He's my boyfriend's father, Mr. Gilbertson! He looks just like Daniel only several years older. And that was Daniel's younger brother. I nearly fainted when they walked in. I've never met them, and they don't know me, but I couldn't mistake who they were."

"Wow. William works for your Daniel's father. That's amazing."

"I know. What else is going to happen today? I'm exhausted already and it's just one o'clock."

When Elise had everything cleaned up from lunch, she took a short break to check on her roommate. Rosa lay across the bed and sobbed in her pillow. "Rosa, I'm sorry."

"It doesn't matter." Rosa sat up and beat her pillow. "They

can have their old rules. I hate Fred Harvey and this whole place. I don't want to work here anyway." She jumped up and wiped her eyes.

Elise sat on her own bed, unsure of what to do or say. She had been afraid this would happen. In spite of Rosa's errant ways, Elise had grown fond of her. The Harvey House would seem less colorful after she left.

Rosa yanked a bag from her wardrobe. "Don't pity me. It's better this way, anyhow. I'm going to get married."

Elise sat forward on the bed. "Rosa, really? That's wonderful. Did Joe ask you?"

Rosa's face colored. "Well no. Not yet. But I'm sure he's going to. We've talked about it."

"I hope everything works out." Elise stood up. "Is there anything I can do to help?"

Rosa shook her head. "No, you better get back to work. Don't want Fred Harvey to come down on you." She paused and looked at Elise. "That'd kill you, wouldn't it? How come you always obey the rules?"

Elise shrugged. "I don't know. I guess it's because my parents taught me to obey. I don't like it sometimes, but I feel terrible when I break the rules. Besides, I fear the consequences. The Fourth of July's a good example."

Rosa looked out the window. "I never had parents to teach me anything. They died when I was little." She turned back to

Elise. "I lived with my aunt. She was so strict, I decided I would do whatever I wanted when I got away from her." She pulled a dress from the wardrobe and held it up. "I'll find something to do, I suppose. I always have."

As Elise went back to work, she felt disturbed. If only she could help Rosa. She'd lost her parents too, but she'd had them long enough to learn from them. Why was it so hard to talk about God? Where once she had had such faith, now there was a void.

The remainder of July flew by in a succession of busy days. No relief from the heat and the grass turned brown. Arnaud stopped by twice, once heading west and once on his way back to Topeka. He was on a tight schedule both times and only stayed through the meal stops.

The last Friday of the month, Elise awoke and sat up in bed. Today she would get her first paycheck. Two whole months she had worked for this. Heat already radiated from the open window, and it was only five-thirty.

She glanced at Betsy asleep in the other bed. After Rosa left, she and Betsy had asked Della, the new head-waitress, if they could room together. Betsy was tall and slender with light brown hair and lively, grey-green eyes. Tidy and quiet, she and Elise complemented each other.

Elise stood, walked to her dresser and picked up Tessa's

letter. She missed her friend. She pulled out the single sheet of paper and reread the hastily scrawled lines.

July 20, 1885

Dear Elise,

I wanted to get a few lines written to you in answer to your letter. I miss you so much.

I know you miss Daniel, but just wait. He'll be back for you. He said he would. Edward sent me a letter. He wants to come see me. It would be nice to see him, but I don't think I want to get serious.

There's a good-looking rancher who comes into the Harvey House here. He doesn't say much, but the story is, he's a widower with four children. I'd kind of like to get better acquainted. I'll let you know if anything develops with that.

It's beastly hot here. We haven't had rain since the storm when we first got here. I've never worked so hard in all my life, including the farm at home. Wheat and cattle trains come through all the time.

The town has grown and is quite modern. Stores have been built along Main Street and there are lots of beautiful houses. Nothing wild has happened so far. I work with a good crew and staff. Fred Harvey built this building two years ago.

I have to quit writing now and get back to work. I hope we can see each other soon.

Your friend,

Tessa

Elise folded the letter and slipped it into the envelope. She splashed water in her face and began to dress for breakfast.

That afternoon, Elise sat with the other Harvey Girls in the parlor and stared at the envelope in her hand. Her name was typed on the front. Tearing it open she looked at the money inside. There it was, seventeen dollars and fifty cents. She had also accumulated three dollars in tips. Excitement raced through her. She could help with the farm payment: the main reason she'd become a Harvey Girl.

She stuffed the envelope in her pocket and walked with Betsy to her station. "Next Monday I start work in the dining room. I served Mr. Ramsey and Della their full, four-course meal today at noon." Elise grinned and gave a small skip.

Betsy smiled. "I heard. Congratulations! Of course, you know you have to come back and take your turn working in the lunchroom."

"I know." Elise wrinkled her nose. "And when I get in the dining room, I'll be expected to serve sixteen people with each train stop. It's kind of scary."

Betsy laughed and punched her lightly on the arm. "You worry too much. It'll be exciting, and you know it."

CHAPTER 18

On Sunday Elise awoke to the sound of raindrops hitting against her windowpane. The fragrance of a summer shower wafted in on the cool breeze. She knelt beside the window and took a deep breath. It would be invigorating to run outside and dance in the rain the way she had as a child. She hoped the rain wouldn't keep them from going to church. She'd begun to look forward to Sunday services.

A few minutes later, she sat down at the lunch counter beside Della. "This is quite a change in the weather isn't it?" She looked out the window at the gray sky and drizzling rain. "The cool air feels good. Are you still planning to go to church?"

"Oh, yes, we're going."

"How're we going to get there? We'll be soaked if we walk."

"I asked Mr. Ramsey to take us in his carriage and he's

agreed." Della picked up her fork as Alma served her a plate of hotcakes, bacon and eggs.

"He's going to take us?" Elise turned her coffee cup right side up and motioned to Alma. "I'll take the same as she has, please. That smells wonderful." Elise spread her napkin in her lap.

Della smiled at her. "He said he was going anyway so a few more riders wouldn't hurt. He'll be at the front door at fifteen minutes before ten."

"I'll be there."

When Elise and Betsy arrived in the lobby, Della and Mabel were already there. "Let's wait on the porch. It's covered so we shouldn't get wet. Then we can see and smell this stuff they call rain. It's been so long since we've had any, I've almost forgotten what it's like." Elise led the way outside.

As Mr. Ramsey drove his horses and carriage around under the train shelter, a loud clap of thunder reverberated across the sky and the rain poured down. He leaned over and gave them a hand up from the platform. "Are you sure you want to get out in this? You might get soaked."

"We're sure." Della climbed in and sat on Elise's lap. "We won't melt."

In a few minutes, Mr. Ramsey pulled up to the boardwalk in front of the church. Before he could alight to help them, Della climbed down and turned to help the others. "Thank you very much for the ride."

Elise picked up her skirt and hurried with the others to the door. Inside, she wiped her feet on the rug provided for the purpose and brushed the rain from her skirt. "Whew, I'm glad we didn't have to go any farther in that downpour."

The pastor stood inside accompanied by a distinguished, dark haired, young man in a dress suit. "Well here, Mr. Johnson. These young ladies are Harvey Girls. They work at the local Harvey House in the depot." Pastor Longford turned to the young man. "Have you had the opportunity to eat there? It's the best food in town."

Mr. Johnson held out his hand. "I'm pleased to meet you ladies. I haven't had the privilege to eat at the Harvey House, but I'll soon remedy that sad state of affairs."

"Ladies, please meet Mr. Benjamin Johnson, our new pharmacist. He's recently set up his business in town." He introduced each girl in turn, ending with Elise. "This is Miss Dumond, one of the latest to join our congregation here."

Elise was disconcerted by Mr. Johnson's direct, appraising gaze, which lingered on her face. Was something wrong with her appearance? Should she check her hair-do after the mad dash through the rain?

"I'm pleased to meet you all." His words were for all of them, but his gaze rested on Elise.

The girls entered the sanctuary and filed into their accustomed pew near the front.

After they sang several hymns and heard the announcements, Elise sat back to enjoy the sermon. She soon leaned forward again. The message was about Christians who didn't receive God's blessing because they didn't read their Bibles and pray. Elise shifted uncomfortably on the pew as guilt pricked her conscience. The pastor seemed to speak directly to her. She never prayed unless she was in trouble or needed help. And, although she had laid Mama's Bible on her bedside stand, she hadn't read it since moving here. Elise stared at her hands, a lump of misery in her chest. At the end of the sermon, when the pastor invited everyone to come forward and pray, she gripped the pew in front of her. She would read Mama's Bible when she got back to the Harvey House.

After the service, Mr. Johnson waited at the door of the sanctuary. "Do you ladies have a ride back to the Harvey House?"

"No, we don't." Della smiled at him.

"I'd be glad to take you in my carriage if you like." Mr. Johnson gazed at Elise.

Mabel spoke up. "We'd appreciate that."

When Elise stepped out on the stairway landing, she was surprised at the bright sunshine. She swung around to the others. "It's so beautiful. I think I'll walk. I need the fresh air." Hopefully, Mr. Benjamin Johnson would get the message that she wasn't interested. Betsy fell into step with her as she started down the boardwalk.

Mabel was waiting for them when they arrived back at the Harvey House. "What did you think of Ben Johnson? He's handsome, isn't he? I think he's interested in you, Elise. He kept looking at you. I wish he'd look at me with such interest."

Elise gestured dismissively. "He's rather handsome. Not nearly as good looking as my beau, Daniel. You can have Mr. Johnson, Mabel. I'm not interested."

"Oh, that's right. Your man is off on a trip somewhere, isn't he? When is he coming back?"

Elise sighed, her heart heavy. "He's on a survey trip for the railroad. I don't know when he'll be back." She frowned as she headed toward the stairs. He'd been gone almost a month and a half. Was he thinking of her? Would he want to see her when he got back? She placed her fingers on her lips. What had his kiss meant?

***

Elise glanced around the large dining room. This was her first day to serve dining patrons instead of the lunchroom crowd. Sunshine flooded in the windows, and the aroma of apple pie wafted in the air. Square tables, which seated eight people, were placed at intervals around the room with just enough space to move between them. Each Harvey girl served two tables.

The noon train had left and local patrons would soon arrive. Elise removed the soiled linen tablecloths and replaced them with fresh ones and then reset the tables, careful to place everything in order.

As she brought water to fill the glasses, she heard a voice behind her. "You do that very well."

Whirling around, she found herself looking at Benjamin Johnson's face. She glanced at the door. "Did Della seat you?"

He smiled. "No. I just came in. I knew where I wanted to go." He pulled out a chair and sat down.

Elise tried not to let her irritation show as she finished filling the glasses and bringing out the salads. She wasn't sure why Mr. Johnson's demeanor irritated her. He seemed like a nice enough man.

The chairs began to fill as Della seated other customers. Pointing to Ben from behind his back, she looked at Elise and mouthed, "I couldn't stop him."

Elise took orders and the meal proceeded smoothly. Several of the townspeople who hadn't met Mr. Johnson were gratified to make the acquaintance of the new pharmacist. One middle-aged man grinned at him. "I'll come see you soon. I'm nearly out of my indigestion medicine."

The dining room emptied except for Ben. He moved his cup so she would refill it. "Are you upset with me?"

"No, why should I be upset?" Elise tried to be polite. In a Harvey House, the customer was always right. She began to clear the other table. "Why did you come to this table?"

"I wanted to get acquainted with you. I hear there's a

Harvey Girl dance next Saturday night. You going to invite me?"

She glared at him. "No."

"Well how do you like that." He grinned at her. "Then I'll just have to get one of the other girls to ask me. I'm going to dance with you, Miss Dumond."

"Mr. Johnson, don't you need to get back to work?" Elise continued cleaning her area, trying not to look at him. Finally when she glanced his way, he smiled at her, then stood and walked from the room, a noticeable limp to his gait.

"Ooh, that man." Elise fumed to the girl at the table next to hers.

"I'd be glad if a good-looking man made eyes at me that way."

Elise shrugged. She'd much rather have Daniel making eyes at her. If only he were here. She didn't need another man.

The next Saturday evening, Elise and Betsy strolled into the parlor. Elise scanned the room. Other Harvey Girls, Margaret, Bertha and Clara were already there. They sat and visited while they waited for the dance to begin. Alma played a rousing southern ballad on the piano.

Earlier, Elise had helped several of the other girls move the furniture back against the walls, and Hans had provided punch, small sandwiches and several kinds of cookies for refreshments. Young men from the train crews, as well as local cowboys and businessmen were in the room. Even though Ben had eaten his lunch at Elise's table everyday through the week, Mabel had asked him to the dance.

Della met the girls as they walked in. "Elise, you and Betsy are finally here. Would you help me pour the punch?"

Elise grinned. "I'd be glad to."

"Sure." Betsy chuckled, lightheartedly. "That way we can watch everyone and not appear to stare."

A grin lit Della's face as she led Elise to the refreshment table. "Look at Mabel and Mr. Benjamin Johnson. She's tried hard to entertain him." She glanced over her shoulder. "He's watched the door ever since they arrived."

Elise laughed. "All the more reason to serve punch."

Betsy touched Elise's arm. "Look, William's here! You know, the cowboy from the Lazy G." She sighed dramatically. "He's so handsome."

Elise watched the tall cowboy. "Too bad Daniel couldn't be with him."

"I wish he could be, too. I'd like to meet him."

Two couples strolled up to the refreshment table. Elise poured punch as they sampled the cookies and sandwiches.

Della walked to the piano. "The dance is about to begin. Everyone find a partner." She spoke to the piano player then stood back with a smile as the introductory chords of "Beautiful Dreamer" filled the room.

Becky drew in her breath. "He's headed this way."

William approached, his gaze focused on her. "Becky, right? Will you dance with me?"

"Yes. I'd like that." She glanced at Elise. "Is that alright?"

Elise nodded as she watched Ben swing Mabel out onto the floor. "You go ahead." She motioned for Betsy to dance with William. "I'll stay here and serve."

At the beginning of the next dance, Ben walked over to the refreshment table. "Why have you ignored me, Miss Dumond? Are you going to stay behind that table all evening?" He picked up a cup of punch.

Elise glanced up at him with an innocent expression. "Ignore you, Mr. Johnson? Not at all. I haven't had an opportunity to talk with you. You came with Mabel, uh...Miss Hartley, not me."

"Why are you giving me such a hard time? You know I want to get acquainted with you." He leaned forward and looked in her face. "Is there someone else?"

Elise smiled. "Yes, as a matter of fact, there is. He's on a railroad survey team down south of Kansas in the unclaimed Indian land."

"That far away? Do you have any promises?"

"He said he'd come back."

"But you're not sure, right?"

Elise straightened her shoulders. "He said he'd be back.

I'm going to wait for him."

Ben grinned. "Well we can be friends can't we? Do things together? At least until you make up your mind about this guy."

Elise didn't smile. "I'm not against being friends, but I have made up my mind about Daniel, and you won't change it."

"We'll see." He murmured quietly. Elise felt uneasy.

As the evening progressed, Elise danced with Ben for several dances. He always found a way to break in or maneuver to become her partner in the group dances. She had to admit, in spite of his limp, he was a smooth dancer.

At fifteen minutes before ten o'clock, Della again stood beside the piano. "It's been fun to have all of you here. I hope you had a good time. We'll have one more dance so pick your partner." Soon the strains of "Good night, Ladies" were floating out across the room.

Elise stood by the refreshment table as Ben danced with Mabel. He turned and smiled at Elise with a wink as he left the room. She looked down at her hands. Was anything wrong with being friends? Although she liked Daniel tremendously, she hadn't made a commitment to him. He hadn't made any promises, either.

A few days later, Elise was greeting customers as Della brought them in when she heard a familiar, husky voice beside her. "Hey, little sis, how you doing?"

Elise swung around to face her brother. It took all her self-discipline and restraint to refrain from a huge hug around his neck. "Arnaud, I'm so glad to see you. Do you have time to visit?"

"I can't stay long. I'm on a schedule, you know." He took her hand. "But maybe we can talk a little bit." He took a seat across from where Ben sat with a scowl on his face.

Elise continued to take orders and deliver them to the kitchen. When she returned, she put her hand on the back of Arnaud's chair. "Mr. Johnson, this is my older brother, Arnaud. He's an engineer with the Santa Fe. In fact that's his train out there," she stated proudly. "And, Arnaud, this is Mr. Benjamin Johnson. He owns the new pharmacy here in town."

Ben smiled in response to the introduction and held out his hand to Arnaud. Arnaud looked at Elise, questioningly, before he returned the friendly gesture.

Elise removed the salad plates and served the meals, but she watched as they carried on a conversation. At the end of the meal Ben stood. "I need to get back to work, and I know you want a little time to visit. I'll see you tomorrow, Elise... Miss Dumond."

After he left, Arnaud pushed back his coffee cup. "Who's that fellow? I thought you were committed to Daniel." He leaned back in his chair and crossed his arms. "How come you're letting this guy hang around?"

Elise frowned. "I told you, he's a businessman. He insists

that he sit at my table. He says he just wants to be friends." Elise gathered the dessert plates with a bit of extra force.

Arnaud sat forward and finished his coffee. "Elise, this guy may be just a friend to you, but that's not how he feels. I can tell by the moony-eyed way he stares at you." At Elise's exasperated look, he continued, "Just be careful. I don't want you to be hurt. Remember, Daniel's a special guy."

"I know." Elise refilled his coffee cup as she tried to calm down. "Have you heard anything from home? I haven't since the first of the month. It sounded like things were alright then."

"That was the last time I heard, too." Arnaud grinned. "I do have some good news, though."

"What?"

"Millie has accepted my proposal and agreed to marry me when she finishes her contract in February."

"Oh, Arnaud, that's wonderful. I'm so excited." Elise forgot her self-discipline and restraint and threw her arms around his neck. "It'll be great having Millie as a sister-in-law." Elise released him. "So Millie will be quitting as a Harvey Girl? Where will you live?"

"We'll live in Topeka. That's where my work is based."

"That's fantastic." Elise gave a little skip.

Arnaud stood. "Well, I better be on my way; have to get back on the road." He paused. "Oh by the way, I think I saw Jerome get off the train here. Have you seen or heard from him?"

Elise shook her head. A sense of dread settled in her stomach. "Not since I was in Topeka. Wonder what his business is? He can't run a saloon here." She glanced at the door. "I hope he leaves me alone."

"He probably will. Don't worry about it." Arnaud gave her a quick hug. "I'll see you when I get back." He patted her shoulder as he turned to leave. "Just keep your head on straight, little sis. Remember, Daniel will be home soon."

CHAPTER 19

Daniel pulled Midnight to a halt and scanned the terrain. The tall grass and scrub brush gave way to a row of trees along the horizon, hopefully, the indication that they had reached the Cimarron River. It'd been two weeks since they'd left Black Bear Creek. They'd only found small springs to fill their canteens. He pulled his handkerchief from his pocket and wiped his brow. The sun bore down. They'd spent the morning and early afternoon surveying. Now they needed to find a good place to make camp.

He pointed toward the trees. "Let's move that way. At least we'll have some shade and maybe water."

Abe guided the mules and wagon off the cattle trail and toward the trees. Carlos followed on his Palomino. He'd bartered a silver crucifix and a turquoise belt buckle for the mare.

Daniel sighed with relief. This must be the river shown on the map. He swung off of Midnight and led him through the thick stand of cottonwoods. The swift flowing river was about twenty-five yards wide and crystal clear water.

The three men stood at the riverbank. "Now that's a sight for sore eyes." Abe knelt and dangled his fingers in the water.

Daniel examined the banks then pointed upstream. "There's a break in the trees. Let's check it out."

Soon they had camp set up and a fire started. Carlos used the water to boil potatoes and cook a rabbit they'd shot and skinned earlier in the day. Abe mixed up a batch of biscuits.

Daniel sat on a small stool at their makeshift table. He studied the topographical map which outlined the borders of the Indian reservations and copied the coordinates along the line they had surveyed. He periodically glanced up and watched Carlos and Abe busy preparing the meal. Carlos took the job as cook reluctantly at first, but seemed to have settled into it.

Abe approached and looked over Daniel's shoulder. He pointed at the map. "This the Cimarron River?"

"It has to be. That means we're well into the unclaimed land."

"It's glad I am that ve finally made it across the Cherokee and the Ponca Reservations. Now ve can concentrate on the unassigned land."

Daniel nodded. "It's a good thing we had Running Bear's

help or the tribesmen and braves might have been more contentious." He studied the area. "We need to watch for an appropriate town site. We're supposed to plat Guthrie near this river so there'll be water for the steam engines. Tomorrow we'll head upstream and see what we can find. There's plenty of unhindered space."

"Señors, supper es ready." Carlos was dipping stew into pewter bowls.

Abe turned toward the fire pit as Daniel rolled up the map and cleared the table. He joined the other men. "This is a meal fit for a king, Carlos. Plenty of water to cook with makes a difference, doesn't it?"

"Sí, and Abe make ze beescuits, very good."

The next morning, Daniel awoke to a spectacular sunrise. Swatches of purple, pink and orange were flung across the horizon. He sat on his blanket for several minutes and basked in the relative coolness of the early morning. A feathered choir of robins, cardinals and finches serenaded him from the trees, with a woodpecker keeping time. They reminded him of the evening walks he'd had with Elise. He closed his eyes and listened. Warmth flooded through him at the thought of the kiss they had shared before he left. *Did she remember?* He bowed his head and prayed for her as he did each morning.

The warmth of the south breeze indicated the approaching

heat of the day. He arose and folded his bedroll then stirred the embers of the fire.

Carlos rolled over, sat up and yawned.

Daniel walked to the river and knelt to wash his face and hands. He was glad he didn't have to conserve every drop of water. When he returned to camp, both Carlos and Abe were up and had folded their bedding.

"Ees beautiful morning, sí?" Carlos waved his arm toward the sunrise.

Abe grunted. "'Tis beautiful now, but vill heat up soon enough vhen zee sun is up in zee sky."

Daniel grinned. "I've been enjoying the sunrise and the birds' songs." He placed his belongings in the wagon. "But you're right, Abe. We need to move out before it gets too hot. We'll follow the cattle trail. It should lead us to a good river crossing."

They ate their breakfast of rabbit stew and biscuits and prepared to leave. Abe drove the wagon back onto the trail and Daniel and Carlos rode ahead. They soon came to a larger clearing in the trees. The trail led to the water's edge. The river had widened and the water was flowing much shallower. Daniel pulled up at the bank. "Let's get some elevations and coordinates so I can get them plotted, then we'll wade across."

Abe arrived with the wagon, and a half-hour later they were ready to ford the river. In spite of the reluctance of the animals, it was an uneventful venture and they exited safely on the other side. The trail followed the river for about an hour then the larger Cimarron River veered to the right and a smaller river continued to the southwest.

Daniel signaled for them to stop. He guided Midnight to the wagon. "I think we should establish the town site for Guthrie in this area where the Cimarron and this smaller creek converge. There'll be plenty of water for the town, and it can be a watering site for the railroad. Let's set up camp here and survey to find the best spot."

They had begun to unpack near some trees when Carlos rode his Palomino to the wagon and pointed up the trail. "Look. Cavalrymen!"

Daniel swung around. There were five U.S. soldiers riding toward them.

The soldiers pulled up in front of the wagon. The one in the middle rode closer. "What're you doing here? This is Oklahoma land. It's not open to settlement."

Daniel met the lead rider. "We work for the Atchison, Topeka and Santa Fe Railroad. The government has given us permission to survey for a rail line through the unassigned land. We are also commissioned to set up water stations and town sites for the railroad."

"Do you have documentation?"

"Yes." Daniel walked to the wagon and retrieved the paperwork from the railroad and the U.S. government.

The soldier examined the documents then nodded and handed them back to Daniel. "Okay. There've been problems with squatters who came in and set up camp. We've had to escort them back to Kansas more than once." He held out his hand. "We're from Fort Reno, west of here, and we patrol this trail. If you need anything let us know."

Daniel shook with him. "Thank you, we appreciate that."

"If you need to stock up on supplies, feel free to come to the Fort."

"We may take you up on that. We'll be here for several days, surveying. We need to set up three railroad depot sites in this area so I'm sure we'll see you again."

The soldiers saluted and rode on down the trail.

Daniel watched them as they left. *Thank you Lord. This is another indication of Your provision and protection.*

Elise looked out the window at the bright sunshine. It was mid-August. A cool tinge accompanied the breeze that blew in the dining room window. Daniel had been gone two months. Loneliness filled her. She missed him and his captivating smile. Where was he, and what was he doing? He was on her mind constantly.

Della walked in with a handful of mail. "Elise, looks like you have a letter from home. Pickens, Missouri, right?"

Elise nodded as she laid down the cloth she'd used to wipe

the table and took the letter. She glanced at the handwriting and frowned. "Justine. She doesn't usually write. I wonder if something is wrong with Marie." She tore open the envelope, pulled out the folded sheets and began to read. After a few moments, she lowered the letter, sat down on the nearest chair and stared across the room.

"Elise, is something the matter?" Della walked back to her.

Elise focused on her. "My brother, Jule, was thrown from a horse. He was unconscious for three days and nobody told me."

"Is he better now? They probably didn't want to worry you." Della pulled a chair up to sit beside her.

"They could've let me know he was hurt." Tears gathered in Elise's eyes and threatened to spill over.

"When did the accident happen?"

Elise studied the letter in her hand. "Last Saturday at the Harvest Festival. That was a week ago." A tear rolled down her cheek. "With the speed of the mail on the railroad, they could have let me know before now."

Della took hold of her arm. "You know the chaos in the middle of a crisis. They were probably concerned about the situation and didn't think about whom they should contact. Is your brother better? Maybe your sister waited until there was something good to tell you."

Elise read the rest of the page. "Yes, he's conscious now and knows them. The doctor said he had a concussion. He also broke his left leg." She gasped. "The doctor thought he might be paralyzed because he couldn't move his legs. Thank goodness that wasn't true."

"See? What would you have done if they'd told you about the accident without any good news? You'd have gone crazy since you couldn't be there." Della smiled. "Sometimes, you're better off when you don't know everything."

Elise nodded. "I guess you're right."

Mr. Ramsey stepped in the dining room. "This telegram just came in. The noon train is on its way. There'll be a full house."

"Will you be alright?" Della hugged Elise.

Elise smiled tearfully as several of the other girls hugged her and patted her shoulder. She wiped her tears and prepared to meet the noon train passengers.

That evening Betsy prepared for an evening with William. She brushed her hair and twisted it into a chignon on top of her head. "Are you alright if I go out tonight, Elise? I can stay if you need me. I know you had bad news about your brother."

Elise shook her head. "No, go on. I need to think." She picked up Mama's Bible from the bedside table and traced the gold lettering with her fingertips. "Betsy, do you think Daniel will want to see me when he gets back? I wish I'd hear from him."

Betsy sat on her bed to tie her shoes. "He said he would, didn't he? He doesn't know where you've been transferred, so it'll take longer for a letter to find you." She shrugged. "You'll just have to be patient, I guess."

Elise laid the Bible on her pillow. "You're right, of course." She sighed. "With Jule's accident, homesickness and my new duties, I feel...I don't know, unsettled." She stood and walked to the window.

"I'm sorry. I wish I could help more." Betsy put her hand on Elise's shoulder. "I'll pray for you."

"Thanks." Elise tried to smile. "Have a good time."

After Betsy left, Elise dropped to her bed and picked up the Bible again. Daniel's letter slipped from the front cover and fell to the floor. Elise reached down to pick it up. She'd almost worn it out when she first received it, but that was over two months ago. She stared at his handwriting bold and angular across the front then held it to her heart. The handwriting was like the man, sure and confident. "I'll wait for you," she whispered.

Elise opened the Bible and thumbed through the pages. If only she could find the peace and joy she had before Mama died. What had happened to her? *Where was God?*

She dropped to her knees and looked up. "Dear God, why can't I feel Your presence? Why am I so confused? Please show me." She laid her head on the Wedding Ring quilt. She had drifted from God after Mama's death. How could she get back? The path seemed overgrown with thorns.

She got up from her knees, walked to the dressing table to pour water into the basin, and washed her face. Listlessly, she brushed and braided her hair, then slipped into her nightgown.

Daniel sat on the bed of his second story hotel room and stared at the playful patterns the rain made on the windowpane. He and his crew had arrived in Gainesville, Texas three days ago. It had rained constantly since they'd arrived. At least they'd slept in a dry bed instead of a soggy bedroll.

He sighed. It was August twentieth, over two months since they'd left Kansas. The second scope was finally repaired, but for two weeks it had rained intermittently, which made it a slow process after they left Oklahoma Country and crossed the Chickasaw Nation. In spite of the less than ideal conditions, they had finished the railroad line survey and had staked out sites for the towns of Guthrie, Edmond and Purcell.

Daniel walked to the dresser. He ran his hand through his hair and pushed back errant strands that fell across his forehead. He needed to meet with George Sealy, the president of the Gulf, Colorado and Santa Fe, and check on the progress of the merger. The other man had been out of town and wouldn't be back until the weekend.

Daniel placed his hands on the dresser and bowed his head. "Father, I want to finish this job and get home." He sat on the side of the bed and put his face in his hands. "I don't enjoy the job like I used to. Maybe because of Elise; the girl of my dreams. But oh God, I don't know what to do about my feelings for her. This job—I'm away so much and for such long periods of time. What kind of marriage is that? If I can't take care of her properly, I won't make a commitment to her. It wouldn't be fair."

A knock on his door brought Daniel to his feet. "Who's there?"

"Just me, Abe."

"Come in, Abe. Door's not locked. How've you occupied this time?" Abe was a short, blond-haired man with a kind face.

"Ah'v been doin' nothin'. Vas pondering vhat you be doing?"

Daniel burst into laughter. "That about says it, doesn't it?" He picked up his hat. "Let's find something to eat. No use to sit here and feel sorry for ourselves." He walked out the door. "Maybe, we can find a checkerboard."

They descended the stairs two at a time. Daniel waved to the clerk at the hotel registration desk. "Guess we'll get something to eat. You seen Carlos?"

"He came through a while ago. I think he was on his way to the saloon."

"Probably so." Daniel walked toward the door. "He's been eye-ballin' one of those good looking little ladies."

"He better be careful. Some of them...ladies is spoken for." The clerk slammed the registration book shut.

"One in particular, maybe?" Daniel's eyes sparkled. "Oh not to worry, it's never anything serious with Carlos. He just likes a pretty face." Daniel grinned as he and Abe walked through the door into the rain. Daniel hated that the saloon was the only establishment in town that served meals. At least the only place they'd found.

"Come on, Abe. We better run for it. Don't step off the boards or I'll never dig you out." They sprinted down the boardwalk past the mercantile, a millinery shop and the bank to the saloon on the far end of Main Street. There were only a few buildings in the whole town. The Land Grant office, the Sheriff's building and the livery were across the street.

A gaudily dressed woman met them as they walked through the swinging doors into the saloon. "Can I get you men something? You wanna drink?"

"No thanks. We need a table and a meal." They followed her across the noisy room. "What's on today's menu?" Daniel asked as he moved a chair around so he could watch the activity. He noticed Carlos at the bar with a girl on each arm.

"Beef stew or beans and cornbread." The girl moved closer to Daniel and smiled coquettishly. "What would you like?"

Daniel leaned away from her. "The stew is probably left-over from yesterday. I'll have the beans and cornbread and a cup of coffee. What about you, Abe?"

"I haf that, too, I think."

"Whew, this town needs a Harvey House and a few Harvey Girls." Daniel rolled his eyes as she sashayed away, hips swaying.

"Yah like one special?" Abe grinned at Daniel.

Daniel grinned back. "Well, I'd like to be with a certain one right now, but I wouldn't want her here." It was difficult to breathe through the haze of tobacco smoke and the pungent smell of beer.

"How much longer, do you think, until we can head back?"

"I have to meet with George Sealy." Daniel drummed his fingers on the table. "I checked at his office. He won't be back into town until Saturday and won't be available to meet until Monday." He looked at Abe. "I checked on the mail service here. It goes by stage on Tuesdays. We should be back home before a letter would get there."

"Ah'm ready to get home to my family."

"Me, too."

After the train passengers left, Elise cleaned and reset her tables. Della placed a child's seat at her table.

"Gram'ma, there's my friend from the train." Elise looked up when she heard the familiar voice.

"Hush Elizabeth." An older woman held the bouncy child's hand. "You don't know anyone here."

"Yes I do. See Lucia, there's Elise." Breaking free, Elizabeth ran to Elise and threw her arms around her. "You're my friend. You know my Uncle Daniel."

Elise knelt and hugged her. "I certainly am your friend, Elizabeth, but I better introduce myself to your grandmother or she'll think I'm kidnapping you."

Elise stood, placed her arm around Elizabeth's shoulders and smiled. "Hello. You must be Mr. and Mrs. Gilbertson. I'm Elise Dumond. I met Elizabeth, Daniel and Lucia on the train coming from Columbia, Missouri, to Kansas City." She nodded to Lucia, who smiled at her. "My brother, Arnaud, is a good friend of Daniel's."

A huge smile creased Mr. Gilbertson's face. Elise once again had the strange feeling she was looking at Daniel several years in the future. He had the same laugh lines at the corners of his blue eyes. "Ah, yes. We've met Arnaud. He came to the ranch with Daniel for a visit." He grabbed her hand in a hardy handshake. "Daniel and Elizabeth also said they had met you on the train when they got home."

Elise lifted Elizabeth into the child's seat as Della indicated the other available seats for the adults. Elizabeth grabbed Elise's hand. "Daniel likes you a lot." She looked at her grandpa. "He said so, didn't he?"

Elise felt her face grow warm. "I'm glad, Elizabeth." She took their orders and moved on to her other customers.

After everyone was served, Elise stopped behind Lucia and

Elizabeth. "How are you?" She placed a hand on Lucia's shoulder.

Lucia glanced up and smiled. "I'm doing well. I love the wide-open spaces on the ranch. Everyone's so friendly."

"She has a boyfriend," Elizabeth whispered loudly, with a giggle.

"Hush, Elizabeth." Lucia blushed and patted Elizabeth on the knee.

Elise chuckled. "I'm glad you're happy."

"I'm gonna get some new clothes." Elizabeth bounced on her seat. "We went to the dressmaker this morning, and Gram'ma has to go to the doctor."

Mrs. Gilbertson reached over and gave her arm a shake. "Elizabeth be quiet. You chatter like a monkey."

"What's a monkey?"

Mrs. Gilbertson sat back in her seat. Her face was red and her breath came in short bursts. She clutched her chest as perspiration broke out on her forehead. Mr. Gilbertson watched her, a worried look on his face. "That's enough, Elizabeth. Be quiet now and eat your dinner."

Elizabeth pouted a bit then picked up her fork and attacked her potatoes and peas. Elise watched Mrs. Gilbertson. Finally after several moments, her breathing returned to normal.

Elise set a plate of apple pie with ice cream in front of Mr. Gilbertson. "Have you heard anything from Daniel?"

"No, we haven't." He picked up his fork and took a bite

of pie. "I thought we'd hear before now. Hopefully he can contact us soon."

Elise sighed. She yearned to hear from him too.

Mr. Gilbertson ate the last bite of pie and finished his coffee. "We'd better go." He stood and assisted his wife to her feet. Elizabeth ran to Elise and gave her another hug before they left. "I hope I get to see you again. I'll tell Gram'pa I want to come back." She looked up at Elise. "You said you'd be my friend."

Elise ruffled her curls. "I'll always be your friend, Elizabeth, and yours too, Lucia."

Lucia smiled shyly as Elizabeth grabbed her hand and pulled her toward the door.

Elise watched as they left the room. It was delightful to see them again. She felt a bit guilty, but was glad they hadn't heard anything from Daniel since she hadn't.

CHAPTER 20

The crimson sun set in the west behind a short bank of clouds, and a slight southern breeze cooled the air as Daniel and Abe rode into Arkansas City. They had made good time traveling back across the Oklahoma territory. Carlos had decided to return to New Mexico to see his family.

"We're here. Can you believe it?" Daniel pulled his handkerchief from his pocket and wiped perspiration from his face. He glanced at the red dirt streaked across it then folded it and returned it to his pocket. "I'm glad to get back to civilization."

Abe nodded. "Ah'm ready to go home to my vife and kids."

Daniel studied him with interest. "You don't talk much about them. How do you keep your marriage and family intact when you're away for such long periods of time?"

"Lots of thinkin' and prayin'." He pointed to his pocket.

"I haf pictures."

Daniel frowned. He wondered if he could do it. He wanted to be around to enjoy his marriage. Besides, what if Elise didn't wait? A troubled pang stabbed through him at the thought of losing her. Could he ask her to live life like that?

After they stabled their horses, Daniel and Abe sauntered up the street toward Mrs. Dickerson's boarding house. "Let's get a room and supper." He studied Abe's appearance then looked himself over. "We could both do with a bath and shave."

Abe chuckled. "Yah, I vill agree vith that."

Daniel stepped onto the porch in front of the boarding house. "I hope there's an eastbound train in the morning. I'm ready to get home."

"You goin' to see your little lady?" Abe removed his large black hat and slapped it against the porch pillar; the dust flew in a red cloud around the post.

"As soon as possible. She was probably transferred after her month of training. I'll have to find out where." He removed his hat then knocked on the door.

~~~

Elise looked out the window of the dining room as she positioned water glasses on the tables. Cool weather settled in overnight and the dining room was drafty. How could it be the middle of September already? Two weeks had passed since Daniel's family came in and still no word from him. No more news from home either. She pursed her lips as she straightened the napkins. Why hadn't anyone written?

Betsy set a pitcher of ice water on a table next to Elise's. She paused, her hand on the back of a chair. "Have you decided if you're going to the opera with us tonight? I'm going with William and Alma, and Maxine and Lydia are going with some guys from church."

"I guess I will. I've wanted to see *Pygmalion* since it came to town." Elise moved a fork. "I asked to get off early."

"Me too. Maxine says the Whitley Opera House is fabulous."

"I know." Both girls stood beside their tables as Della ushered the train passengers in.

Later that afternoon, Elise walked with Betsy up to their room. then gathered her toiletries and clean clothes. "I'll take my bath first." She hurried down the hall to the bathroom. She hummed a tune as she undressed and filled the bathtub with warm water from the reservoir. She hadn't been anywhere fancy for a long time. It would be perfect if Daniel were here to go with her.

Afterward she returned to the room. As Betsy left, Elise took her dark green brocade dress from the closet and slipped into it. Not overly ornamented with ruffles and lace, it was elegant in its simplicity; appropriate wear for the opera.

Della knocked on the door. "Elise, you received a letter

today. I'm sorry I didn't get it to you earlier. You were busy when it came, and then I forgot."

Elise whirled around. "Is it from Daniel?"

Della frowned. "No, I think it's from your family."

Elise sighed. "I've wondered about Jule." She took the letter. "Thanks for bringing it." She ripped the envelope open and sank down on her bed.

September 12, 1885

Dear Elise,

Sorry I haven't written sooner. Things have been crazy around here. I knew you'd want to know that Jule isn't doing well right now.

We thought his leg was healing although he continued to have fevers and swelling. However, Sunday the wound broke open and discharged a horrible, foul-smelling drainage. He's developed an infection in the broken bone wound and it's not healing properly. Doctor Harris wants him in town so he can observe him closely. We took him to Uncle Henri and Aunt Victorine's. Justine has cleaned and re-bandaged the wound twice a day for the last three days.

Pray that we can stop the infection. If it doesn't clear up soon, the doctor says he'll have to amputate the leg. The infection could spread to the rest of Jule's body. If that happens, he could die. Jule vows he will not let his leg be taken. If it comes to that, I'd rather have Jule with one leg than to lose him.

Elise felt faint. She stared out the window. Surely this

couldn't happen. Visions of her mother's death from intestinal infection flashed through her mind. She'd assisted the doctor when he attempted the surgery. Slowly she returned to the letter. Tears blurred her vision. She could hardly read.

Paul and his father are harvesting the oats with assistance from our neighbors. Thank goodness for their help. We should have a fairly good yield, though the price to sell isn't very high. I'm afraid with all of Jule's doctor bills; we won't have enough money for the farm payment. At least we have the money to take care of him. That's the most important thing right now.

No! Things couldn't get worse. She'd left home to be a Harvey Girl so she could help save the farm. Now it was hopeless. Tears stained the page as Elise finished the letter.

I had to start school in spite of Jule's illness. August has spent some evenings with me. I think he'll ask me to marry him soon. I hope so.

Everyone says to tell you "Hello." Keep praying. We'll keep you updated on Jule's condition. I've written to Arnaud, but if you see him before he gets my letter, please tell him what I've said.

Love, Marie

P.S. We received a letter from Papa's cousin, Julius Montague. He said he's traveling to France to investigate Papa's robbery. Justine says nothing will come of it. I'm afraid to get my hopes up.

Elise folded the letter and tossed it on the bed, then snatched her handkerchief from the dresser and mopped her eyes. What else could happen? She covered her face with her hands and heaved a huge sigh.

When Betsy came in a few minutes later, Elise sat on her bed and stared at the floor. "Come on, Elise. What're you doing? You need to get ready. The others will be here shortly."

Elise turned, misery etched on her face. She held up the letter. "I can't go. Della just brought this letter from my sister. My brother has infection in his leg and it may have to be amputated."

Betsy sat on the bed beside Elise and put her arm around her. "Oh Elise, how awful." She gave her a hug. "I'll pray for him."

"Thanks, Betsy. He'll need all the prayers he can get." She looked at her hands. *Oh, God. I need to pray. Why do I feel so far away from You?*

Betsy touched her arm. "I know you're discouraged, Elise, but it won't help to sit here and worry. Come on. Maybe the opera will take your mind off your troubles for a little while. You're already dressed."

Elise stared at her. "Oh, all right. I'll go crazy if I sit here alone all evening." Standing, she glanced in the mirror. Her eyes were red and swollen from crying. She washed her face and patted her hair into place.

When she and Betsy entered the parlor, Lydia, Alma, and Maxine were there visiting with three men from church. William greeted Betsy. Ben stood and strolled toward Elise from the chair by the window. His limp was quite pronounced. "Hello, Elise. It looks like the others have all paired up. That leaves you and me to go in my carriage. Is that alright?"

Elise frowned as she considered the other couples. They were ready to leave. "I...I guess so."

Ben winced. "I can tell you're ecstatic. It's not a date, you know." Elise allowed him to place her light wrap around her shoulder and took his arm. "You do look nice if I may say so."

The evening train pulled into the depot as they strolled together from the Harvey House to his carriage.

Elise pointed toward the setting sun. "The days are getting shorter. I hate that. I like summer."

"I do too, but that's part of living in Kansas. We have the four seasons. It'll start getting cold before we know it." Ben offered his hand and helped her step into the carriage.

A lump formed in Elise's throat, which made it hard to breathe. She wanted to be in Missouri with Jule, not in Kansas! "I...I'm sorry, Ben. I can't go to the opera, not tonight. I feel sick." Her voice broke. She closed her eyes and grimaced with the pain in her chest. She glanced up. "I...I received a letter today from my sister. My brother... may have to have his leg... amputated." Elise felt tears building behind her eyes. She blinked hard, but they tumbled down her cheeks. She covered her face with her hands.

Ben placed his arm around her shoulder and pulled her close as he handed her his handkerchief. "Elise...don't cry."

~~~

Daniel grabbed his satchel and peered out the train window as he walked toward the door of the passenger car. Emporia looked like an oasis after spending three months in the wilderness. Anticipation welled up in him at the thought of seeing his family. He'd spend a few days here then go to Topeka. He wanted to find out where Elise had been transferred.

His pulse raced with a mixture of excitement and anxiety at the thought of seeing her. Would she be happy to see him? He pressed his lips into a straight line and let out an exasperated sigh. If only he hadn't been away so long.

He stepped from the train and scanned the familiar scene. He'd arrived and departed from this depot many times, but he never lost the thrill of home. This was where he saw his first locomotive and fell in love with the railroad.

He glanced toward the Harvey House next to the depot, then stopped and stared in shock. *The young woman in the carriage. She looked like Elise...in another man's arms!* No! It couldn't be. Just then she pulled away and looked his direction. His chest constricted. *It was her!* He couldn't believe it, but there she was in plain sight.

~~~

Elise wiped her eyes and regained control of her emotions. She pushed away from Ben. "I...I'm sorry. I didn't intend to do that." She smoothed her skirt and looked around to see if anyone had observed her crying.

She stiffened and sucked in her breath. "Oh-h no." Her heart seemed to stop beating for a second then her pulse pounded in her ears. Daniel stood in front of the depot staring at them. "Oh no." A sob tore its way out of Elise's throat.

"It's alright, Elise." Ben reluctantly removed his arm. "We don't have to go if you'd rather not."

"No... I mean... No. I can't go." Elise almost fell as she stumbled out of the carriage.

"Elise, wait." Ben jumped down and followed her, but his limp impeded his progress. He frowned as she ran away from him between the passengers along the deck calling Daniel's name.

When Elise reached the spot where she had seen Daniel, he was gone. Frantically, she looked around. She had waited all this time for him, and he'd come at the precise moment she'd had a crying fit on Ben's shoulder. She covered her mouth with her hand as another sob choked her. Why, oh why, had she agreed to go with Ben?

Elise searched around the passenger cars and along the platform. No sign of Daniel. She stopped. Maybe she'd dreamed he was there. Maybe she'd mistaken him for someone else.

"Elise, what's going on?" Ben walked up behind her and took her arm. "You're acting peculiar." He looked around. "Come on, I'll take you inside."

Elise pulled away. "No! You go on. I'll be alright." Whirling around, she ran toward the Harvey House entrance. *Dear Lord, please.* Her heart cried out. *Please, don't let that have been Daniel.* Tears started again. Maybe it hadn't been him. But she knew in her heart it was.

No! Oh God, why? Daniel felt like Midnight had kicked him in the stomach. He spun around, swung onto the platform at the end of the train car and jumped off on the other side of the track. He heard Elise call his name as he hurried toward the caboose, away from the Harvey House. He couldn't face her, not now. He'd come back later for his baggage.

CHAPTER 21

Daniel sat astride Midnight and watched the sun rise. Its heat warmed his body, but his heart felt as cold as stone. He'd awakened long before dawn, rode the hills and replayed the times he and Elise had spent together before he left. He'd been certain she'd felt as strongly as he had. Their kiss still burned on his lips.

All those months in the Oklahoma Territory, he'd held Elise close to his heart and remembered her beauty and goodness. Her memory had carried him through many cold, wet, dark nights.

He'd had no right to expect her to wait. He'd freed her from promises or commitments when he left, and she'd found someone else. A sigh escaped him. He should've known better than to let his heart get involved again, but he'd thought Elise was different. He bowed his head, the pain of rejection washed over him; with it came the realization that he'd fallen in love with her.

Daniel swung off Midnight beside a fast flowing stream. He knelt on the ground and stared at the clouds that floated lazily in the sky. "Father in Heaven." He paused. His voice cracked. "Why, oh why, did You allow this to happen? Why did You bring this beautiful, wonderful woman into my life only to let me lose her? I'd hoped she'd be the one You had for me." He buried his face in his hands. "I should have learned, I can't expect a woman to wait month after month while I'm gone. Please guard my heart, Lord. No matter how much it hurts, I want to do Your will. I place my life and my relationships into Your keeping. In Jesus' name, Amen."

Sitting back on his heels, Daniel rested for several minutes as the peace of God seeped through the pain. Standing slowly, stiffly, he remounted Midnight and rode toward the ranch house. He'd continue to be Elise's friend as they were before they parted. There could never be more. An aching void invaded his chest.

Monday morning Daniel rode Midnight into town. He had to catch the train to Topeka. A drizzling rain, which matched his mood, fell from a gray overcast sky. He pulled his greatcoat around himself and grimaced. He'd worn it the day he met Elise in a similar rainstorm. Elise, beautiful Elise. Why hadn't she waited for him?

He hadn't been very pleasant company for his family over the weekend. It saddened him to see his mother's condition worsen. She was much weaker than when he'd left. He brought his fist down against the saddle. Midnight whinnied and looked back at him. "Sorry friend. You're the only one who hasn't changed." He patted the horse's neck. "Of course, you were with me so I could keep an eye on you." He touched his heel to the stallion's flank. "Come on. Let's get into town before we get completely soaked." Midnight broke into a gallop as Daniel continued his monologue. "I need to talk to Elise before I go to Topeka. Might as well get it over with. right, old fellow?"

Daniel left Midnight at the livery stable and jogged the two blocks to the Harvey House. As he entered the depot lobby he shrugged off his outer coat and hung it and his hat on the coat rack. Thankfully his dress jacket wasn't too wet. He pushed his damp Levi's down over his boot tops then sauntered up the stairs to the door of the dining room.

He took a deep breath and steeled himself against the sight of Elise. Quickly his eyes sought her out. He stood and watched as she took lunch orders from the train passengers. She was so graceful, so sure of herself, as she moved around her assigned tables. His eyes feasted on her dark-haired beauty. *Why, why did he want her so when she had chosen someone else?* He'd wanted her to get this job so he could be close to her, spend time with her.

He leaned against the doorpost as he waited for the head waitress to seat the people ahead of him. Elise turned and looked at him. His breath caught in his throat. She was stunning. It was a mistake to come so soon after he saw her with another man. He straightened as the head waitress returned.

"Hello. How may I help you? Do you prefer the dining room or lunchroom?"

Daniel gestured toward Elise's tables. "Dining room. I'd like to be at Elise... er, Miss Dumond's table."

Della gazed at him, a pleased expression on her face. "Miss Dumond? Elise? Are you, by any chance, Daniel Gilbertson?"

Daniel looked at her in surprise. "Yes. How did you know?"

"Just a wild guess." Della grinned as she led him across the room.

Daniel's gaze engaged with Elise's as he neared her table.

"Daniel. You're finally home." She continued to stare. A myriad of expressions crossed her face from gladness to uncertainty. Was she happy he'd come, or did she wish he'd stayed away?

"It's wonderful to have you back." Elise stepped back as Della seated him at her table and asked his drink preference. Elise took his order and served his salad, then with a lingering look, moved away and took orders from the other customers.

Daniel watched her walk to the window at the back of the

room and turn in her orders. Jealousy flashed through him. It wasn't fair that some other man had won her devotion while he was away, unable to give her the attention she deserved. He finished his salad and laid down his fork as she approached.

Elise traded his empty salad dish for his dinner plate. Daniel watched her as she moved to serve the man beside him. "Elise, did you get my letter?"

Elise swung around. "You sent a letter?" Her shoulders sagged.

Frustration surged through him. "I mailed it from Arkansas City. I didn't know where you were transferred, so I sent it to Topeka." Maybe if she had known he was coming...

"I've waited to hear from you. I've missed you deeply."

Daniel raised his eyebrows, but said nothing as she served her other customers. Obviously she hadn't missed him too much. Or else she'd made up for her loss with another man. He continued to watch as she served the meals. She moved with grace and confidence. She'd make a wonderful wife. He closed his eyes against the pain sweeping through him. *Get a grip, man, it's over.*

As she removed his dinner plate to serve the dessert, he spoke to her. "My folks enjoyed their dinner here."

Elise smiled. "I enjoyed meeting them."

Daniel chuckled. "Elizabeth told me all about it. She was excited to see you."

Elise placed his dessert in front of him. "She's a sweetheart. It sounds as if Lucia is doing alright, too. Elizabeth said she has a beau." Elise stepped back as one of the other Harvey girls filled his coffee cup. "Are you back to stay?"

"For a while, in and out. I travel to Topeka today. I'll work there most of the time to map our route." He looked at her. "My mom's heart is worse. The doctor thinks her time is short so I need to be with her as much as possible." He finished his pie and drank his coffee. "I better go. Can't miss the train. I'll try to see you when I'm back to visit my family." He stood and pushed his chair under the table. "Don't worry, though. I won't interfere with you and your new beau."

"Daniel, wait." Elise stared in consternation, her hand over her mouth, as he walked briskly toward the door.

Numbly, she whirled back to her tables. Most of the customers had returned to the train. After the stragglers left, Elise cleaned and reset her tables in a daze. Her heart had become a lump of lead. She'd waited with such anticipation for Daniel to return. Now all her dreams lay in shards around her feet.

When Della ushered the locals in, Ben took his usual place at the table. Elise wanted to ignore him but knew she didn't dare. How had she given him a second thought compared to Daniel? Elise shook her head and tried to put the thoughts from her as she served the diners from force of habit.

When she served Ben's dessert, he grabbed her arm.

"What's wrong with you? You've been ignoring me." He pulled her around to face him.

"Wrong? There's nothing wrong." Elise gritted her teeth at the sarcastic tone.

"Are you going to the talent show tonight? It starts at seven-thirty."

She pulled her hand away. "No, Ben. I'm not going. Don't ask me ever again." Elise spoke softly, but firmly.

Ben frowned. "It's that surveyor guy, isn't it? Daniel. Is that his name?" He said the name mockingly. "Why wasn't he here when you needed him?"

"Yes, it's Daniel. I told you when we first met that I was waiting for him. His work takes him away. Now I have to get busy." Elise turned away and placed the dessert plate in front of her next customer. Her hand trembled so much she nearly spilled the coffee. If only she could tell Daniel she'd waited for him. He probably wouldn't believe her now. Maybe he would avoid her altogether.

Instinctively, Elise worked through the lunch rush. She straightened her tables and prepared them for the next meal, then walked to the window and watched the rain pour off the depot eaves. She closed her eyes and hugged herself. Her neck felt tight and her head pounded. *Lord, what are You doing? I can't take anymore. You've gotta show me the way. I can't pray. Oh God, where are You?*

Betsy touched her arm. "Are you alright, Elise? Maybe you better take a break. Go to your room for a while. I'll have Della get someone to take care of your tables." She glanced around. "You have them ready for supper anyway."

"I think I will. I'll try not to be gone long." Elise walked toward the entrance of the dining room. Della stood just inside the door. "I need to take a break. I've got to get away."

Della nodded. "Will you be alright?" She handed Elise a letter. "This came in the mail today."

Elise glanced at the envelope and recognized Daniel's bold handwriting. It had come a day too late. She hurried to her room and shut the door. She wanted to be alone. She sat on the bed, dropped the letter on the pillow, and gazed out the window for a few moments. Then she threw her cloak around her shoulders, picked up her mother's Bible and the letter and hastily moved down the stairs. The rain had changed from downpour to a light drizzle as she walked from the Harvey House.

The church. She'd go to the church. She walked up the street beside the Harvey House. She'd prefer to go to the park, but the chilly breeze blew from the North, and the drizzly rain persuaded her that wasn't a desirable choice.

The church door opened easily when she pressed the handle. She shivered and pulled her cloak closer around her. There wasn't any heat in the building.

Elise made her way to the front. She stood and stared at the wooden cross; the Bible clutched to her heart. She believed Jesus died for her on the cross, and she had asked Him to forgive her sins and be her Savior, but somewhere along the path she had lost her way.

She dropped to her knees at the altar and laid Daniel's letter beside the pulpit. "Why, God? Why have You brought so much misfortune to me? First You took Papa and Mama. They loved You and served You. Then the money and the farm and Jule's accident. He might have to have his leg amputated." Elise burst into harsh sobs as tears flowed down her face. "Daniel's gone and he thinks I love Ben."

Elise clenched her fists. "Where are You, God? Why can't I pray?" Shoulder-shaking sobs racked her body for several minutes before they subsided. She fumbled in her pocket for a handkerchief and blew her nose.

Completely spent, she folded her hands on the Bible and remained kneeling. She looked again at the cross.

"I will never leave thee, nor forsake thee." The words formed in her mind as clearly as if she'd just heard them from God's mouth.

"But where, God? Where are You?" No sooner had she cried out the words than she understood. God hadn't deserted her. He'd been with her all along. She'd slipped ever so slowly away from Him.

With sudden clarity, she realized she'd deliberately rejected God's love when her mother died. Marie always quoted Romans 8:28. "And we know that all things work together for good to them that love God..." But Elise had refused to accept it. She'd refused to believe that God would bring good from her parent's death. In fact, she had never forgiven Him for taking them.

Elise put her hands over her face and sank back onto her heels. She had never forgiven God! What would God do to a person who refused to forgive Him, especially one who was His child? The Bible said something about God chastening His children that He loved. Mama used to quote that verse when she was about to spank them for doing something wrong. Was that why she had suffered so much loss?

Elise opened the Bible with trembling hands and began to thumb through the pages. There were many underlined verses, but she needed to find a particular one. Somewhere near the end. Not Revelation. There it was. First John 1:9. *"If we confess our sins, He is faithful and just to forgive us our sins, and to cleanse us from all unrighteousness."* Mama had heavily underlined that verse.

Dropping her head on her hands, Elise prayed as tears streamed down her face. "Dear Father in Heaven, please forgive me for doubting that You know what is best for my life. I'm sorry I didn't forgive You when Papa and Mama died. I realize now that they're much better off with You. I just missed them so much. Please forgive me, too, for my stubborn pride. I thought I could do everything myself. You said in Your Word that You'd forgive me and cleanse me. I want that, dear Jesus. Please."

Elise continued to kneel, her head bowed. A feeling of calm and peace that she hadn't known for a long time flowed through her. "Thank you, Jesus," she whispered.

Opening her eyes, Elise looked at the cross again. God had led her all along. If she hadn't needed money for the farm, she might never have left Pickens, Missouri. She'd thought God had forsaken her, that she needed to do something on her own. He'd given her the Harvey Girl job. Filled with awe, she whispered, again, "Thank you, Jesus."

Bowing her head, she cringed as she thought of all the trials God had allowed to open her eyes and draw her back to Him. "Dear, Father, my stubborn pride has caused a terrible mess for everyone. Jule's sick, we're about to lose the farm, and Daniel...well I may have lost Daniel for good. I'm sorry, God. I turn this disaster over to You. I pray You will work good out of it. I know I can't do it. Dear Father, please lead me in the right path from now on. Amen."

Elise picked up the Bible and sat on the first row of seats. She leafed through the pages and read the underlined verses. She grinned as she read Psalms twenty-three. God had prepared a table for her on the prairie.

She pulled the ribbon marker. The Bible fell open to Jeremiah, thirty-three. The third verse was underlined. *"Call unto Me, and I will answer thee, and shew thee great and mighty things, which thou knowest not."* Would God do great and mighty things for her?

Elise sighed, slipped Daniel's letter in the front cover, and closed the Bible. Her feet were frozen, but she didn't care. An amazing peace filled her heart. Her problems remained, but now she could pray and wait for God's help through them. His presence was real again.

She pulled her cloak around her, let herself out of the church, and walked back to the Harvey House ready to work.

CHAPTER 22

October scurried by. Leaves turned to red, gold, and brown. After the first hard frost, they carpeted the boardwalk along Fourth Street. The original group of four girls who walked to the church on Sundays had grown to eight or nine, quite an entourage. Elise went on the Sundays she didn't work. The sermons took on new meaning for her.

She was relieved that Ben was interested in Mabel. He now spent his lunch hour at her table.

Elise enjoyed working in the Harvey House. She met senators and actors who traveled the rails, but her thoughts often strayed to Daniel. Where was he? What was he doing? Her heart lurched at the thought of seeing him in the dining room door. Would they ever get together again?

Twice she'd seen him in the lunchroom on his way to and

from the ranch. She'd wanted to talk to him, but her responsibilities kept her from it. The knowledge that he ignored her caused a heart-piercing pain. She'd known that he'd come back when he was on the survey trip. Could they get past the misunderstanding?

Another letter came from Marie the second week in October. Elise kept it in her pocket for two hours after Della gave it to her. Finally at her afternoon break she walked slowly up the stairs to her room.

She shut the door, opened the letter and began reading.

October 10, 1885

Dear Elise,

I have good news to tell you. The doctor thinks Jule's infection has cleared up, and his leg has begun to heal at last. He's still in town with Uncle Henri and Aunt Victorine so Doctor Harris can keep a close eye on him.

Jule is ecstatic that he'll keep his leg. He says to send thanks to you for your prayers. He'll have a huge, deep scar on his left thigh, but he can live with that.

"Oh thank you, Lord." Elise clasped the letter to her chest. "Thank you for answered prayer." She lowered the letter and read on.

We won't have the money now to make the farm payment. God knows our need; He will provide.

Elise nodded, thankful for the peace only God could give.

August has asked me to marry him. Can you believe it? It's a dream come true. I want you to stand up with me. It will be Sunday, December 27. I hope you and Daniel and Arnaud and Millie can all come to Missouri for Christmas then be here for our wedding. I want to be married here, in our house, before we have to move.

All the family love you very much and look forward to seeing you at Christmas.

Love,

Marie

Elise smiled though the tears sprang to her eyes. She rejoiced for Marie and August. The wedding would be perfect on the farm. She'd ask permission to be off two weeks at Christmas since she'd have worked six months by then. She needed to ask soon. Christmas was a busy time for train travel.

She looked out the window. It would be devastating to lose the farm, but Marie was right, Jule's health was of utmost importance. It was amazing how God could change a person's values. Elise folded the letter and hurried back to work with a lighter heart.

Elise strode through the depot lobby. She was excited. Mr. Ramsey had informed her that she was approved for time off at Christmas!

Ben surprised her as he rose from one of the lounge chairs.

"Elise." He called her name as he hobbled toward her. She noticed his limp was more pronounced. "I need your help."

Elise stopped and studied him. "My help, Mr. Johnson?" She put her hands behind her back.

"I'll be out of town for a few days. I expect a shipment of pharmaceutical supplies to arrive on the train, probably Friday. I wondered if you'd pick them up and store them for me until I return."

Elise frowned, bewildered. "Why me? Can't they keep them at the depot?" She placed her hands on her hips. "Besides, why aren't you asking Mabel instead of me?"

"I just thought you'd understand. Couldn't you keep them in your room? The station master prefers I find someplace else to leave them since it's medicine." Ben smiled, coaxingly.

"I suppose I could." She frowned again, uneasiness gnawing at her. "How long will you be gone?"

"I'm not sure, maybe a week." He smiled at her. "Thanks, Elise. I appreciate it." He walked from the lobby before she could reply.

Elise watched him disappear. Something wasn't right. A thought niggled at her conscience, something about his limp.

Frowning, Elise walked into the dining room.

Later, Elise, Betsy, and Alma polished silverware after they'd finished the breakfast cleanup. Alma rubbed the bowl of a spoon. "Have any of you heard talk about the local men having liquor?" She glanced at the others. "This morning, Mrs. Bidwell and some of the other Temperance Union ladies were sitting at my table. They were furious. Someone has sold illegal liquor. They said some local ranchers are upset, too. Their ranch hands have bought it somewhere and come to work drunk." She laid down the spoon she'd been working on and picked up another. "I thought we were through with drunken behavior when the Prohibition Act was passed."

Mabel spoke from the next table where she polished her salt and pepper shakers. "You can bet they'll find out where it's from. With those Temperance Union ladies on the job, it won't go on for long."

"It must've all started the Fourth of July." Betsy gathered up a pile of spoons and stacked them in their holder. "Remember, someone got drunk at the Randolph's dance. There was quite a row about that, but the culprit got away."

Coldness gripped Elise's heart. Yes she remembered all too well! She bit her lip and rubbed hard on the fork with her polishing cloth.

"There's a rumor Ben Johnson has sold it on the side." Alma spoke up. "Of course, that's only a rumor," she amended as Elise and Mabel both looked up and stared at her.

"Oh no. Ben wouldn't do that." Mabel walked over and picked up some spoons. "He's a good Christian."

Elise sat and gazed at Alma. Could Ben be involved with

alcohol? A cold chill shivered down her spine. What was in that shipment he'd asked her to pick up? Elise straightened. Arnaud said he saw Jerome get off the train here. She hadn't seen him so she'd put it out of her mind. Suddenly a picture crystallized in her thoughts. The man with Jerome at the Columbia, Missouri depot had walked with that peculiar limp. Was Jerome stalking her through Ben? He'd certainly been determined to make her acquaintance when he'd first met her. Elise shivered.

She'd wait and see if the shipment came in. Arnaud should arrive Friday afternoon. She'd talk to him about it. Daniel might come for the weekend too. Would she see him? Elise's heart constricted at the thought. She ached to see him. Why couldn't he understand she loved him and would be willing to wait for him? He hadn't given her the chance to explain.

Friday afternoon, Arnaud walked into the dining room. Elise hurried to meet him. He smiled and took her hand. "Mr. Ramsey said you wanted to see me. I don't have much time. I have to take the train into Topeka tonight."

Elise stepped back and glanced around to make sure none of the other girls were close to them. "I need to show you something." She pulled him out of the dining room and toward the door that led to the dormitory.

Arnaud laughed. "I can't go in there."

"Yes you can. Just for a minute. Everyone's at work."

Elise led him down the hall to her room and shut the door behind them. "See that crate? Ben asked me to pick it up and keep it for him. He was going out of town for a few days and couldn't leave it at the depot."

Arnaud looked at her sharply. "Ben again! Why are you doing what he wants?"

"I don't know." She hugged herself. "I don't feel right about it. It says pharmaceuticals on it, but I wonder if there's liquor in there instead of medicine?"

"That's a serious accusation. What makes you think that?"

Elise sat on her bed. "Someone's sold liquor around here. The rumor is it's Ben." She looked at her hands. "I may be wrong, but something about Ben's limp has bothered me since I met him. The other day I remembered. When I was on my way to Kansas City, I saw a man who had a limp like Ben's. He was with Jerome at the Columbia train station."

"Are you certain?"

"I wouldn't swear to it, but I'm pretty sure. It seems odd, in hindsight, that Ben made such a determined effort to flirt with me when he first arrived. He wouldn't leave me alone even when I told him I was interested in Daniel."

"When did he say he'd be back?"

"He said a week, but I don't trust him."

Arnaud frowned. "I have to go to Topeka today, but I'm off duty tomorrow. I'll come back in the morning and take this to the sheriff. Let's go talk to Mr. Ramsey now. He needs to know about your suspicions. I would feel better if this crate wasn't in your room any longer than necessary."

The next morning Elise watched the dining room doorway as she prepared for the second breakfast crowd. Her breath caught in her throat, and her blood raced through her veins as Della brought Daniel and Arnaud toward her tables. Daniel's deep blue eyes sparkled with laughter at something Arnaud had said. The dimple in his chin deepened. He sobered as he looked at her. Elise grabbed the back of the nearest chair to bolster her weak knees. Her gaze caught Daniel's. Was there desire in his eyes? He looked so good!

Elise curbed a sudden impulse to reach up and push aside the strands of sandy blond hair falling over his brow. Her heart ached for him to understand how fervently she wanted to be a part of his life.

"Hello-o-o. Elise. I'm here too." Arnaud chuckled as he touched her arm. "Daniel and I came to have breakfast at your table."

Elise felt her face grow warm with embarrassment as she turned to her brother. "I'm glad to see you both." Her glance returned to Daniel and she was disconcerted to see his gaze on her. She motioned to two empty chairs. "Are you on your way to your family's ranch? How is your mother, Daniel? I think of you all often."

Daniel grimaced as he sat down. "She's not well. The doctor said she doesn't have long. I take every opportunity I can to be with her. We thought we'd lost her a couple weeks ago, but she surprised everyone and pulled through. You just never know."

Elise nodded. "Tell her I'm praying for her."

Daniel smiled. "I will."

Elise found it difficult to keep her mind on her work. Twice she forgot an order and had to have the customer repeat it. Arnaud caught her eye and winked.

Daniel left much too quickly for Elise. She watched as he walked to the dining room door. Would he be back? Would they ever reconcile? Hope flared in her heart.

After breakfast, Arnaud waited until all the other patrons had left then gestured to Elise. "Have you heard anything else?"

Elise shook her head. "I've watched for Ben, but he hasn't come in."

"Good, I'll get that box from your room. I don't want it there if Ben comes back early. I'll get Mr. Ramsey to help me. Don't worry." He touched her arm. "Will you have a break this morning?"

"I can take a break after I get set up for the next train."

"Good, I'll meet you in the parlor."

Elise's hand trembled as she cleaned her tables. What kind of illegal activity was Ben involved in?

Thirty minutes later, Elise walked to the entrance of the dining room where Della stood. "May I spend time with my brother?"

"Go ahead. There are a couple of hours before the next train."

Arnaud strode up the stairs as Elise left the dining room. He took her hand and pulled her to the parlor. A fire blazed in the fireplace and the morning light shone in the windows. Elise looked around. They were alone. She turned to Arnaud. "Did you talk to the sheriff?"

"Yes. He's extremely interested. He's going to check the crate." They moved to the window. "Guess who I saw in front of the livery?"

"Ben?" Elise stopped as a tremor shivered down her spine. "I was right then."

"You definitely did the right thing, sis."

"If only I hadn't let him talk me into getting into his carriage. I didn't think clearly. I'd just heard about Jule." Elise's voice quivered. "Why did that have to be at the very time Daniel came home?" Tears welled up in her eyes.

"You like Daniel a great deal don't you?"

"I love him, Arnaud. I'd wait forever for him."

Arnaud nodded. "He loves you, too. He'll come around. He's been miserable away from you."

Hope leaped in Elise's heart. "Do you truly think so?"

"He couldn't take his eyes off you this morning." Arnaud chuckled and patted her arm. "You better go back to work. I'll check with the sheriff."

Chapter 23

Later in the afternoon, Elise and Betsy were sitting together in the depot lobby when Arnaud stepped in from the outside, accompanied by a blast of cold air. He walked toward them, rubbed his hands together to warm them, and sat on the couch. "You were right, Elise. It was liquor. He must have tried to set you up. The sheriff and his men will raid the pharmacy tonight. Some of the ranchers are coming in too. It could get nasty."

"I suppose you have to go?" Elise grabbed his hand as he nodded. "Be careful."

"I will."

Elise, Betsy and Della waited with Mr. Ramsey in his office off the depot lobby as the night hours wore on.

Elise put her face in her hands. "Arnaud said he'd let us

know what happened. I hope no one gets hurt. If Ben is bootlegging, there's no telling what he'll do." She shuddered and silently prayed a quick petition for everyone's safety.

A few minutes before midnight the door to the Depot flew open. Elise jumped to her feet. A tremor of fear skyrocketed through her as Jerome strode across the lobby and into the office toward her. "Jerome, what are you doing here?"

"Hello, cousin. Didn't want to see me, did you? You little two-timing cheat." He grabbed her arm and smiled menacingly. "You agreed to keep that box, knowing full well what was in it. I told you that you'd end up working for me."

"You're lying, Jerome. I've never worked for you, and I never will. I did not know the contents of the box. I just started putting two and two together." Elise struggled to pull free. Her voice quivered in spite of her effort to speak calmly. "You won't get away with this, Jerome."

Suddenly Mr. Ramsey threw his arm around Jerome's neck and thrust his knee into his back. Jerome lost his grip on Elise's arm. The sheriff and Arnaud rushed in as Elise stumbled backward against Mr. Ramsey's desk. Arnaud's face was white. "You alright, Elise?" He relaxed when he saw she didn't have any serious injuries. "We've got Ben and a lot of evidence. Jerome was in on it too, of course." He put his arm around Elise and glared at Jerome as the sheriff handcuffed him. "There's been a shooting, though."

"Who...?" The color drained from Elise's face as she stared at Arnaud. She grabbed Mr. Ramsey's desk for support. "It's Daniel, isn't it? He came in with the ranchers. I can tell by your face. Is he...?"

Arnaud took hold of her shoulders. "It's Daniel. I don't know how bad the wound is, but he's alive. They're taking him to Doc Warren right now. Ben had a gun and Daniel lunged for it. I don't think Ben intended to shoot. The gun just went off."

Elise picked up her cloak and threw it over her shoulders as she headed toward the door. "Where's the doctor? Take me there. I've got to know how he is."

Betsy hurried to her side. "Wait a second. Let me get my coat. I'll come with you."

They followed Arnaud through the dark streets to a building with a burning lantern in the window. Several men were milling around outside.

Elise pushed her way to the door. "Excuse me. I've got to get in. I need to find out how badly Daniel's hurt."

"Don't you think that's what we're waitin' for lady?" one of the men spoke. "They'll let us know soon's they know somethin'."

Elise didn't listen. She pushed the door open and walked in with Betsy close behind. The smell of alcohol permeated the air. Daniel was lying on an examination table in a small side room. Doc Warren leaned over him. Elise closed the door and made her way across the small outer waiting room to the head of the table. Daniel's eyes were closed tight, his teeth clenched. The doctor was sewing up a wound on his side.

"Daniel?" Elise spoke quietly.

He opened his eyes and squinted trying to focus on her. "Elise, is that you? What're you doin' here?" His voice was slurred from the medicine. He grimaced as the doctor took another stitch.

Elise's heart nearly stopped. "Arnaud told us. I had to come."

"You...din't have ta' come. I'm a'right. Just got a flesh wound on my side." He closed his eyes and muttered. "Sorry about Ben."

Elise frowned. "Daniel, I don't care a whit for Ben. I never did." A sob rose in her throat. "It's you I love, no one else."

He opened his eyes and looked at her, a small light flickered in their depths. "You sure?"

"Of course, I'm sure. That's the way it's always been."

Daniel gazed at her a few moments, then smiled and drifted off to sleep.

Doc Warren stood up and wiped his hands. "You girls go back to bed. This guy's tough. He's gonna be fine, just needs to sleep this off." He grinned at Elise. "You don't have to worry."

Arnaud met them as they walked from the doctor's office. "How bad is it?"

Elise nodded and grabbed his arm to steady herself. "He has a wound on his side. The doctor stitched it up. He said Daniel would be okay."

William stepped to Becky's side. "Glad to hear it wasn't serious. He insisted on riding in with us." He took Becky's hand. "I'll accompany you back to the depot."

Betsy placed her hand on Elise's shoulder as they walked with Arnaud and William back toward the Harvey House. "It'll all work out, Elise. I'm sorry about your cousin, though."

"It was bound to happen sooner or later." Arnaud spoke up. "Jerome's been in trouble since we were kids." He turned to William. "How will you get Daniel back to the ranch? He won't be in any shape to ride for a few days."

"I'll head out with the other hands and let his dad know what happened. Then we'll probably bring the carriage in to get him in the morning. He'll need his sleep tonight."

"Do you want me to ride out with you? Back you up?"

"Would you? I'd appreciate that." William relinquished Becky's hand.

"Sure." Arnaud gave Elise a hug as they reached the depot. "See you in the morning."

The girls watched as they hurried toward the livery. Elise sighed. "Whew. I'm exhausted! That was way too much stress for one night." She turned to open the depot door.

"Me too. Who would have thought Ben was involved in

bootlegging? I'm glad Daniel wasn't hurt any worse."

Elise wasn't sure she would make it to their room without collapsing. Ben and Jerome captured and Daniel wounded! It was too much to process. Hopefully, she would be able to sleep.

⌒⌒⌒

A week had passed since Daniel was shot in the raid. He sat on the examination table in Doc Warren's office. He winced as the doctor took out the stitches on his right side. "My elbow hurts every time I try to move it, Doc."

"That bullet grazed it, probably chipped the bone. Nothing we can do for it." Doc felt the elbow joint. "I don't think there are any other breaks. Just keep it in the sling until it heals." He shook his head. "You may have problems with that elbow the rest of your life. I hope not, but it's hard to tell."

"Can I travel to Topeka? I need to get to work."

Doc washed his hands in a basin of water and dried them on a towel. "I don't see any reason why you can't travel by train. Your side is healing nicely, and you've almost recovered from your blood loss. You need to be careful of that arm, though. Have it checked by a doctor up there, make sure it heals right."

Daniel nodded. "Doc, I have another question. I may be crazy, but the night of the shooting was there a lady in here? I was so doped from that medicine that dulled the pain, it seems like a dream, but I thought someone was here."

The doctor leaned against his worktable and crossed his arms. "Yep, there were two young ladies in here. One was frantic, dark haired, pretty face. Said something about you being the only one she ever loved." He chuckled. "In fact, she checked on you after you went home."

Daniel grinned as excitement filled him. It was Elise. "Thanks, Doc. I'll stop in when I get back."

Daniel walked slowly up the boardwalk toward the Harvey House. Thomas had brought him into town. They'd agreed to meet for lunch at eleven so Daniel could make the train to Topeka.

As he passed the park, he decided to stop and sit on a bench near the street. He groaned as he rested his good elbow on his knee and ran his fingers through his hair. Elise said he was the only one she'd ever loved? Could it be true? Maybe he'd jumped to a hasty conclusion, but he'd seen her in Ben Johnson's arms, hadn't he? The anguish of that scene washed over him. He covered his face with his hand. Why had she reported Ben to the law? He had to find out.

He sat up and looked at his pocket watch. Fifteen minutes before ten. He'd have time to talk with Elise if she could take a break.

Daniel hesitated in the doorway of the Harvey House dining room and watched Elise as she prepared her tables for the noon rush. His pulse raced at the sight of her. She moved around the tables with practiced ease. Her dark hair was pulled up on her head. It framed her classic features. Her eyes were bright with laughter and her lips were curved in a teasing smile as she joked with the girl at the next table.

Elise swung around as Daniel walked toward her. An expression of welcome leaped into her eyes, followed immediately with a look of cautious questioning. "Daniel." She walked toward him a timid smile on her face. "Have you recovered from your wounds?" She touched his sling. "Does your arm still hurt?"

"The bullet grazed the elbow. Doc thinks it chipped the bone. Hopefully it'll heal quickly." Daniel watched her face. "Elise, do you have time to talk? I have to leave on the noon train."

Elise glanced back at her tables. "Yes, I can take a few minutes. I have everything ready for lunch."

She led the way into the parlor and sat in a chair near the window. Daniel sat facing her.

"Elise, I barely remember you in the doctor's office the other night. Doc had me so doped up. What did you say? I need to know." Daniel's voice was gruff with emotion. "Is there another man in your life?"

Elise leaned forward. "No, Daniel. There isn't anyone else. No one. That's what I told you."

"What about Ben Johnson? It must've been hard turning

him in." Daniel watched her. "Do you love him? I saw you... in his arms."

"Oh Daniel. No. I never cared for Ben. He tried to get me to go with him, but I wouldn't. The day you saw us, the day you came home..." Her voice broke and she had difficulty going on. "I had...just received news that Jule...might lose his leg. Ben was trying to comfort me."

Daniel raised his eyebrows. "In his carriage?"

Elise looked down at her hands clasped in her lap. "A group of us planned to go to the opera. The others paired off and left me to ride with Ben." She glanced up, pain evident in her eyes. "I looked so forward to your return. Then when you got off the train at the precise moment I was crying on Ben's shoulder, I thought I'd die. I tried to find you, but I couldn't." Tears glimmered in her eyes. "I didn't go to the opera."

Daniel groaned. "I'm sorry, Elise. I thought you..."

Elise bowed her head. "I know. It's not your fault. I never should have agreed to go with him, but I wasn't thinking straight."

She glanced up. "When you walked out of the Harvey House thinking I liked Ben, I was devastated." The words came in a choked whisper. "It turned for good, though. It drove me to my knees. God used it to bring me back to Him." She gave him a teary smile. "I realized I had drifted away from God when my parents died. He was there for me all the time, but I wouldn't acknowledge Him. Your leaving, the loss of our farm, and Jule's illness, made me realize I had to ask forgiveness and get back into fellowship with Him."

Daniel leaned forward and took her hands in his good one. He was unashamed of the moisture in his eyes. "Elise, please forgive me. I've been such a chump, the world's worst bungler. God gave you to me, and I almost let you slip away with my jealous assuming. I'm sorry. I want to spend time with you; get better acquainted. Will you forgive me? I love you." The words tumbled out.

"Oh yes, Daniel." Elise laughed, joyously. "You're forgiven, and yes, I want to spend time with you, every chance we get. I'll wait for you as long as it takes. I love you too, Daniel."

Daniel stood and gathered her into his arms. Pain shot up his arm from his elbow, but he hardly noticed it as he covered her lips with his. All the pent up passion from the last few months was wrapped up in that kiss. His heart felt as though it would burst with relief and happiness. Elise responded to his kiss with all the fervor of her being.

Finally Daniel raised his head and looked into her eyes. "I better let you get back to work. They'll think I kidnapped you."

Elise gasped. Her eyes sparkled with happiness. "I lost track of time. What time is it?"

Daniel took out his watch and looked at it. "Fifteen minutes before eleven."

"Gracious, I have to go." Standing on tiptoe, she kissed him lightly before she ran from the room.

Daniel watched her go then slowly walked back to the dining room. Thomas stood near the dining room entrance staring at Elise as she walked quickly across the room. He turned as Daniel approached, a perplexed look on his face. "What's with her? She just gave me a hug."

"I think she's happy." Daniel chuckled.

"I'd say. Her smile would light up the room. Did you two finally talk things out?"

Daniel nodded. "I was such a fool. Glad I finally came to my senses."

Thomas slapped him on the shoulder. "It's about time. Maybe you can get on with life now."

Daniel couldn't keep from smiling as Della came to seat them.

CHAPTER 24

It was almost Thanksgiving. Elise looked up from setting the salads on the table to see Della escort Mr. Harvey and two other distinguished gentlemen toward her.

She straightened and waited to greet them. A quiver of anxiety raced through her. Della smiled, reassuringly.

"Miss Dumond, I'm sure you know Mr. Harvey." At Elise's nod, she introduced the other gentlemen. "This is Santa Fe President, Mr. William Strong and Chief Engineer, Mr. A. A. Robinson."

Della gestured toward the table. "Gentlemen, you may have a seat." She took their drink orders and adjusted their cups accordingly. Soon she was back with more customers and the tables began to fill.

Elise tried not to let her distinguished guests distract her as she took orders and followed the routine she knew so well. When Mr. Ramsey brought in the main course, Elise smiled at the attentiveness with which he served Fred Harvey and the other men.

As Elise removed the dinner plates to serve desserts, she overheard Mr. Strong speak to Mr. Harvey. "The purchase of the GCSF railroad in Texas is almost complete."

The word, Texas, caused Elise to focus on the conversation. She couldn't help but eavesdrop as she continued to serve the pie and ice cream.

"That means we'll need to establish Harvey Houses in Texas in the near future." Mr. Harvey picked up his fork and began eating his pie.

"I would say you could start late next year. If negotiations go as planned, we may be able to close the deal with the Gulf, Colorado, and Santa Fe Railroad early in the new year. Then we'd have to build the railroad across Indian Territory, but I expect that to go according to our schedule."

"That'll take us to Galveston on the Gulf, won't it?" Mr. Harvey turned to Elise. "Tell the chef, this pie is excellent."

"Thank you, sir. I will." Elise smiled as she continued serving desserts.

"Yes, it'll be an excellent acquisition. I predict if we have a route from Kansas City to the Gulf of Mexico, it will end the railroad trade monopoly in Texas." Mr. Strong ate a bite of pie. "We have a brilliant young man, Daniel Gilbertson, from right here in Emporia, in fact, who has been in on the negotiations since we first contacted George Sealy, the president of the GCSF, in 1884."

Elise's heart skipped a beat at the mention of Daniel's name. She quickly asked if anyone would like seconds on dessert.

Mr. Strong shook his head as he continued. He took a drink of coffee and another bite of pie. "He'll work with us on the final negotiations since he started them almost two years ago. There are promotions in store for that young man if he pulls this off, possibly to vice president over the Gulf line."

Mr. Harvey pushed his plate back and drank the last of his coffee. He shook his head at the girl serving drinks. "You'll let me know, then, when we can open the Harvey Houses in the Oklahoma Territory and in Texas?"

"I'll definitely let you know." Mr. Strong finished his pie and swallowed his coffee. He turned to Mr. Robinson. "We better go. Don't want to miss the train." Standing up, he laid a dollar on the table. "Very good. Thank you for a delicious meal, well served."

Mr. Harvey stood also. Giving Elise a wink, he laid two dollars on the table. "Good job." He followed the other two men from the room.

Elise stood and watched them in a daze. She'd received a

coveted compliment from Mr. Harvey himself, but her mind was on Mr. Strong's words about Daniel. She leaned against the table and stared at the dollar bills. Happiness filled her. She couldn't help but smile. Daniel had dreamed about being a vice president of the ATSF. Would that really come to fruition?

~⋘

Thanksgiving morning Elise awoke to the jangling of her alarm clock. She sat up, turned it off then threw back the blankets. Brrr... A shiver raced through her. She slipped her feet into her slippers and peered out the window. The sun wasn't up yet, but it was surprisingly light outside. A full moon shone on a sparkly, white world. Elise gazed at the beauty; the first snow of the season. The steam in the radiator hissed and popped as she held her hands over it to warm them. She shivered again.

Betsy sat up, her blanket still wrapped around her. "It got cold in the night."

"Come, look out the window."

Betsy padded over and peeked out. "Isn't it pretty? I wish I was back home in Ohio to enjoy it."

"Me too. I miss my family." Elise washed her face. "I hope this snow doesn't prevent our trip to the ranch this afternoon."

"I know. I've been looking forward to the visit. William said they always have a Thanksgiving meal for the ranch hands and their families. We'll be stuffed after eating the noon meal here."

Elise dressed in her uniform and arranged her hair. "Daniel's coming in on the early train. When are you expecting William?"

"It'll probably be closer to noon. This snow may make it harder to get the carriage through."

"Let's plan to eat dinner together." Elise sat on her bed to put on her socks and shoes. "It still amazes me that William works on the Lazy G, Daniel's family ranch."

"It works out good for us." Betsy smiled as she pulled her hair up into a chignon. "We better hurry since we both work the early shift. I'm glad everyone has time off today for the holiday."

They walked together to the lunchroom for breakfast.

Later, Elise watched the dining room door as she prepared her tables for train passengers. Her heart leaped as she heard the whistle and the rumble of the locomotive as it pulled in.

Elise stood beside her tables as people began to enter the dining room. Della was working quickly to get them seated. Disappointment filled Elise as her tables began to fill. Maybe Daniel hadn't made it after all. Then she saw him in the doorway, his coat over his left arm and the sling on his right arm. A smile lit Daniel's face as Della led him to her table. "Thank you." He spoke to Della as she turned his cup over.

Elise felt a wild urge to hug him, but knew she had to work steadily to get everyone served. "What would you like?" She put her hand on his shoulder as she took his order.

Daniel grinned mischievously. "A kiss."

She slapped his arm. "Daniel! You know what I mean." She looked around and felt her face grow warm as she saw smiles on the faces of the other diners at the table.

"You asked." Daniel laughed. "I'm sorry. Actually, I'd like the French Toast." He reached up, took her hand and kissed it.

Elise took orders as Alma served the drinks. Though embarrassed, her heart sang as she served the meal.

After the locals were fed, Della approached Elise. "Daniel came to spend Thanksgiving with you. Go get ready. I'll have one of the other girls cover your tables." She grinned and gave Elise a light shove. "Wear something pretty."

"Thanks, Della. I appreciate it." She hurried to her room and slipped into her green brocade dress.

Daniel stood at the window of the parlor as he waited for Elise. The gaslights had been lit and a fire roared in the fireplace giving the room a rosy glow. Outside, the snow covered rooftops, trees and even the blackened gravel along the train tracks. The morning sun turned it to sparkling diamonds.

His pulse raced as Elise stepped up beside him and slipped her hand under his elbow. "It's so good to have you here."

Daniel turned and took her in his arms. "I'm sorry I embarrassed you. Will you forgive me?"

Elise laughed softly. "Oh yes. You're forgiven."

Daniel leaned down, pulled her close and gently kissed her. A thrill shot through him as she leaned against him and returned the kiss.

A few moments later, he pulled away and gazed into her eyes. "I love you, sweet Elise, and I'm glad I'm here too." He took her hand. "Come on, let's go eat that turkey dinner. Then we'll head out to the ranch."

Elise stopped him with a touch on his arm. "Daniel, I have something exciting to tell you." She pulled him over to the couch. "Two weeks ago, Fred Harvey and Mr. Strong came to the Harvey House and sat at my table. Mr. Harvey asked when he could build Harvey Houses along the railroad to the Gulf. Mr. Strong said they could probably be built the end of next year. He was sure negotiations would be completed after the first of the year. Then he said he had a brilliant young man who was working on the negotiations, and he said it was you."

"Really?"

"Yes. He said you were from here, in Emporia. He said if you get the merger finalized you'd probably get promoted to a vice president position."

Daniel stared at her, hope flared in his heart. "Are you positive he said that?"

"Yes, I shouldn't have been eavesdropping, but I couldn't help hearing." She chuckled. "Maybe I took a little longer than usual to serve the dessert."

"Do you know what that would mean? I could be home more." He sat back against the cushion. "It'd be a dream come true, but I won't get my hopes up. He may forget he said it."

Elise smiled. "I couldn't wait to tell you. When I heard him give you such high praise I nearly burst with pride. I wanted to shout, 'That's my man you're talking about!'"

Daniel laughed and pulled her into his arms. His emotions were mixed. Part of him wanted to get up and dance a jig; the other part was scared to believe. "Thanks for telling me. I'll do my best to get the merger done and then we'll see what happens."

Elise gave him a hug, then stood and pulled him up beside her. "All right. Let's go eat, Mr. Doubter."

William and Becky were waiting by the dining room door when Daniel and Elise walked up. Della returned from seating some other patrons. "Would you four like to sit together?" She glanced back into the room. "We're pretty busy, though mostly locals today. There weren't many train passengers. They all traveled yesterday, I guess."

Elise nodded. "They're probably home today. Becky and I discussed this morning how nice it would be to see our families."

Daniel stepped forward. "We'll be family today." He glanced at William and Becky. "Good fellowship will make the meal even better."

Della seated them at Lydia's table. Hans and his crew outdid themselves on the Thanksgiving dinner. The turkey was roasted to perfection, tender and juicy, with potato soufflé', candied sweet potatoes and seasoned green beans. There was Royal Chocolate layer cake for dessert. Elise pushed her empty dessert plate aside and took a drink of iced tea. "Whew! I'm full. That was delicious."

"Yes it was." Becky scraped the last crumb of cake from her plate. "How are we going to hold another meal?"

"That's what Thanksgiving is all about, I guess." Daniel finished his coffee and looked at William. "Did you bring the sleigh into town?"

"Yes. Your dad said it would travel better on the snow." He paused while Lydia removed their plates. "Mom Gilbertson is excited to see you all." He chuckled. "She gave me a list of instructions before I left this morning." He focused on the girls. "She's a second mom to all us cowhands. I wish her health was better."

Daniel turned to Elise. "This is a big day for my folks. Every year they plan this evening meal for all the ranch hands and their families. Cecelia has probably cooked enough for the whole county."

William faced Becky. "Are you ready to go?"

She smiled and nodded. "Yes. It'll be good to get away from the Harvey House for a while."

"Well then, let's be on our way."

The four of them were soon bundled in the sleigh. Daniel and Elise sat in front and William and Becky in back.

Elise laughed. "I think we need bells to ring."

The rolling hills were beautiful, covered with freshly fallen snow that glistened in the afternoon sunlight. Cattle were huddled under the few trees and along fences.

After about twenty minutes, Daniel pointed to a group of buildings in the distance. "There's the Lazy G."

As they got closer, Elise could see the lovely, white two-story ranch house. The jewel of the prairie, it had an elegant arch over the front entrance and a large side porch. There were gables and a round tower room. "Look Becky, isn't that gorgeous?"

"Yes it is! I'm delighted we get to visit."

"Thank you." Daniel chuckled as he guided the horses up the lane. "Can you believe Dad and Mom started out in a sod house down by the creek? Dad worked hard to build this house for her."

An impressive red barn and other ranch buildings were situated around the farmstead. Carriages and sleighs sat near the barn and several children were playing in the snow. "Looks like lots of people are here already." Elise shaded her eyes to look for Elizabeth.

"Many of Dad's ranch hands have families. They'll all be here today."

As Daniel pulled the horses to the hitching post in front of the house, Elizabeth left the other children and ran toward them. "Uncle Daniel! Elise! You're here!" She jumped up and down while Daniel stepped from the sleigh and turned to help Elise. "Grandma said you were coming." She threw herself into Elise's arms. "I'm so happy you're here."

"I'm glad, too." Elise gave her a hug.

Elizabeth grabbed her hand. "Come on. Grandma's waiting to see you."

"Slow down, Elizabeth. Give us a chance to catch our breath." Daniel held her arm. "Is Grandma in her sitting room?"

Elizabeth nodded and gave a little skip. "She said for you to come up right away, when you get here."

"Okay. Why don't you go back and play, and we'll go see Grandma."

Elizabeth pouted as Daniel took Elise's hand. He motioned toward William and Becky and led the way to the front door. They walked across the spacious entry hall and up a grand oak spiral staircase. At the top of the stairs they turned right and walked to a room at the end of the corridor. Daniel knocked lightly. "Mom, we made it." He guided Elise into the room and motioned for the others to follow.

The sunny, welcoming feel of the room struck Elise. One wall was lined with floor-to-ceiling bookcases. An elegant white marble fireplace occupied the far wall. A fire blazed on the grates. Overstuffed chairs with bright colored pillows invited one to enter and relax.

Mrs. Gilbertson sat in a cushioned rocker with a small writing table in front of her. She set the table aside and held out her hands. "I'm so happy to see you all."

Daniel put his arm around Elise. "Mom, this is Elise Dumond. I've wanted you to get acquainted."

His mother took Elise's outstretched hand in her own frail one. "We've already met, though not formally. Alas, I regret I was not good company that day at the Harvey House. I wasn't feeling well. I'm pleased to make your acquaintance, Elise." There was a decided twinkle in her eyes, and Elise was surprised by the strength in her grip. "Believe me, I have heard of your many favorable qualities."

Elise smiled. "Thank you. I've wanted to get acquainted with you, too. Your son speaks very highly of you."

"I'm sure we'll get along well." Mrs. Gilbertson held out her other hand to Becky. "And William, this is your young lady. Becky, right?"

"Yes. Becky Stephens." William stepped forward.

"I'm so glad to meet you, Becky. I understand you are Elise's roommate, and you met William in the Harvey House lunchroom."

Becky nodded.

"I'm glad William found you. These young ranch hands

are like sons to me. I like to see them settled. I pray daily that they'll find the right mates." She glanced at Daniel and Elise. "Had to pray extra hard for these two."

Becky took her hand. "It's a pleasure to meet you and to enjoy your beautiful home. Thank you for inviting me."

Mrs. Gilbertson settled into her chair and shooed them with a wave of her hand. "Now you go on and enjoy yourselves. I don't feel up to joining you for dinner, but I will have pleasure thinking about all the activities. This is the highlight of my year."

Esther's weakened condition saddened Elise. Occasionally, her thoughts wandered to Daniel's mother the rest of the afternoon. In spite of it, Elise found herself enjoying the time with Daniel's family and the sumptuous meal.

CHAPTER 25

December flew by in a happy haze for Elise. Daniel had agreed to travel with Arnaud, Millie and her back to Pickens for Christmas and Marie's wedding.

A week before Christmas, as Elise prepared for the noon meal she heard Elizabeth demand. "We need to sit at Elise's table."

Thomas, Lucia and Elizabeth crossed the room. Elizabeth broke loose from Lucia's restraint and ran to throw her arms around Elise's legs. "Hi Elise. We went Christmas shopping, and I got some things for your hair."

"Elizabeth, you're not supposed to tell." Lucia grabbed her arm.

Elizabeth stuck out her lip. "I didn't tell her what it was."

Lucia grinned at Elise and shrugged her shoulders.

Elise hugged Elizabeth. "Uncle Daniel's train should get here any minute. Won't that be fun?"

The train whistle sounded. Daniel was among the first to walk in. Elise's heart leaped with joy as he smiled at her. When he joined them at the table Elizabeth threw her arms around him and jumped up and down. "Uncle Daniel, we're gonna have Christmas tomorrow at Gramma and Grampa's house. We went shopping." She peeked around him at Lucia. "I can't tell you what we got."

Daniel's eyes twinkled with laughter. "I know, sugar. I'm excited, too. Let's eat dinner then we can go."

That afternoon, they traveled to the ranch in the carriage. Elizabeth sat between Daniel and Elise. She chattered excitedly until she fell asleep with her head on Elise's lap.

The snow had melted leaving winter brown grass. Elise caught her breath at the sight of the exquisite ranch house as they approached across the prairie. How had Daniel left all this to work on the railroad? She was glad he had or she might not have met him. Yet it seemed a dream that she could be a part of this beautiful family and the legacy of the ranch.

The next day, they exchanged gifts and had Christmas dinner with Daniel's family. Charles had carried Esther down to enjoy the celebration. Her emaciated body and pallor disheartened Elise.

After the noon meal, Elizabeth crawled onto Elise's lap and

snuggled close. "I love you, Elise. I wish you were my mommy."

Elise drew in her breath as love for the small girl rushed through her. She glanced at Daniel. He was watching her, an intrigued expression on his face.

Elise's gaze traveled to Esther Gilbertson. She sat propped with pillows. To Elise's surprise, Esther smiled and nodded slightly.

Elise hugged Elizabeth to her and spoke softly. "I love you, too, sweetheart, but now your grandma and Lucia will care for you. I have to work at the Harvey House." She glanced again at Daniel. Maybe someday, if she and Daniel married, Elizabeth could be their little girl. Elise hugged her again. "We'll wait and see how God works."

~⋙≺~

Christmas Eve afternoon, Arnaud drove Uncle Henri's carriage up the drive to the farmhouse. He, Millie, Daniel and Elise had arrived at the Pickens depot two hours earlier.

Elise scanned the farmyard. Everything looked natural. She couldn't believe the family would move in a matter of weeks. A lump rose in her throat as she looked toward the creek where tall, leafless trees stood sentinel. It would be a bitter experience to lose this home. There were so many memories here.

So much had happened since she'd left to become a Harvey Girl. One thing was certain; she'd matured and changed tremendously.

Justine and Marie ran out to greet them as they pulled up to the front door. They made their way into the house where Paul and Jule were waiting. Jule stood on his crutches; a huge grin on his face. When Elise embraced him, he whispered, "Thanks for all your prayers, Sis."

Elise stepped back so she could see him better, her hands on his shoulders. "You look wonderful, Jule."

"I feel wonderful. My leg is healing now."

Elise hugged him again as tears rushed to her eyes. His well-being was worth all the trials they'd endured.

Justine hurried to the kitchen to finish supper. The aroma of baked ham wafted into the sitting room.

The next morning when Elise awoke, snow had covered her beloved farmyard with a mantle of white. Star and Star Fire stood in the barn lot.

After the sumptuous breakfast Justine had prepared, everyone gathered in the parlor around the decorated tree. Paul lit the candles, and they sang their favorite Christmas carols. Daniel put his arm around Elise and pulled her close. They sang *Away in a Manger.* His strong tenor blended with her clear soprano.

Marie distributed the gifts. Elise had shopped with Millie in Topeka and bought Daniel an inscribed pocket watch on a chain. Daniel gave her a diamond and sapphire pendant necklace. "It's beautiful, Daniel. Thank you." Elise smiled, although disappointment touched her. She'd hoped for an engagement ring.

While the men visited in the parlor, Elise and the other girls prepared the Christmas meal. August arrived mid-morning and Uncle Henri and Aunt Victorine came out for dinner. Elise peered into the parlor from time to time. It made her happy to see Daniel in conversation with Paul, Arnaud, August and Jule. He would be a perfect addition to the family.

Sunday morning, they all bundled up and rode into town for church. Elise enjoyed the opportunity to see friends and neighbors and introduce them to Millie and Daniel.

Her eyes followed the path, which led to the cemetery behind the church. It was a relief to be free from the anger and bitterness she'd felt after Papa and Mama's deaths.

She sat between Daniel and Arnaud in the family pew and gazed at the stained glass window at the front of the church. Jesus, the Good Shepherd, had taken care of her. The winter sunlight illuminated the compassion in His eyes. How could she ever have doubted His care and goodness?

Daniel reached over and squeezed her hand as they began to sing. Elise looked at him and smiled. It was incredible to sing in harmony with him. As the message began, Elise felt God's presence. The minister spoke about the Shepherds' and Wisemens' worship of Jesus. She learned that her most important duty and privilege were to worship Jesus and give Him her life.

When they arrived home, Elise and Marie hurried upstairs to dress for the wedding. Soon, friends and family arrived in carriages and wagons.

"Stand still, Marie. How do you expect me to get your veil pinned if you keep fidgeting?" Elise chuckled. "You're usually so calm and collected, what's the matter?"

"I don't know. I want everything to be perfect; this is so important."

"It will be. The Lord led you in your love for August. He'll take care of the details."

Arnaud appeared at the top of the stairs. "Elise, it's time for you to go."

As Elise slowly descended the stairs, her eyes sought out Daniel. He watched her. The adoration in his smile touched her heart.

As Mr. LaFayette, Paul's father, played the *Bridal March* on his violin, Marie walked regally down the stairs on Arnaud's arm. Elise fought tears. Papa would have loved to give Marie away.

Elise listened as Marie and August repeated their vows. Would she repeat those vows with Daniel soon?

The next morning, Justine and Elise packed dishes in the

dining room in preparation for their move. "When do you meet with the banker?" Elise wrapped a bowl in a linen towel and placed it in a box.

"Thursday, the thirty-first. He'll tell us how long we have to move out." Justine sat on one of the dining room chairs. "Paul, Jule and I will move into the house we lived in when we first got married. It's small, but it'll be large enough for the three of us."

Jule hobbled over to the table and sat down, his shoulders slumped. "If I hadn't insisted on riding that stallion, all this wouldn't have happened. We wouldn't lose the farm."

"Jule, it's not your fault." Elise put her hand on his shoulder. "God used this to draw us together as a family. Each person in this family is more precious than any earthly possessions we have. He'll continue to care for us."

She put her hand under Jule's chin and raised his face to look at her. "You're more valuable than this farm could ever be."

Paul called from the front porch. "Someone's here. A carriage is coming up the drive."

Justine and Elise hurried to the window and looked out. Paul walked to the edge of the yard to greet the two men as they pulled to a stop.

Justine started toward the door. "That's Mr. Parker, I don't know who the other man is. I suppose it's someone to buy the farm."

As they stepped onto the front porch, Mr. Parker and the other gentleman climbed from the carriage and accompanied Paul up the walk. Elise thought the stranger looked vaguely familiar. Mr. Parker shook hands all around. "Paul, Justine, Elise, I have someone here you'll want to meet." With a friendly gesture and a huge smile, he indicated his traveling companion. "This is Mr. Julius Montague, your cousin, I believe. All the family should hear some extremely interesting news he's discovered."

Elise stared at the visitor; their cousin? The one with the shipbuilding company Papa wanted to invest in? He had left France to settle in America when Justine was just a baby.

Justine invited the men into the house and directed them to the parlor, as Paul called the others to join them.

When everyone had assembled, Mr. Montague sat forward on the sofa. "I have fantastic news for you. Your father's money has been found."

"What do you mean, found?" Wide eyed, Justine sat down on the nearest chair. "We were told he was robbed."

Mr. Montague nodded. "The authorities thought that, too. But a few weeks after your father's murder, I received a cryptic message by post in his handwriting. I recognized the code as one we used to write messages to each other as kids. He must've written it in a hurry. I could hardly make it out." Digging in his pocket, he pulled out a crumpled piece of paper and handed it to Arnaud.

"As you can see, if you study it, it says something about the sea and a secret treasure. Your father had written to me earlier about an investment in my shipbuilding business. So I determined that the note had to do with the money, but I couldn't figure out what he was trying to tell me. I contacted the authorities in France and they began an investigation into the matter but couldn't turn up anything.

"One day this fall I was puzzling again over the note, and it came to me: As boys, Louis and I had had a secret hiding place in a cliff by the seashore not far from our homes. We often left messages for each other there.

"I'd supposed it had disappeared long ago but felt I should check it out. I traveled to France, and sure enough, found the money, safe and sound, in the little niche in the rock. He knew he was followed and wanted the money invested so you and your mother would have it to live on. The childhood hiding spot was the only safe place he could think of."

The occupants in the room sat, dumbfounded, unable to speak.

Julius smiled. "I know this is a shock; more than a year after your parent's deaths. I've invested most of the money but thought you'd need some to defray your costs until it begins to pay dividends." He pulled an envelope from his pocket and handed it to Arnaud. "Here's a thousand dollars, and I can get more if you need it."

Arnaud opened the envelope and pulled out a handful of bills.

Tears welled up in Elise's eyes as she held on to Daniel's arm. "You don't know what this means to us. We were about to lose our farm."

After Mr. Parker left, Daniel touched Elise's arm. "Would you care to go for a walk?"

Elise turned to him and nodded. "Let's go down by the creek? I've wanted to go since we got here."

They stopped to pet Star and Star Fire for a few minutes on their way across the farmyard. When they got to the shelter of the trees, Elise led the way down the path beside the stream. She threw out her arms. "I love it here. I'm so glad we'll keep the farm in the family."

Daniel followed as she led the way to the fallen log. After brushing off the snow, Elise sat down, made room for Daniel then leaned against the tree. "I was sitting here when I read Arnaud's letter with the application for the Harvey House." She looked at him. "I'm glad you suggested it."

"Me too." Daniel said, fervently. He sat for several moments, gazing across the slowly flowing water before he turned to her. He took her hand. "I have to leave again right after the first of the year. I don't think it'll take long for the railroads to come to an agreement on the merger, but I'll have to stay until negotiations are finished." He looked back across the stream.

"I know. Remember, I heard Mr. Strong and Fred Harvey talking about you. Mr. Strong called you a brilliant, young man."

Daniel grinned at her. "He didn't say that."

"Yes, he did, and I agreed, but of course I didn't tell him." She smiled. "He said if you see this merger through you have a good chance for a promotion. He said something about the vice presidency over the Gulf operation."

"Do you think he really meant it? I've been afraid to believe it."

"I'm positive he meant it. He was talking to Fred Harvey and I heard every word."

Daniel took her other hand and swung her to face him. "If that's true, do you know what that would mean? We could live in Topeka, have a big house and raise a large family. I wouldn't have to be away so much." He stopped and gazed at her uncertainly. "That is, if you want a large family."

Elise laughed as joy surged through her. She spoke shyly. "I want lots of children, Daniel." She hesitated. "Do you think your parents would be hurt if we took Elizabeth and raised her as our little girl? If you want to."

Daniel nodded, relief shining in his eyes. "I do want to, and I know Mom and Dad would be thrilled. In fact, Mom asked me if we might." He took Elise in his arms, drawing her close, as she raised her face for his kiss. His lips were warm and tender, sending her blood surging through her veins. Elise felt a happiness she hadn't thought possible.

When he released her, Daniel looked into her eyes, the blue color deep with emotion. "I love you, Elise."

"I love you more than I could ever tell you, Daniel. I'd wait for you until the end of time, but haven't you forgotten something with all this talk of a large family?" Elise's eyes sparkled with mischief.

He drew back and gazed at her. Then he grinned as a flush spread across his face. He took a small box from his pocket and handed it to her. "I almost forgot. Open it."

Elise's breath stopped as she saw the gorgeous diamond and sapphire ring winking at her in the afternoon light. It matched the pendant perfectly. "It's beautiful. Oh Daniel." She threw her arms around his neck.

"Elise, will you marry me? I want to share my life with you." Daniel slipped the ring on her finger.

"Yes, yes, I love you! I want to be your wife more than anything in the world."

Daniel pulled her close and kissed her again, deeply and fervently. The world stood still, and neither of them noticed the setting sun.

Finally Daniel stood and pulled Elise up to stand beside

him. "We better get back before they send out a search party."

Hand in hand, Elise and Daniel walked along the narrow path. Her heart felt light, and her feet barely touched the ground. She couldn't remember being so ecstatic.

When they arrived at the house, the family visited with Julius in the parlor. Elise rushed into the room holding out her left hand for all to see. "Look what I have." The smile refused to budge from her face.

Daniel laughed. "As you can tell, I've asked Elise to marry me, and she has accepted."

"I wondered what was taking you so long." Arnaud pounded Daniel on the back. "Welcome to the family."

Looking around the room, Elise knew they had gained much more than the farm and money. They had gained a greater appreciation for each other and a fuller knowledge of God's provision. "Thank you, Lord." She whispered. "Tell Papa and Mama we are blessed!"